LIVERPOOL

Ged Melia

Grosvenor House
Publishing Limited

The right of Ged Melia to be identified as the author of this
work has been asserted in accordance with Section 78
of the Copyright, Designs and Patents Act 1988

The book cover is copyright to Ged Melia
Book cover design by Claire Marsden

This book is published by
Grosvenor House Publishing Ltd
Link House
140 The Broadway, Tolworth, Surrey, KT6 7HT.
www.grosvenorhousepublishing.co.uk

A CIP record for this book
is available from the British Library

Paperback ISBN 978-1-80381-435-3
Hardback ISBN 978-1-80381-436-0
eBook ISBN 978-1-80381-438-4

https://dmscollectables.co.uk/novels/

PREFACE

Novels about life in the mid-nineteenth century written from a working-class perspective are rare beasts. The classics of that period are typically authored by the middle classes, for the obvious reason that few in the 'lower' class could actually read or write. They had more immediate matters to contend with: namely, feeding themselves. Where middle-class life did interact with workers, the latter's experience would often be sugar glazed; the stark realities of their misery perhaps unworthy of mention, or perhaps deemed too wretched.

Like many people, I have undertaken the now well-trodden path of exploring my ancestral history. I did not have to travel far before discovering their horrendous life experiences. The tiny fragments of record that have survived suggest lives of abject poverty ended by premature death. Real characters from my own family history have been used as anchors in the story, but it could be the tale of many Irish families escaping cultural, economic, and religious oppression, and starvation, in their homeland. It's a theme that still resonates in the twenty-first century.

The novel is largely set in 1840s and 1850s Liverpool. It tells of one family's escape from a bare subsistence world to one that was hardly better. Some of the people and events are real; some are invented. In writing the novel, I have tried to capture their experience, but have to admit to likely failing, at least in part. I am, after all, the product of a comfortable middle-class world well over a century-and-a-half later. Nonetheless, despite its faults, I felt that an attempt at the story had to be made. The experience of the 1840s Irish diaspora and the famine years may not have been erased from history, though the subject certainly does not attract the attention and study it fairly deserves.

I did not set out to shock, but seen through the prism of a twenty-first century view of the world some aspects of life in 1840s Liverpool are disturbing. Not least of which are the ages young girls had children and were married. Recorded details in marriage and census records are unreliable, notoriously so in the age 'rounding' approach used in the 1841 census. By 1851, record-keeping had improved, so I have treated that as a more reliable source of reference. Not that it changes anything. A working-class ancestor having a child at the age of 13 might be worthy of further comment today, but in 1842 it would not have been unusual.

Thank you to those who have read and commented on early drafts and have helped proof it, especially Oliver, who has painstakingly been through the story. Your Irish language skills and knowledge of Ireland has been especially helpful.

Although informed by research, and inspired by actual people, actual events, and conditions of the time, the book is a work of fiction. Throughout the novel, characters, scenes, and incidents have been created or altered for dramatic purpose.

Entwistle, Turton, December 2022

PROLOGUE
1839

'Raithe an ocrais.'

Spring had been better than most years. Food had been plentiful and bellies were full, but now it was summer; it was the hungry season. Every year it was the same, and every year Edward swore that this year would be better than the last. Food would be stored to tide them through the lean months between the last potato crop and the next.

But they never seemed to have enough.

'Mam, I'm hungry.'

It was John again. Bridget briefly glanced at his emaciated form, but then quickly looked away towards the twins sitting on the earthen floor opposite the doorway. It was so difficult to maintain eye contact. How could she fully explain their predicament to her young son? Should she even try to?

'Later, John. Before sunset.'

'But I'm hungry now, Mam.'

The twins, Cecilia and Anne, knew better. They were hungry too, but had learned not to ask. Bridget could not bear to look at her two daughters either; there were no words, but she could see the desperation in their eyes.

There was nothing worse than a hunger that could not be met.

* * *

It had been a fine afternoon, and the evening promised no worse. Edward and Austin, his son, had set out over the hills the previous day to find some work. If none could be found within a day's walk, one, or both, would return. Edward had been as far as Murrisk, almost to Westport, but to no avail. There was nothing to be had.

Uggool came within view, and beyond it the sun was slowly edging towards the Atlantic horizon. A distant silver white pencil of sand marked the boundary between land and a deep blue sea. The view was stunning and could lift the heart in good times. But these were not good times. Edward was returning empty-handed. He just hoped that Austin had been luckier than him.

He tried to console himself; they would manage as they always had.

Edward had tasked his wife to check the crop while he was away. Bridget did not really need to be asked, but there was always the risk that someone might take advantage. Their neighbours were good people, but even good people might be tempted when they were hungry. And everyone but the landlord was hungry at this time.

A few more yards and he could see for himself. Standing above their potato crop, planted in terraced ridges on the hill aside the bay, he saw that it was untouched. Good. Perhaps relief would soon be at hand. Only a few weeks now.

Some more steps further up and around the hill and he would be home. He could see the smoke escaping from the chimney already. Bridget would have started supper.

'*Daidi!*'

John had seen him and tried to run towards him, collapsing after only a few steps. He had not the strength, and Edward knew it. A flush of guilt and concern ran through his mind.

'Mind the midden,' shouted Edward, rather belatedly.

It was close to the cabin, and John had fallen in it before now. Edward picked up his son and carried him towards the open doorway.

Unlike some Edward had seen, their cabin had been partly built of stone recovered from clearing the crop terraces. Its walls reached shoulder high, before scrap wood, grass, heather, and sods of turf had been used to create a roof. At least they had a roof and a chimney. Many travellers had naught but ditches to sleep in; not that many visited Uggool.

Edward entered their tiny room, lit only by the cooking fire and the diminishing strength of the day's fading sun penetrating the darkness through the open doorway, and a tiny aperture in one of the stone walls acting as a window. He placed John on the floor next to his twin daughters.

'Bridget.'

His wife, her back facing the fire, turned towards Edward, hope in her mind.

'No luck. Is Austin back?'

'No.' A momentary wave of panic and despair crossed her mind.

'That's good. Perhaps he's found something,' replied Edward.

'Perhaps.' Bridget resumed her task, stirring the pot.

'Where's Bridy?' asked Edward.

'She's been looking for berries all afternoon. I'm sure she'll be back soon,' replied Bridget.

Bridy, their daughter, had the same given name as her mother. They nicknamed her Bridy to avoid confusion.

'There are too many looking for work. More than last year. We'll have to make what we have last longer,' said Edward.

'We can't, Edward. We can't keep doing this. The children are starving. What happens if the crop fails again like last year?' she replied.

'I know it. I know it. But what can we do? Austin will bring food. And the summer is better this year,' said Edward, more out of hope than reason.

'It's every year it happens. One meal a day. It's not enough. The flax and oats are eaten. I'm frightened we will truly starve to death one of these years,' replied Bridget.

'What to do then?' said Edward.

'Leave,' replied Bridget.

'And go where? To Westport? There's nothing there,' said Edward.

'To wherever the work is that can feed us. Oh, and there's more,' replied Bridget.

'More? What do you mean?' he asked.

'McNulty was evicted yesterday,' replied Bridget.

'His family have farmed here for generations. Why?' asked Edward.

'Can't pay the rent. Landlord's put it up. And he owes the gombeen man. I think they want rid of us all you know,' said Bridget.

Edward's face changed from horror to fear.

'They said the tithe... I haven't—'

'I know it,' replied Bridget, interrupting his reply.

'Then there is no choice,' replied Edward.

'We should go after the summer crop but before the next six months' rent is due. I've thought about it. The money will be needed, and that bastard will get none of it. The McNultys were good people,' said Bridget, showing uncharacteristic anger.

'They were,' agreed Edward.

Chapter 1

LEAVING HOME

'Bridget.'

Edward whispered into her ear, accompanying it with a gentle shake.

'Bridget. It's time.'

She turned over to face him, rubbing her eyes in the pre-dawn darkness.

'I'll wake Austin,' he said.

He sat up and swung his legs to the floor, away from the wooden cot they used as a bed. Their cloth undercover had loosened during the night, allowing strands of straw to stick to his legs. He pulled them off before standing and walking towards a tiny annex to the main room. Austin slept there with John in the summer, while the twins and his daughter Bridy slept with them.

There was no need. Austin was already up. He must have heard them, thought Edward, while examining his son's form standing at the annex's entrance. He was difficult to see with only night vision as an aid.

1

'Wake John. Quietly,' instructed Edward.

Young Bridy stirred, not quite awake but aware something was going on.

'Mam.'

'Bridy. Wake Cecilia and Ann,' whispered Bridget.

Her daughter complied, whispering in like manner to her younger sisters. Cecilia and Ann groaned, reluctant to leave the meagre warmth provided by their straw bedding, a few ragged covers, the closeness of each other, and the almost dead embers of the previous night's fire.

'Girls. Remember what I told you yesterday. Be very quiet. We are away today on our adventure. Get up and pack what I told you. We will be leaving before light,' said Bridget.

'Mam, I'm hungry,' said Ann.

'We'll eat later. Do as I say,' replied Bridget.

'Mam, I need to pee,' said John, appearing behind Austin who seemed prepared to leave.

'Use the midden but be quiet,' replied Bridget.

It was not unusual to have to do a necessary, as Bridget called it, during the night.

'Anyone else?' Bridget had to ask.

'Yes, me,' replied Ann.

'And me,' added Cecilia.

2

'Wait until John's finished,' instructed Bridget.

Edward sighed. 'Quickly. It will be light soon.'

Austin and his older sister, Bridy, could understand the secrecy, but the younger ones seemed bemused by it. Edward had told them to see it as an adventure, a bit of fun.

The plan was to leave before dawn. It was decided unwise to say much to the others in the settlement, not even to Bridget's cousins. Only Patrick, Edward's brother, knew. Well, someone had to know, and he might follow them one day.

The younger children had been told just before bed on the day prior to their journey, and Bridy and Austin had been sworn to secrecy. There were less than a hundred in Uggool, and everyone knew everyone; and everyone knew everyone's business much of the time. Most would help where they could, but in harder times they had naught to give. With such a small community, gossip was always there, and there was always the risk that something might slip, risking the landlord discovering their intentions. Neither Edward nor Bridget thought that any would deliberately share their secret, but there was always someone you could not be sure of. It was a shame not to tell, but there were other considerations. Secrecy was unavoidable.

Austin had been brought in on the plan very early on. After all, he had a vital part to play. His task was to go into Westport and use the rent money to buy a hand cart for the journey. He was to hide it as close to the road as he could then return home. Dublin was at least a week's long walk – hard, and likely dangerous in places. Edward knew that the children would soon tire, and he also knew that he and Austin would have difficulty carrying their belongings and the children very far. The hand cart would be acquired in Westport and sold in Dublin, its purpose served.

'Have you got everything?' asked Bridget of her younger children.

Each nodded in unison.

There was not that much to carry, and all the younger children had to do was to wrap their spare dresses in a blanket and tie it together. All three would also have to carry a cooking utensil, and at least a spoon and a bowl as well. Austin would take their two pots, and Edward the family's only piece of furniture – a three-legged stool; the one that was used for everything. He would also take a small sack of food they had managed to accumulate – mostly potatoes, some flax seed, and oats. Bridget hoped it would be enough to see them through to England at least. As for Bridy, she would bring her spare skirt, blouse, and shawl.

Almost all their money had been sewn into the garments each member of the family was wearing. There was too much risk in using only one.

The plan had originally been to leave the previous year, but events had taken their toll. John had been unwell for months, and it had been considered unwise to leave until he had improved. Fortunately, 1839 had been a better summer than the previous year. Even with the effects of the 'Night of the Big Wind', the family had fared well. Austin had found work in nearby villages, and their savings had improved. So much so that Edward had been able to buy a pair of shoes a few months earlier – second or third hand, of course, from one of Uggool's few visitors. He was so proud of them. Not many in the Uggool's community wore shoes, nor many in Westport for that matter.

'Quickly.' He instructed everyone to move.

Edward, followed by his wife, led each member of the O'Mhaille family from their small cabin. It was still dark, but as they started to walk, a half full moon had appeared from behind a cloud; it seemed to improve visibility.

'This way,' he whispered.

Bridget put her finger to her lips, reminding the children of the need for silence.

Not many minutes later, they were away from the settlement. Another half hour or so and they would be halfway round the mountain, and likely out of sight of any early risers. Everything seemed to be going to plan.

Edward stopped and beckoned them all to turn and look back.

He almost shed a tear. The morning air was still cool, not cold and wet like winter, but invigorating; it was clean and fresh. The sun had started to rise, illuminating the landscape, and highlighting the different shades of green, grey, and blue that were the colour of Uggool, the valley, sea, and the more distant Killary Fjord. It was a beautiful sight and one that he would certainly miss.

'Take a good look at it. We may never see its like again,' said Edward.

The younger children seemed puzzled. What did he mean?

'Mam?'

It was Cecilia.

'I'll tell you about it later. We have far to walk yet. But we'll eat soon,' replied Bridget.

Five minutes was all they had. Edward wanted to get past Westport and be on the way to Castlebar before the day was done.

* * *

The cart was where Austin had left it. Undisturbed and intact, it took only minutes to load, and they were soon on their way. Relieved of their burdens, the children were happier, and began to skip on their bare feet. They could not always eat a breakfast, but Edward knew that each would need their strength for the journey, and he and Bridget had ensured that two meals a day would be available. There was even enough money to buy some bread – not in Westport where there was a chance they might be noticed, but perhaps in a village on the way. Westport was where the landlord's man lived and would have to be avoided; they would walk around it.

Edward and Austin had never been out of Murrisk. Their whole world had been lived on the lands between the Killary Fjord and Clew Bay, and most of that in Uggool. As for the other children, not one of them had even been to Westport. Their world had always been Uggool, and a walk even to Barny or Gross was unexplored territory. It was an adventure for them indeed. Beyond Castlebar, and Edward would have to ask the way to Dublin. It might appear foolish to some, but he thought most would look at their ambition kindly, as he had with other less fortunate travellers he had come across on his own forays beyond Uggool.

The first day went quite well, at least as far as Edward was concerned. They made it to Westport and on to just past Clogarnah. He had hoped they might make Castlebar, but Clogarnah was close enough. If they could keep up this pace, they might make Dublin in just over a week. But the warnings of possible delay were already there. By the end of the day, the younger ones were exhausted and had been complaining for the last hour, with John and the twins having to ride the cart on top of their luggage. Even with Austin sharing the task, it had become too much. They had to stop.

Austin was sent on ahead to find a place to rest, with Edward suggesting the tip of the Castlebar Lough; it was about the only landmark he knew in these parts other than Castlebar itself. He had slept near there once before on his only visit to the town, on an errand for his own long dead father. Within an hour, Austin returned. He had found a sheltered place amongst some trees, some distance from other travellers who had apparently already settled for the evening. It would be their first night away from home, sleeping under the stars and reassuringly familiar moonlight. They slept that night with the sound of the gentle lapping of lough water against the shoreline, whipped up by a light breeze. Its action acted as a natural sedative – a vague reminder of the sea shore not far from Uggool.

* * *

Austin woke first.

The cart had been emptied of its load and used as a shelter in case the weather should turn overnight. Spare blankets, luggage, and whatever brushwood they could find had helped fill the gaps around the makeshift refuge. But it was not enough. The gentle breeze of the previous night had transmuted into something much stronger, and with it some rain. The younger children had slept in a line underneath the base of the cart and in between its wheels, fully covered. Edward, the two Bridgets, and Austin, slept underneath its handles, a blanket being laid across, lengthened and supported at either side with some additional long wooden stakes. A blanket was meagre protection, but it was the best they could do. Austin had been the most exposed. Stretched out at the opposite end to his father, the two women in between, he lay with his head against some flapping cloth; it was the side most exposed to the direction of the wind. A sudden gust had lifted it out of what they had thought was a secure hold, exposing him to an unwelcome damp blast. The weather had indeed changed overnight, and their precautions had been wise. But they were not enough.

'Ugggh,' grunted Austin.

He turned away from the weather, disturbing his sister who was lying by his side.

'Ouch,' groaned Bridy. Austin had caught her arm.

Within seconds they were all awake.

'It's raining. Wind as well. Looks like a shower,' said Austin.

'Rain or no, we have to be on our way. We can't stay here. Is the fire still in? Ann, check,' instructed Edward.

A fire had been lit the previous evening at what was now near the feet of the adults.

'It's still warm. An ember. It should light,' replied Ann, after placing her hand above the ashes.

'We'll have the herring for breakfast. It hasn't been salted, and it won't keep. Austin, use the dry twigs we brought with us and get it going again. And see if you can find some wood that is still dry,' instructed Bridget.

This would be the pattern of their journey, thought Edward, as he stood up and inspected the sky and landscape. Austin had been right. The clouds were not a threatening deep grey colour but more like an April day. With luck it would be a summer shower. Perhaps in an hour they might see the sun breaking through, just in time for the day's travel to begin.

'I'll need to ask someone the way to Dublin. I'll be back soon. Don't eat it all!' said Edward.

Beyond Castlebar was a mystery. He just hoped nobody would try to fool him and send them the wrong way. Asking more than one would be the answer; that is, if he could find anyone.

A half hour or so later, Edward had a direction at least. The only traveller he had come across had never been to Dublin and could only provide a broad direction. It would have to be enough for now. Returning to their resting place, he found the herrings still cooking in a pot over what had become a healthy fire.

'I found a man. He didn't know for sure, but he said we should go on the road to Ballyhaunis, and ask again near there. Let's hope he is right,' announced Edward to his waiting family. In truth, they were more interested in breakfast than what he had to say, the smell of the frying herrings teasing their senses with anticipation.

With breakfast eaten and the cart packed, they were soon back on their way.

* * *

Ballyhaunis proved to be a little too far. After a hard but uneventful day's walking, they stopped a little short of the town in a place a local seemed to call Bacon. Edward had never heard of it, but the area had a useful lough, just like the previous night.

9

GED MELIA

'Mam. Look. Where are the walls?' asked John, pointing at what looked like three shelters.

'They're cabins, John. Just like ours was,' replied Edward.

'But there's no stone. The walls are like our roof,' said Cecilia.

'That's true. They're built like that around here. We had the stone from the hills. We'll leave them be and stay over this side tonight,' replied Edward, a little wary of the dwellings.

The cabins John had seen were built completely of turf, sods, and bits of wood. Nothing more than pieces of raised earth, with holes at the top of their windowless cabins serving as chimneys. Only one smoked – the only visible sign of habitation.

As dusk fell, the light of their fire must have attracted some attention. A child, not much older than John appeared.

'Sir, can I have some food?'

Edward was taken aback. He had never been addressed like that before.

'Be off with you. We have none to spare. Ask your mam,' said Austin.

'Leave the poor mite be, Austin. I'm sure we can give him something,' interjected Bridget.

'But, Ma. There's barely enough for us. What if they all want some?' replied Austin.

'We can't feed everyone. But we can feed this one. It's what we'd do in Uggool,' said Bridget.

Edward remained silent. For the first time in his life, he felt better off than someone else. It was an uncomfortable feeling even thinking about turning a child away. How could he face his god? He examined the child more closely. Judging by his cadaverous form, it was clear the child had not eaten for some time, perhaps not even for days. He looked like he would be better off in a workhouse than roaming the countryside begging.

'Where's your mam?' He finally decided to ask.

The boy pointed in the direction of the turf cabins at the other side of the water.

'Has she not fed you today?' asked Edward.

'She's sick. No food. Da's gone looking for work,' replied the boy.

A wave of guilt rippled through his thoughts, but what could they do? They could feed the boy, yes, but what about the mother? And what about the other cabins? Did they hold starving occupants as well?

'Alright, Bridget. Share our food with the boy. But then you need to be off back to your mam. Is that clear?' said Edward.

The boy nodded, brightening up at the prospect of a meal.

With the meal over with, and the family settled for the night, Edward felt the need to address his family.

'He won't be the last. Things are worse than I thought they would be, if the boy's an example. We can't feed everyone. As Austin said, we've barely enough ourselves for the journey. There'll be times when we have to say no. And there may be times when we have to protect what we have. There will be thieves as well as beggars on the road to Dublin. I'm sorry to say it, but times are hard. This is why we are going to America.'

'America?' Cecilia chirped up.

It was the first time anyone had said anything to her.

'Yes. America. We are going to Dublin, then Liverpool, and then to America. Things will be better over there, so they say,' answered Bridget.

Drifting off to sleep amidst the occasional crackle of the cooking fire's receding flames, Cecilia, Bridy, and John wondered just what this America thing was. Too tired to ask any more questions, each resolved to return to the subject at a later time.

* * *

Passing through Ballyhaunis, Castlereagh, and Plunkett proved to be uneventful. After nearly twelve hours of hard walking, they settled down for a third night not far away from a lough on the road to Strokestown. The family had made good time again. The weather had stayed clement, and the children were already starting to become used to the long days on foot.

Crossing the Shannon was next; the bridge at Tarmonberry. If they could make that by midday, they would be close to halfway; at least, that was Edward's estimation. Not having ever travelled to Dublin, he had only the vague estimates of visitors to Uggool as a reference. Some said it would be seven or eight days, and others ten or twelve. Edward felt optimistic. It was summer, the weather was good, and the children were as well as could be expected. And the whole family was in good spirits, excited even, at the prospect of a new life.

An island in the middle of the Shannon acted as an intersection between the two bridges connecting Connaught with Roscommon. Edward and Austin could not fail to be impressed with the seven bridge arches on one side, and four on the other. It was the largest they had ever seen.

'Is there a toll?' asked Austin.

'I don't know. I can't see anyone paying. Perhaps there is no bridge-keeper,' replied Edward hopefully.

The family proceeded to cross at a leisurely pace, taking time to admire the flowing Shannon as they did. They stopped at the end of the causeway on the island, Austin and the younger ones on one side, and Edward, Bridget, and Ann on the other. There was little to see on the island, but it just seemed like a good place to stop. As Edward and Bridget started to cross to join the children standing on the northern side, a horseman suddenly appeared.

'Out of my way!' called an approaching voice with an unmistakably English accent.

Bridget quickened her pace to join her children, but Edward inexplicably froze, staring at the rapidly advancing horse and well-dressed rider. Austin's placement of the hand cart had reduced the width of the passageway, and Edward's position, although a few yards away from the cart, was in the way.

'Out of my way or you'll taste the whip, Irish scum. And move your cart!' the man shouted.

But there was nowhere for the cart to go, nor was there the time to move it. Edward blinked, recovered his senses, and began to move. But it was not quick enough for the rider. Increasing his speed, he raised his horse whip, his intent clear.

'I'm sorry, sir!' shouted Edward.

But it was too late. His few seconds hesitation had a cost. The rider whacked Edward on the side of his head as he passed the group, knocking him to one side.

'Edward!' shrieked Bridget. 'Are you alright?'

'I am too. There was no harm done. It was my fault; I should not have blocked the way,' replied Edward.

A red line started to appear on Edward's cheek, marking the place where the end of the whip had come into contact with his skin.

'You could have lost an eye. There was no need for that,' said Bridget.

'Who are we to say? What can we do? It's a master's world,' replied Edward.

'It shouldn't be like that. It shouldn't be like that at all,' said Bridget.

'I'm alright. We should be on our way,' said Edward, now more composed. 'And let that be a lesson to you all. Keep away from the masters and all will be well,'

Austin took the cart and began to move it. But there was silence for a time. The children had seen their father horse-whipped, treated no better than an animal. It had indeed been a lesson that none would forget, but perhaps not for the reasons Edward had given.

* * *

'Well then. You could take the road East to Longford, Edgworthtown, and Mullingar, then on to Killegad, Killcock, and to Dublin. I would say three or four days. Or you could take the towpath on the canal.'

At last. Edward had managed to speak to someone who took the road to Dublin on a regular basis. The names and places were all unfamiliar, but it felt reassuring to have a route.

'Which is the best?' asked Edward.

'I use both. I can't see the difference, if you ask me. You would have been better going to the harbour after Tarmonbarry rather than walking to Longford, but you can still find the canal from here. They call it the Royal Canal, and it goes all the way to Dublin. It would save you asking the way if you just follow the water,' replied the traveller.

'Thank you, sir,' said Edward.

'I'm not a sir. Good luck with you. Are you going anywhere after Dublin?' enquired the traveller.

'To America,' interjected John, pleased to show his knowledge.

'Ahhh. You won't be the first. There's many going now,' said the traveller.

'I'll thank you for your kindness,' replied Edward.

'Not at all. Good day to you. Oh, and just follow that road over there if you want the canal,' said the traveller.

Edward surveyed the potential route pointed out by the traveller before announcing his decision.

'We'll go by the canal.'

By the early evening, they had reached the canal near a village the locals called Barry. A day later it was Mullingar, where they spent a fifth night under the stars. At Enfield they were told it was only two days to Dublin, but to beware of the thieves who preyed on travellers, rich and poor.

A seventh night was spent close to Leixlip.

'I think we'll be in Dublin before the day is out tomorrow,' said Edward.

The children were already asleep, tired from the day's, and the week's, travelling.

'Will we need to find lodgings?' replied Austin.

'I think we will. We'll have to see when the boat goes to England. It might be a few days or a week. I dunno. We have enough money for a few days. And we can sell the cart,' replied Edward, now more confident in his estimations.

Austin did not reply, sleep already getting the better of him.

* * *

The Royal Canal towpath was narrow on both sides, so the hand cart they had used was too wide for anyone else to pass. Stoppages were therefore quite a regular event, especially for the horses pulling the flyboats and other trading vessels that frequented the waterway.

'There's another,' said Ann, who was walking ahead of Austin and blocking his view.

'Not again. It's not more than a few minutes since the last one,' replied Austin.

'Don't be too long. They're coming quickly. Children, out of the way,' interjected Bridget.

'It's that passenger boat again,' said Austin, now scrambling to increase the speed of the loaded cart.

'I'll get the other handle, Austin. We'll have to run with it. Bridget, Ann, grab the younger ones and run ahead,' instructed Edward.

There was a long stone wall to their right, and they were already too far ahead to turn the cart and return to a clearing they had recently passed. They had no choice but to rush towards the two rapidly approaching horses, one of which was being ridden by another canal man.

Fear suddenly spread across both men's faces as the enormity of the problem they faced sunk in.

'It's that fast boat, the one between Dublin and Mullingar. We saw it yesterday going both ways. It's even quicker today. Twice the pace of a walking man,' shouted Edward.

'I can see it,' replied Austin.

'Faster, Austin,' said Edward.

'Move! Move!' Move!' cried the boat steerer in the distance. He was remonstrating with his arms and could see what was happening; he also knew that he would not have the time to stop, even if he wanted to. In fact, neither of the two canal company men seemed in a mood to stop, or even to slow down.

'We'll be in the water, cart, belongings, and all. They're not going to stop,' said Edward, now in fear or being drowned and crushed, as well as losing the cart.

'Made it,' shouted Bridget, only yards ahead.

Splash!

A poorly secured cooking pot had flown off the cart as it encountered a small ridge on the towpath. Meanwhile, the two approaching horses relentlessly marched ever closer, their sweating skins and flared nostrils signalling both exertion and danger.

'Faster!' Edward shouted. The instruction was unnecessary. Both could clearly see the details of the draft horses – a black bay and a liver chestnut – and they seemed to be accelerating, not slowing. To make matters worse, as if they could be, they were being scowled at by most of the two dozen or so passengers, who were by now also participants in the spectacle.

'We can do it,' shouted Austin, desperately trying to suppress panic.

Fifty yards, forty yards. And then the two tethered draft horses could not have been more than thirty yards ahead, the gap shrinking by the second.

'Tip the cart when I say,' shouted Edward.

'Now!'

Austin and Edward tipped the cart over and leapt, one on one side, and one on the other, just as the horses sped past. They had perhaps no more than ten yards to spare and less in seconds.

'Fools!' shouted the boatman.

The boat's occupants laughed as it raced past the two sweat-soaked men, now lying on their backs amongst grasses, weeds, and the luggage littering the area, their faces flushed red by the experience. Austin and Edward stared back at them, helpless in the knowledge that there was nothing they could do. A minute or two after the danger had passed, Edward suddenly started to laugh, soon followed by Austin. It was a nervous laugh but no less welcome, a relief from stress induced by what might have been a disaster or even a tragedy. The women in the party looked on, amused and smiling, but not quite ready to join in. It was a good five minutes before Edward declared an end to the incident, and a return to their task.

'It's over. Let's be on our way.'

Austin lifted himself off the ground and pulled the cart back to its loading position.

'The right wheel's loose. I'll need to tighten it before we can go anywhere,' replied Austin.

'Can you repair it?' asked Edward.

'It's not broken, just loose. I'll use a stone to knock it back,' replied Austin.

'We'll need the money for it in Dublin, Austin,' said Edward.

'I know it. It will be good. Fear not,' replied Austin.

'We can carry something if we need to. You said Dublin's not far,' added Bridget.

'It will be fine, Ma. Just give me a bit of time,' replied Austin.

The fixing took longer than expected and defeated Edward's ambition to be in Dublin by nightfall. When they finally got moving, there was not enough time to get into Dublin and find some lodgings, so Edward made a decision to stop near the small village of Blanchardstown.

'For sure, this will be our last night without a roof over our heads,' he announced as they settled down for the night.

'Tomorrow we will be in Dublin, and soon on a boat to Liverpool, and then America.'

'America?' John enquired. He still had not asked what it was.

'Tomorrow, John. Get some sleep,' said Bridget.

Like the rest of them, he needed little persuasion.

* * *

'Make way! Make way!

They had left the towpath and were making their way down the new road towards Dublin. A rapidly moving jaunting car had appeared behind, its driver ferrying two well-dressed passengers, a man and a woman, to what they obviously considered an important appointment. It was not the first time the family had been in the way of their betters.

Edward swivelled his head and looked back. It was his turn to push the cart. They were still some distance away, so there was little danger of a collision. Unlike the incident by the canal, all he had to do was to move the cart to one side and let the vehicle pass.

'Need a hand?' asked Austin.

'No. I'll be fine,' replied Edward, as he removed their cart to a space amongst the weeds and cottoneasters which lined the road.

The jaunting car sped past, its driver and passengers ignoring Edward and the children, all of whom were becoming increasingly curious about Dublin.

'How long before we get there, Mam?' asked John.

'It won't be long now; half a day's walk, so I was told last night,' replied Edward.

The road became busier as they neared. All manner of life was there to be seen – rich, poor, and wretched. At the Observatory Gate there were beggars spaced every few yards, all hoping to catch a coin or something else of value from the wealthier types entering Phoenix Park, perhaps to view the exhibits at the recently opened zoo.

'Is this the road to Dublin?' Edward asked of an old woman, dressed in what even Bridget would have called dirty rags.

She looked at Edward, her expression clearly searching for the prospect of some reward.

'It is so. Or you could take Black Horse Lane, that way,' she replied, pointing in its direction.

'Have we some bread to spare, Bridget?' asked Edward.

'A little,' replied Bridget, while delving into a pouch containing food. She pulled a couple of bites worth off and handed it to the woman.

'God bless you all,' announced the old woman.

'We'll take this Black Horse Lane,' said Edward, turning towards it. The rest of the family followed as he pushed the cart through Observatory Gate and by the park.

'Watch for the beasts that way,' shouted the old woman as they continued.

'Beasts?' asked Cecilia.

'I dunno. Murphy once told me they had strange beasts in Dublin City. Perhaps that's what she means,' replied Edward.

With the exception of a few strange noises emanating from the zoo area, there was little to see. If they did have strange beasts, then it wasn't for the likes of the O'Mhailles' pleasure.

'What's that?' asked John. Dublin was already proving to be a place of wonder.

John and the rest of the family had stopped to examine a partially constructed column. Edward shrugged. It was baffling to him, as it seemed to serve no purpose.

'We'll need to move on if we are to get there before the afternoon is over,' said Edward.

Less than a half hour or so later, the river was in sight.

'That'll be the Liffey. We're here, in Dublin,' announced Edward.

To the former residents of Uggool, Dublin appeared a vast metropolis, far bigger and more intimidating than Westport or any of the small towns and settlements they had seen on the way. The Royal Barracks, a stone edifice of English military might, towered above them as they passed. Its mere presence exuded the power and control it had over Edward and Austin's fellow Irishmen. There was no way they could fight the British Army, even if they wanted to.

'We should find some lodgings for the night before we do any more. And we need to sell the cart. No need of it now,' said Edward.

'Stay close to me,' said Bridget, addressing the younger ones. 'There are many people here. I don't want to lose you.'

She grabbed John with one hand and Cecilia with the other, who was already holding Ann's hand.

It did not take long to find somewhere. A few questions to fellow travellers and they were directed to the Brunswick Street area, close to the lunatic asylum and workhouse – 'House of Industry', they seemed to call it. Flashing coin in front of a potential landlord soon did the trick; there was always space for someone with a bit of money.

'Tonight, we stay here. Bridy, help your mam unload the cart. Austin, see if you can sell it today, or you'll have to sleep with it tonight. We can't have it stolen; we need the money from it. And I'll go and find the docks,' said Edward.

Instructions given, Edward left the rest of his family to go and explore Dublin. He needed to find the docks, yes, but he also had to satisfy his curiosity about the place. Dublin was a wonder indeed, but it was also just a staging post. Or was it? Might there be work here as well?

* * *

'Follow Church Street down to the Liffey, then follow the river and the quays to the sea.' His impromptu guide pointed in one direction, and was then instantly on his way, clearly in no mood for a longer conversation.

They were simple instructions, but Dublin was an overwhelming mass of people and unfamiliar places. Edward had to admit to himself that he was a little afraid of getting lost, but he had no choice but to do it. They had enough money for lodgings in Dublin for a few days, perhaps a week. Anything more and they would be spending what had been reserved for Liverpool and New York. Perhaps if he could find a bit of work in Dublin, they could manage a little longer, but to do that he had to explore the city.

The flow of people and traffic seemed focused on the Liffey and its various quays. His walk down Chapel Street was relatively short, and he soon found himself standing by Arran's and Kings Inn Quays. In his anxiety to get into Dublin, he had not really noticed the river. It was dirty, black even, nothing like the sparklingly clear colours of the Killary on a fine summer's day. Already he could sense that the city's main artery had paid a price for its success as a centre of commerce. The detritus and waste of its tens of thousands of inhabitants constantly poured in, defeating even the supposed cleansing effect of the ebb and flow of sea tides.

Turning away from the Liffey, the 'Four Courts' dominated the river front. Six Corinthian columns stood on a platform, ascended by a number of steps. Each helped support a triangular pediment, the apex of which in turn supported a statue of Moses, with two others – 'Justice' and 'Mercy' – at either end. Behind the portico sat a large dome, with two wings of complementary character on either side. But the architectural details of the structure were lost on Edward; he was simply dumbstruck by its scale and grandeur. Nothing in his life so far had prepared him for anything like this.

'Move on.'

An official had spotted Edward staring at the court's towering form, and had grown suspicious. It was starting to become a habit. Wherever he or the family went, they seemed to be in the way of something or someone.

Capel Street's commerce caught Edward's eye, an amalgamate of characters plying their various offers and trades to an eclectic mix of Dublin's best, and its worst; a tatterdemalion mass of the unwashed and the desperate. Each of this latter company apparently hoping to acquire the scraps left over from the city's naked mercantilism. The prospect of obtaining some work faded before him; he walked on. If Capel Street had been a marvel, Sackville Street was a spectacle indeed. Its broad thoroughfare, perhaps as much as one hundred feet wide, had been designed to impress. It was lined on either side by rows of five-storey terraced buildings, their ground floors acting as hosts to a myriad of retail ventures, all apparently catering for Dublin's wealthy.

A statue of Nelson stood atop a tall pillar in the centre of the avenue, somewhat overshadowing what would have been the street's most imposing construction – the General Post Office. This was the world of the aristocracy. There was nothing here for Edward amongst uniformed men on horseback, expensive carriages, and other gentlemen, women, and children, each dressed in fabrics and colours he had never seen before. Dogs of various kinds patrolled behind these small groups of the well-to-do. But these were not the scavengers of the streets of Westport, or those of the city's wretched suburbs. They were well fed and doted upon by their masters and mistresses, quite obviously better treated than Edward or the thousands he had already seen searching for the gift of a day's nourishment.

The more Edward saw, the less he liked. Dublin surely was a busy and thriving centre for trade and commerce. Its buildings were no doubt a testament to its success, and perhaps a match to any in Europe and the Empire, but it was also a disappointment. It was a city of contrasts. The rich, likely the English, were thriving and enjoying the fruits of the city's success. But little seemed to have rippled down to its poor. Even in the short time he had been in Dublin, he had already seen the thousands of destitute families, many evicted from their cabins or, like him, voluntarily escaping from a life of near serfdom to find something better. Likely every single one of them had migrated to Dublin in the hope of securing an improved life here, or at least as a step towards hope elsewhere. But the city seemed to offer very little. There were too many like him and Austin looking for a steady income, and it was difficult to see where that might be had. Dublin, for all its finery, its wealth and splendour, could not even feed its current populace. What it did offer he could have just as easily obtained in Westport – a life on the streets searching for scraps to feed himself and his family.

He turned away from Sackville Street and took in the view from Carlisle Bridge, before journeying towards the Customs House and the Old Dock. The saltiness of the sea air reminded him of home, Uggool. It was a fond memory, and although it had only been a couple of weeks, it seemed like a lifetime already. But this was not the time for despondency. He reminded himself that Dublin was simply a step on a long journey to a new world, America. It was a time for hope not despair.

Checking himself, he surveyed the area and began to ask who he thought might be those in the know.

'Where can I get passage to America?' he asked of a passing stranger.

'It'll be better from Kingstown Port,' came the reply.

'Kingstown?' queried Edward.

'Aye. Ten miles down the coast. That way,' replied the stranger, pointing in a southerly direction.

'You could get the train; you'll soon be there,' he added helpfully.

'Thank you kindly,' replied Edward.

His heart sank as he absorbed the significance of the interlocution. There was no money for fancy modes of transport like the railway. They would have to walk; it would be another day on foot. He just hoped Austin had not managed to sell the cart, or they would have to carry everything on their backs another ten miles or so. His mission partly accomplished, Edward decided to return to their temporary lodgings and share what he had discovered.

* * *

Alas, Austin had been successful in his quest to sell the handcart and had returned with several pounds. Prices in Dublin for this sort of thing were much better than in Mayo, and he seemed pleased with himself.

'It's only ten miles or so down the coast road. We'll get there before the light goes tomorrow,' said Edward to Bridget and Austin.

'What about our belongings?' asked Austin.

It was an obvious question with an obvious answer.

'We'll have to carry them. Cart's gone. There's nothing we can do. We can't spend money on a train without knowing the cost of passage to America,' replied Edward.

'Well. At least we only paid for one night's lodgings, and we now know where to go,' said Bridget.

'We do so,' replied Edward.

There was little need to ask for much in the way of directions the following morning. Edward now had knowledge of the Liffey bridges and knew the direction. And they were not alone. There were dozens of his fellow countrymen all apparently heading in the same direction, and most using the same means of transport, their feet. All they had to do was to follow the flowing mass of itinerants using the coast road.

For much of their journey they were accompanied by the Dublin to Kingstown train. The railway had only recently been opened, but had already become popular with those that could afford it. Here and there the railway ran parallel to the road, and when a steam train passed, the family were treated to the amused stares and gawping of the railway travelling class. But there was no point in being envious. The world was as it was, and they had to live with it. So long as they stayed healthy, all would be well. That had always been Edward's philosophy.

Edward had underestimated their ability to walk while carrying luggage, and had also slightly underestimated the port's distance. Nonetheless, despite a couple of rest stops, they made it to Kingstown Port before the end of the afternoon.

'They must both be a mile long,' said Austin.

The family had caught their first sight of Dunleary Harbour. Like everything they had seen in Dublin, it was an impressive sight. There were two piers, both reaching far out into the sea where they almost joined. Due to their relative start positions on the coastline, the West Pier looked to be a little longer than its opposite, the East Pier.

'Look at all them ships,' shouted John, excited by what he was seeing.

'I've never seen the like,' said Bridget, stating the obvious, though they all thought the same.

The harbour was teeming with seafaring ships and smaller boats, and even larger vessels were visible further out to sea. Some were already in full sail, heading off to England or America, while others were bearing in their direction, likely readying themselves for port.

'We'll be on one of them, John. Maybe tomorrow. We'll have to see,' replied Edward.

Ann and Cecilia put down what they were carrying, and each made a grab for one of their mother's hands. Bridget had to place her own baggage down, after which she got hold of both her daughters and hugged them.

'Yes. As your father says, we'll be off to a new country soon. It's exciting, isn't it?'

'Yes, Mam,' both replied in unison, as was their habit.

'What next?' Austin asked of his father.

'They say we have to find a booking agent for tickets. There were some in Dublin, but there must be more here. We'll try that new building over there,' replied Edward.

Edward was pointing at the Harbour Master's House. It seemed to be a focal point for activity around the harbour. Amongst the crowds of people more like them, were other well-dressed types entering and exiting the building on a regular basis.

'Book here for America!'

'Book for Liverpool!'

'Book for London town!'

As they approached the building, the cries of the booking agents became obvious. Some called for America, and others for ports in England and Scotland. Two or three of the loudest invited business for Liverpool.

'Book here for Liverpool and America. Passage to America is cheaper if you go from Liverpool!'

That caught Edward and Austin's attention. In the short time they had been here, they had already learned that booking passage would not be as simple as handing the money over and buying a ticket. Some ships seemed to be bound directly for America, but many seemed to stop in Liverpool where they took on additional supplies, passengers, and sometimes goods destined for the new world. What were they to do? They would have to ask.

Edward led his party to the agent who happened to be shouting that it would be less costly to go to Liverpool than to catch a ship from Kingstown to America.

'How much to America?' His question to the booking agent was direct and to the point.

'Well then. They'll charge you more to go from here than for you to catch a boat to Liverpool and book passage to America from there. You see, there are more ships leaving from Liverpool to America than there are from here to America. Them people over there know it, but they won't tell you. I'll take your money for Liverpool only, and you can catch any ship you like for New York. They have ships leaving for New York every day from there, you know,' said the agent, with the full knowledge that there were no emigrant ships leaving directly from Kingstown to New York. But his prospective customers did not need to know that particular fact.

'But how do I know that?' asked Edward, wary of being cheated.

'Well, you can ask anyone. They'll all tell you the same,' replied the agent.

Edward looked around. There were hundreds of people, but who should he ask? He turned back to face the agent.

'I will. We'll be back if what you say is true,' said Edward.

'Well, don't be long. You can see there are many here wanting tickets to the good life. Passage soon gets filled. We have a ship going at high tide tomorrow, and I'll be here till seven tonight,' replied the agent.

'Before I go, what will be the price of passage to Liverpool?' asked Edward.

'I'll tell you what they want from you to America first,' started the agent, while raising an accusing finger at his competitors.

'They want four pounds for each adult, and two pounds and ten shillings for each child under fourteen. It's robbery, I tell thee. You'll get there for much less from Liverpool. All you have to do is pay me for tickets for Liverpool...'

Sensing custom, he continued with a question. 'Do you have luggage? How many of you?'

'Just what we are carrying. Four fully grown and three children,' replied Edward.

'Seven then. I'll tell you what I'll do. It's getting late, so I'll give you a price to Liverpool for all of you. Two pounds. I can't say fairer than that, can I? You'll not regret it,' said the agent, now hungry for Edward's money.

'Let me have a think,' replied Edward, obviously unsure of whether he had a bargain or was being cheated.

'Don't be long then. I'll be selling to others,' said the agent.

Edward nodded in response and led his family away.

'What do you think, Austin? We could try asking, but why would they know? Most look to be the same as us.'

'I dunno. It's a lot of money,' replied Austin.

'It's getting late, Edward. The children are tired, and we have to find somewhere to sleep,' interjected Bridget.

'I think we'll be under the stars tonight, Mam. I can't see a lot of lodgings, and what there is will probably be full already,' said Bridy.

Edward's wife looked towards the buildings near the harbour. There were some, but it was nothing like Dublin itself.

Her daughter was probably right. They would likely have to sleep by the sea that night.

'Wait for me over there with Austin. I'll get the tickets from him,' said Edward. He had made a decision. On this occasion, he had decided to trust what he was being told.

'You're back then,' said the agent.

'I am. Two pounds you say for seven tickets,' said Edward.

'I did. It will leave at half past two tomorrow, at high tide. The ship's called *Queen Victoria*. It's a fine ship, a fast paddle steamer. You'll need to board before that. Say, half past twelve, or you'll miss it,' replied the agent, while taking Edward's money and writing out a passage ticket for each person.

Edward took the seven pieces of paper and pocketed them. There was no turning back now.

* * *

It had not been the best of nights.

They had slept some way from the village, next to the sea, with the continuous and hypnotic lapping of waves falling on the area's rocky coastline acting as soundscape. The evening had passed without interruption, as the family sat beside a hastily constructed open fire and ate the last of the food they had brought with them. Without even the cover of the cart, each was exposed to what nature could throw at them. The stillness of the previous evening changed in the early morning. The wind had picked up and brought with it some less amenable weather. Perhaps about four, a sudden blast of warm summer rain accompanied by the slowly brightening sky woke all except John who, still deep in sleep, seemed oblivious to it. The rain was no more than a light summer shower and lasted no more than ten minutes, but it was enough to raise most of the family from slumber.

Austin was the first to stand.

'It's getting light,' he said, stretching in an attempt to relieve the discomforts of a night sleeping in the open. They were now used to it, but it was no less uncomfortable.

'Check the fire. It's too early yet to go,' responded Edward, who was still sitting.

'I'm hungry,' said Cecilia.

'So am I,' added Ann.

'We'll see if we can find something later. I have none to give you,' replied Bridget.

'I'm hungry as well, Mam,' said John, now also suddenly awake and alert to the possibility of eating.

'Do you think you could catch anything?' asked Edward of Austin, as he surveyed the sea.

'I've a line. We could try. What else are we to do?' he replied.

'You never know. Maybe there are some crabs or shellfish to be had,' added his sister. 'I'll go look,' said the younger Bridget.

'I'll find some more wood,' said Edward.

'I want to pee,' announced John.

'Go with your da and do it. Ann, Cecilia, and I will try and get the fire going with what we have,' said Bridget.

Each assigned a task, the morning began.

It took what felt like a couple of hours, but both Austin and his sister had been successful in their undertakings to find something to eat. It was not much when divided between seven, but it was enough to take the edge off the morning hunger. By seven or eight, they were ready to leave, though it was still too early.

'What now?' said Bridget.

'We could walk down there for a bit,' suggested Austin, pointing at a Martello tower about a half mile away.

'No. We should keep away from the English soldiers,' replied Edward.

'I don't want to carry anything longer than I need to,' added Bridget.

After some further discussion, they agreed that it would be best if they just stayed where they were until the sun was a little higher in the sky. Out of sight of a clock, and people to ask, it was not long before Edward's anxiety got the better of him. Without the benefit of a timepiece, he estimated eleven o'clock by looking at the height of the sun in the sky. The passing of time had never been a great concern back in Uggool, the seasons meaning more to him, but here it had suddenly become important. They left at what he thought was eleven, only to find it was eleven when the family arrived at the West Pier. Although surprised, he was more relieved than concerned, and continued to lead his party towards a large wooden ship docked about halfway down the jetty.

'There it is. The *Queen Victoria*,' announced Edward, pointing at a nearby vessel.

'There are people getting on already,' said Austin.

'We were right to leave early,' replied Edward, clearly pleased with his decision.

'It's called a paddle steamer,' he added, cementing his status within the family as someone with knowledge.

'It's a big boat,' said John, marvelling at its size relative to several other smaller vessels docked on either side.

The ship was of a strange composition to eyes that had only seen sailboats. Amidst two furled sail-carrying masts stood a single large iron funnel, about half in height of the foremast and mizzenmast. On either side of the deck, and in alignment with the funnel, two large wheel arches had been attached to the ship's wooden sides. Within these covers hung huge wheels with paddles, which served to propel the vessel when in motion. It was a marvel of the age, thought Edward. And they were about to sail on it.

The family joined the queue to board, and soon found themselves standing on its deck along with at least fifty others by the time their embarkation process had completed. The advice provided by the booking agent had been good. It had made a lot of sense to be early. At best, the ship might carry a hundred passengers, and it was at least half that when they sat down a good two-and-a-half hours before they were due to leave. Ten minutes or so after they had embarked and had been subject to a series of inspections and questions, they were instructed to go down below.

It was just as well. Austin was the last to climb down the stairs. He achieved three steps, and was still waist above deck, when a distraction above caught his attention. There was a sudden commotion. From his vantage point, and from what he could tell, there was a problem with a man's ticket. A Dublin man, clear from his accent and somewhat the worse for drink, had been refused access by an appointed deckhand.

'This ticket is for last week. You missed it. You'll have to buy another. You can't come on here,' advised the deckhand.

'I will and you, you, you won't stop me,' replied his slurring adversary.

Stepping in front to block access, the deckhand repeated his assertion.

'Not today. Leave now, or I'll have to throw you off.'

For the half-drunk would-be traveller this proved too much. On another day, and with less drink inside him, perhaps his reaction would have been different. But not today. He lashed out at the deckhand with a poorly aimed fist. Anticipating a problem, and with the advantage of a clear head, the deckhand swerved to his left, thus avoiding contact. The momentum of the flying fist, combined with a slight movement in the ship, caused the prospective passenger to lose his balance. He fell flat onto the deck, at which point the captain's mate and another deckhand rushed over to assist. As the man attempted to recover, the other deckhand thumped him in the face while his two companions held him down. Dazed and subdued, it was down to the captain to issue a final instruction.

'Get him off my ship. If he argues, throw him in the harbour.'

The mate and the two deckhands grabbed the man, lifted him, and then carried him back to the jetty, some yards away from a half dozen remaining passengers who had been patiently waiting to board. It took a minute or two for the man to return to his senses. Although defeated in his immediate quest, he had still not finished.

'I'll have you! I'll, I'll have the lot of yee, I will,' he shouted, waving and pointing his arms.

Not that the crew took any notice. Normal service resumed the instant the situation had been dealt with. He had become irrelevant. To be ignored; barely worthy of even an eye.

The whole incident had begun and ended in less than five minutes. Austin, along with others who were still on deck, had watched what had transpired with a mix of interest and fear. All normal deck activity had stopped for a time. However, what had struck Austin was the captain's authority. When he spoke, everyone listened. There was no questioning his word; it was to be followed by all, and that meant crew and passengers.

He momentarily caught the captain's eye as the latter noticed that Austin had paused his descent. It was not a comfortable few seconds. You never wanted to catch a master's eye lest he take a dislike to you, least of all someone who had real power. The captain was about to say something. Austin intuitively knew it as he inspected the skipper's leathery, wind worn, ruddy face. As he raised an arm and pointed a finger, his cap seemed to slightly raise itself, as if it was too small for his head. The captain's eyebrows raised, he pointed at Austin.

'You there. Get down below!' he boomed, from a distance of at least twenty feet away.

'Yes, sir,' replied Austin, quickly moving below even before he answered.

Safely down below, Austin joined his father, mother, and siblings, all of whom were anxious to hear about what had transpired. The story told, all they could now do was to wait, sitting amongst their luggage on the hard wooden benches that would be their resting place for the journey.

Finally, it was time to leave. The captain's orders to cast off could still be heard, even amidst the sound of the steam engine, which had been fired up earlier in time for departure. When the vessel was deemed far enough away from the jetty, the engine started, which jerked the ship forward, and then the paddle wheels began to turn. As the ship moved, an elderly woman, a fellow passenger, fell to the floor and began to pray. It was not immediately clear why she was praying or whose help she was invoking, but then it became obvious. She was praying for safe passage, clearly worried that the ship might be lost at sea.

It had not occurred to any of them that the ship might sink. Bridget looked at Edward and then her children, a mild wariness of strange surroundings now transmuted into tangible fear. Edward sensed the atmosphere.

'It will be fine. Ships leave for Liverpool every day. There's nothing to fear.'

The truth was he knew no more than his wife. He had no knowledge, only hope, and the help of the Lord, his God. But this was something new, and for the first time he wondered whether a journey to America was such a good idea after all.

A diversion was called for.

'We might be in England tomorrow. Let's pray for some good luck, and for the people we have had to leave behind.'

39

All the adults put their hands together, and in true Catholic tradition started to pray out loud to the Blessed Mary. No mention of ships, or the sea, but of the luck they were bound to have in their new life overseas. As the vessel departed the harbour, the same feelings returned as the day they left Uggool. Excitement and optimism tinged with melancholy, and a mild yearning for an irretrievable past. Huddled around the two portholes they were able to access, no-one seemed to have the words. It was left to Bridget to speak, though none would force her. But she could not speak either. The most emotion she could manage was a single tear, which striated down the side of an unwashed cheek. Each minute took them further away, as the rhythmic sound of the splashing paddles increased the distance between them and their homeland, while also reducing the distance to their destination.

Edward could feel it; he knew it, but could not bring himself to utter it.

They would never see Ireland again.

Chapter 2

LIVERPOOL

'Bridget, look!'

Passage had been relatively short and uneventful. The Irish Sea had been clement, and the paddle steamer had made good time. Indeed, according to the crew, they were slightly ahead of their expected arrival time. For most of the journey fellow passengers had stayed huddled below deck, but once word had been received that they were to land 'within a few hours', many climbed the stairs to take in the view. Edward, Bridget and family had been among the first, and had found a good vantage point towards the bow of the ship. When Edward called out, the port was still something of a blur on a still relatively distant coastline. But what was noticeable were the sails seemingly criss-crossing their path. There were dozens of them, of all shapes and sizes. It was not a single vessel that had caught his attention but the amalgamation of nautical traffic. Kingstown Port had been busy, but it had been nothing like this.

'There's so many of them,' replied Bridget.

The children stared, wide-eyed and fascinated by the unfolding scene.

'Yes, but we won't be in Liverpool for long. It's America for us. New York,' said Edward.

By mid-afternoon the pace of the steamer had slowed as it prepared to enter port. Liverpool was no longer a speck on a distant shore. It was a complex mass of timber poles embedded in the decks of a myriad of ships, all lined up within a suite of docks built along the city's waterfront. The types of vessels they had seen from a distance now had more definition. There were iron and wooden ships, briggs, clippers, schooners, screw steamers, paddle steamers, and dozens of other smaller service craft. Some were being loaded, others unloaded; yet others being painted and maintained. Ships were leaving just as they were arriving. Each had a role to play in Liverpool's growing reputation as a global centre of trade, perhaps matched only by London, the nation's capital.

Clarence Dock had been built as the port's most northerly dock only a few years before. Named after the Duke of Clarence, the late King George, it had been created as a steamship-only dock. And for good reason. Like many ports, Liverpool had been plagued by fires, particularly within its warehouses, and it was reasoned that it was best to keep the predominantly iron vessels away from those wooden-hulled to reduce the risk. The Irish paddle steamers fell into this category, and so by association the primary disembarkation point for Irish immigrants became Clarence Dock.

The squawking gulls, banging, shouting, and carts clattering on the dockside road created an aural backdrop as the vessel negotiated a complicated manoeuvre into its designated berth area. Salty sea air mixed with the assorted smells of a city bustling with life and commerce. The tangible sense of anticipation that had emerged amongst the waiting passengers offshore, had suddenly changed to one of excitement, as the fore and aft mooring lines, or hawsers, were thrown towards the dockside employees of the steamship company. Each passenger suddenly had something to say to his or her fellow, the sum of which seemed to be, 'Well, we have arrived. Now what shall we do?'

With the ship moored, passengers began to collect their luggage and assemble in a rather disorderly line close to the gangway, which had been rapidly assembled between the ship and the dock.

'Form a straight line. And no more than three on the gangplank,' ordered the first mate.

They had arrived. Edward led his family off the ship, with Austin at the rear of their family troupe. Bridget held John, while Bridy held the hands of her two sisters. It was not easy carrying luggage and acting as ward to the younger members, but they were fortunate in that the transition from ship to shore took less than five minutes.

'Let's sit down over there and decide what to do next,' said Edward, pointing towards a windmill a few hundred yards north of the city line.

They had barely moved ten yards from the ship when the group was accosted by two strangers.

'Welcome. We can help you with that.' It was a fellow Irishman, sounded like a Dubliner to Edward. The man was pointing to the miscellaneous luggage, baggage, and clutter the family were carrying.

'We are well. We don't need your help, thank you,' replied Edward, already on his guard against the unsolicited offer.

'Have you got somewhere to stay? It's hard in Liverpool. We can always help a fellow Irishman. We know people. You know you can't be sure of people around here. They'll cheat you, you know.'

Edward had been told to be careful by another passenger on their way over, but he was not too sure of what he should be careful of.

'We do need to find somewhere, Edward,' interjected Bridget.

'Well, er, I dunno,' replied Edward. He had lost his footing. The stranger's intervention had circumvented his admittedly unclear plan. What he did know was that he needed to take the initiative, to ask questions.

'What's your name?'

'O'Brien. Paddy,' replied the stranger.

'And your friend?' questioned Edward.

'Oh, that's Murphy. We just call him Murphy,' replied Paddy.

Edward was not sure what to ask next and turned towards Bridget and Austin, as if to say 'What do you think?'

They both shrugged.

'Where are you from? You sound like you are from the West Coast,' asked Paddy.

'We are. And you?' replied Edward.

'Dublin,' replied Paddy.

'Why did you leave?' asked Edward.

'It's a world of opportunity here. Men can make their fortunes in Liverpool,' replied Paddy.

Edward nodded. 'Yes, I've heard that.'

'Look. I know some top-class lodging houses, the best in Liverpool. And not at all costly. We can take you there,' said

Paddy, now anxious to seize the initiative and make an arrangement.

'I dunno,' replied Edward, echoing his answer to Bridget.

'Ahh, you'll regret it if you don't come with us. It rains a lot in Lancashire, much more than the old country. I wouldn't want my family out in that. And there are thieves as well. You wouldn't want to get robbed, would you? Liverpool can be a violent place,' said Paddy, increasing the pressure. He had made a point of looking at Bridget rather than Edward when mentioning the risk of assault.

'Perhaps we should take Paddy's offer, Edward. What else are we to do?' said Bridget.

'Well, er...' started Edward.

'Look. There are other passengers. We'll leave you for today and ask them,' said Paddy, now starting to walk away.

'No wait,' said Bridget.

'Edward, what else are we to do?' She repeated her earlier question.

Feeling cornered, Edward relented. 'Alright. What do you have in mind?'

'There's a place near here called Vauxhall. We'll take you there. Murphy, help the ladies with their luggage,' ordered Paddy.

Murphy approached the two Bridgets, immediately relieving them of their baggage and some of their most precious belongings, including coats.

'Murphy, you go on ahead to Kitty's. We'll catch up with you,' ordered Paddy, before turning to Edward and Austin.

'He's quick, but not very strong in the head.'

Murphy ignored the clear insult and proceeded to leave, while Edward and Austin laughed at Paddy's observation. Neither saw the smirk on Murphy's face as he darted off down Waterloo Road.

'Will you be going to America?' asked Paddy.

'We are,' replied Edward.

'I'll go there myself one day. But first I'll make my fortune here,' said Paddy.

Edward looked at him, a little puzzled.

'Liverpool's a good city once you know your way around. There's plenty of work at the moment. Look, I'll tell you where we are going. This is Waterloo Road. Up there is Regent Road and down there is Bath Street.'

Paddy pointed in the direction of the city before continuing.

'It's growing fast. They say there will be more docks, more ships, and more work. Aye, fortunes will be made here, and I intend to have one of them.'

Murphy moved surprisingly quickly given his load, and soon disappeared into the maze of streets that was Liverpool. As the group lost sight of him, Bridget started to express disquiet. Some of their money had been sewn into a coat she had been carrying; she had forgotten about it in the melee of leaving the ship and meeting their new companion. It had all happened too quickly.

'Where's he gone?' she asked.

'Ah, don't worry. Murphy knows his way around Liverpool. You'll see him soon,' replied Paddy.

'But I am worried. He's got our belongings,' replied Bridget.

'We'll soon catch him. Kitty's is the next left and a few hundred yards up to Gibraltar Street. It's near the prison. Not long now,' said Paddy.

Edward quickened his pace. No member of the family could read or write, so all he had to go off were the still vague directions of their guide. He remained a little nervous, unsure of whether to trust Paddy or not. But it was too late now. A decision had been made, and all they could do was hope for the best.

'This is Denison Street. Gibraltar Street is there.' He pointed towards the other end of two opposing rows of grim looking and clearly poorly maintained and unloved housing.

'Kitty O'Reilly is the landlady. She's a good woman; very fair,' suggested Paddy, attempting to reinforce his earlier words of reassurance.

'Nearly there. Kitty's is the fifth in that row over there.' Paddy had stopped at the top of Denison Street.

'This is Great Howard Street. The pig market is over there, and the building to the left is Liverpool Gaol. You don't want to find yourself in there. Not everyone comes out. Wait outside after we cross. I'll go and find Kitty,' said Paddy.

'Where's Murphy?' asked Bridget.

'I'll get him too. He won't be far away. I can tell you that,' replied Paddy.

As instructed, they crossed the road, walked up to the fifth house and waited. Paddy knocked on the door and was invited inside by an as yet unseen occupant. With Paddy out of earshot, Bridget spoke.

'Edward, I'm sorry. Murphy has some of our money. It's in the green coat. I forgot about it. I'm sorry.'

Edward looked askance.

'Bridget.'

'I know, I know,' she replied. 'I'm so stupid.'

'Paddy seems like a good man. I'm sure it will be alright,' replied Edward.

'Yes. Of course, he is,' said Bridget, attempting to hide her mood. The last thing she wanted was to frighten the family.

Paddy emerged.

'All is well. Kitty doesn't know you, so will need to take payment in advance. You'll be here for at least a week. You know you can't just turn up at a transatlantic ship and go. You have to book in advance. I might be able to help you with that as well. Give me a week's lodging and a few shillings for my services, and I'll sort it out with Kitty.'

'Where's Kitty?' asked Edward.

'Oh, she's inside dealing with another customer. She has lots of rooms, you know. If you give me the money, I'll pay her, and then we'll get you inside. You must be tired after the long journey. Murphy has already left your belongings upstairs,' replied Edward.

Bridget suddenly felt a sense of relief. Perhaps it would work out after all.

'Edward, pay him. I want to go inside and rest. The children are tired as well.'

'But we haven't even met her. I don't know, Paddy. I think we should meet her,' said Edward to Paddy.

'Don't you trust me? Haven't I done right by you today?' replied Paddy, feigning offence.

'It's not that. It's just that it's a lot of money, a week's lodging. I don't begrudge you a shilling or two,' said Edward.

'Edward. Pay him,' said Bridget, alarmed at the possibility she might not be reunited with her coat.

Edward took some coins out his inside pocket and started counting them out. The instant he finished, Paddy took them and disappeared back inside the house.

They waited. Five minutes, then ten. After fifteen minutes, Edward became impatient. He walked up to the door and knocked. He needn't have. The door was open, and the vigour of his knocking opened it further. He pushed it wide open.

'Hello there. Is Kitty here? Paddy?' shouted Edward.

He turned round to speak to his son. 'Austin. Let's go inside and look.'

They walked in and down a dark and dingy corridor. There was nobody on the ground floor.

'Austin, take a look upstairs. I'll go out the back.'

Austin leapt up the narrow wooden staircase, taking two steps at a time. He shouted for 'Paddy' on the first and second floors. There was no answer there either. The building was completely empty. Returning to the ground floor, Austin called out for his father before meeting him at the back door.

'There's no-one here, Da.'

'I know it. We've been cheated,' replied Edward.

The enormity of their predicament abruptly hit him.

'They've taken some of our money and belongings as well. We've not enough to go to America,' said Edward.

Austin seemed more pragmatic.

'What's done is done. We'll never find them in this city. I suppose we'll have to find some work to pay our passage.'

'We will. We'll have to sort it out as a family as we always have. Let's tell them our plan, and don't let your mother feel too bad about it. She will feel responsible, but it happened to all of us. I should never have trusted that bastard Paddy. If anything, there is one silver lining to this cloud. This place looks like it's empty. Well, we did need a roof over our heads, and after sleeping under the sky for weeks, this will more than do.'

Austin chuckled. There was no point in being angry or depressed about the episode. If they were to survive, they would just have to deal with situations like this. Life was not always very fair.

* * *

'The money is running out, Edward,' said Bridget.

'I know it. I'm trying,' replied Edward.

He had no need to be told, but there was also no need to answer back. Even with the 'free' accommodation they had tripped over, the money saved on rent was nothing like a wage. And it was only a matter of time before they would be found out. There must be a landlord somewhere.

Edward and his family had been sleeping in the rooms they entered on the day of their arrival for almost two weeks. Two weeks without being disturbed or caught. Even if they were, Edward and Austin had concocted a story. They would tell the owner, landlord or landlord's man, that they had been robbed and were staying there on the chance that the thieves would return. It was half true. Whether or not they were believed was by the by; at least they had an explanation for their unofficial presence.

Both Edward and Austin had been out every day looking for work. It was not easy. Liverpool's business was being a port. Its fortunes ebbed and flowed with the shipping traffic that arrived and departed. One or two ships arriving meant work. All had to be unloaded, and that meant manual labour as a porter. It was hard labour, but even harder to actually secure a job. Appearing at the dockside in the hope of being picked by a captain's mate or his shore agent was not enough. Work on the docks was controlled by the lumpers, who took dockers on in accordance with owners' and agents' needs. The lumpers would profit, often excessively, on the difference between what they agreed with a merchant and what they agreed with the dockers. Neither Edward, nor Austin, knew this when they arrived. It would be days of fruitless questioning before they were eventually tipped off that in order to get any work they needed to know the lumpers. And to get to know the lumpers they would have to drink in one or more of the pubs that lined the Dock Road and the areas close by.

Selling the idea that drinking ale in Murphy's, The Dewdrop, or the Crow's Nest was an investment in getting work would be a difficult conversation for Edward, so he resolved to take the whole family with him on the second Sunday. They would go to morning Mass at St. Anthony's, and then straight on to The Baltic Fleet, an old pub on the Dock Road close to the site of some new docks that were being rumoured – another opportunity for more regular work. It was not one of the nearer beerhouses, but Austin and Edward had been told that it was a good place to meet the work bosses, the lumpers.

A waiter wearing what they had been told was a 'pork pie hat' – a fairly new innovation in Liverpool – came over to their table as soon as they seated.

'What will it be?' he asked.

'A half-gallon jug of fourpenny ale,' replied Edward.

The waiter nodded, slightly disappointed. Fourpenny beer was the lowest quality due to the lower quantity of sugar that was added during the fermentation process. Sixpenny ale would have meant that little bit more in his pay that evening, but that was not to be.

Glasses for each member of the family were brought and set down on the table, soon followed by an almost full half-gallon jug. With many drinking, perhaps his 'loss' might be assuaged by quantity, mused the waiter as he returned to the bar.

Edward poured each glass and passed them around. Even with the smaller portions given to the younger children, the jug was almost empty.

'Now what do we do?' asked Austin.

'Keep an eye out. We need to look for people who look like they are doing business, not just drinking,' replied Edward.

Everyone started to look around. It looked unnatural and suspicious.

'Don't make it too obvious. Austin and I will look. You just enjoy the ale,' added Edward.

A roar of laughter from a far corner interrupted the family's discussion. What looked like half a dozen men, already the worse for drink, were becoming increasingly louder. Four they could see, but two had only their backs in view.

'Austin, go and stand nearer. See if you can hear what they are talking about. It might be work,' suggested Edward.

As Austin sidled over, one of the men stood up and turned. It was Edward who recognised him first.

'McCabe! Michael McCabe!'

The man turned towards the source of the shouting, Edward. In an instant he recognised an old friend.

'Malley. Edward. How ist thee?' asked McCabe, not expecting an answer from that distance.

Austin waved, now also catching his fellow countryman's attention.

'Austin. So, you made it over here as well. Wait there. I'll come over.'

The man the family now knew as Michael McCabe, twisted round to his table, said a few words to his companions, and then came over to join Edward and Austin, who had already returned to their seats with Bridget and the rest of the family.

'Well, I never. I never thought I would see you over here, Edward,' said McCabe.

'No, it never was the plan, Mikey. But times are hard back in the old country. I think more will follow; that's for sure,' replied Edward.

'I see your family's here as well. Where are you staying?'

'Nowhere fixed. We need to find another roof. But first Austin and me, well, we need to get some work,' said Edward.

'It's difficult to be sure. But perhaps I can help. You helped my father once. I'll pay his debt,' replied McCabe.

'There's no debt. But help would be welcome. We were robbed on the docks,' said Edward.

'Oh no. It happens to many. It's a hard lesson to be learned. You can't trust every man you meet. I bet it was an Irishman. There are too many out for themselves. Look here. I'll make an introduction. You'll only get work from the lumpers. You know that, yes?' replied McCabe.

'We've learned as much,' said Edward.

'Can you wait here, Bridget? It's not for women and children,' said McCabe. It was more of a command than a request.

Bridget nodded. 'We can.'

'Follow me,' instructed McCabe.

Edward and Austin accompanied McCabe, taking the few steps over to where the now rowdy group were sitting. McCabe said a few words to whom they assumed was the leader, most of which was inaudible to Edward and Austin. McCabe turned back towards Edward.

'I've vouched for you and Austin. He says there could be something tomorrow. He's expecting a certain ship to arrive and has agreed to try you out. It's hard graft, unloading. Something I said you'd be used to. It's best if I take you there tomorrow. It will be early. Where shall I find you?' said McCabe.

'Can we come to you?' asked Edward.

McCabe gave Edward a puzzled look, but then shrugged his shoulders.

'If you want to. Meet me outside the Iron Foundry near Stockdale Street up in Vauxhall at five,' replied McCabe.

'We will,' replied Edward.

'Now go back to your family. We'll meet and talk some more tomorrow. They'll need to get used to you,' said McCabe, nodding in the direction of his companions.

'Thank you, Mikey. This will be a great help,' replied Edward, before following Austin back to the family.

'That was lucky,' said Edward.

'It was. I don't know McCabe that well. I remember him, sure. But it was an age ago. Yes, it was. I think—.'

'Well? What did he say?' interjected Bridget, cutting Austin short mid-sentence.

'We may have some work. He's made an introduction,' replied Edward.

Bridget looked relieved.

'Let's order another jug. I think our luck may be about to turn,' suggested Edward to his very receptive family members.

Coming here surely had been a gamble, mused Edward, as Austin started to pour the fourth jug of the day. Perhaps Liverpool could offer what America promised. They just needed to give it some time, although he did think it better to keep that thought to himself for the time being. They would just have to see. Thoughts of work and the future slowly receded as the effects of the alcohol started to work through, and the noise of the public house increased.

A drunken woman at the far end of the room stood up to give a bawdy rendition of 'The Lively Flea':

Oh! a dainty old chap is the lively flea,

As he creepeth o'er young and old;

His choice food is fat, no lean liketh he,

And he's not very fond of the cold.

You can't be too warm when he finds you in bed,

To pleasure your dainty skin;

Off a nice young kid wot's been veil fed,

Is a very good meal for him.

'Another jug!' shouted Edward, as the family and the rest of the room joined her in the chorus:

Creeping where no light there be,

A dainty old chap is the lively flea;

Hatching, scratching,

All over your body at night he'll be;

Creeping, hopping,

A dainty old chap is the lively flea.

Today was for making merry; work was for tomorrow, Edward decided, as the immediate joys of the present supplanted the trials of the past and fears for the future.

* * *

Edward and Austin had no means of telling the time, but a farming life by the sea seemed to have given them the ability to wake without a clock. They left their temporary accommodation, without any breakfast, keen to avoid being late. It was early, and yet there were many about. Lucky for them as it happened, as neither knew the exact location of Stockdale Street. Neither had thought to ask, both sharing a misplaced confidence that it could be easily found.

Minutes after leaving, they were walking up Earle Street, past the yellow sandstone edifice of St. Paul's, it's four Ionic columns supporting an imposing pediment entrance to a domed interior. But there was no time to reflect on the merits of Liverpool's architecture; they had to ask for some directions. Passing over Edmund Street, they reached Tithe Barn Street. There was no need to ask for Vauxhall Road, as they knew that already, but that was where their knowledge ended. At the junction of Vauxhall Road, Marylebone, and Great Crosshall Street, they stopped and asked a passer-by.

'Would thee know the direction to Stockdale Street?' asked Edward.

The man looked surprised, fearful even, perhaps afraid he was about to be robbed.

'Up there.' He pointed to one of the many streets running off Vauxhall Road without stopping to take another question.

'That one?' questioned Edward, in the direction of the rapidly receding man.

There was no answer; if anything, the man quickened his pace.

Edward, followed by Austin, marched off in the direction they had been given. There was nothing to indicate which street was Stockdale Street. The help had been vague, though better than none at all.

'He'll have to walk this way to the docks. Perhaps we should just wait here,' suggested Austin.

Edward stopped, barely three streets away from the foundry, and sat down. It was a sensible suggestion. Their wait was short. Within minutes, McCabe appeared from a street twenty or thirty yards further away.

'You got here then. Good,' said McCabe.

'We did indeed. It was no problem,' replied Edward, feeling decidedly lucky.

'This way,' said McCabe, leading them back in the direction they had just come from.

'Straight down to St. George's, past St Nicholas,' added McCabe.

'Is there anything we should know?' questioned Edward.

'Work hard, don't slack, don't answer back, and do as you are told. Munroe says what goes, and he'll be testing you; both of you. If he likes you and thinks you are good for the money, he'll hire you again. If not... Well, I won't be able to help you. It's down to the both of you now,' replied McCabe.

Edward and Austin stayed silent until they reached the docks.

'Prince's Dock today, not St. George's. I can see him over there. Good luck to you both,' said McCabe.

'Thank you, Mikey,' replied Edward.

* * *

'A shilling a day. You won't get any more than that around here. There's maybe three or four days work this week. You'll be paid at the end of the day in the pub,' said Munroe, before immediately walking away to talk to a gang leader. Both men were surprised at the paucity of detail and looked towards McCabe for more information. They waited a moment until Munroe was out of earshot.

'You'll work with me today. You're both in my gang. But he'll be watching,' said McCabe, fully aware that Edward and Austin would have to work as hard as the rest. An old friend he may be, but that was as far as it went.

'It's cement today. Heavy as hell, but you'll have to carry it as best you can. Don't let him see you slow down. If Munroe thinks you can't take it, there'll be no more work. Don't rest until I say so. Don't do anything to make him think you are a slacker, or too weak for this work. There's many around here that'll do it for a shilling, less even,' added McCabe.

He then introduced Austin and Edward to the rest of his gang before leading them onto a wooden sailing ship, clearly fully laden.

'Oh, and don't try and steal anything. Munroe is fair most of the time, but if he thinks you are robbing him, he'll have you. Rumour has it that the last one to try ended up with a knife in his back in the Mersey. And forget the Watch Committee Police. They would not be interested,' continued McCabe.

McCabe beckoned his gang to line up and then gave them instructions for the day. They were to move what appeared to be large bags of cement piled high across both sides of the ship's capacious amidship cargo hold. Austin and Edward held back, watching the others pick and lift the sacks. There was little to learn. It was unskilled labour, moving material from ship to shore. After watching the other eight members of the gang pick and lift a bag of cement, first Austin, then Edward, bent down and lifted a sack onto their backs.

'God forsake me, this is heavy,' whispered Austin, careful not to be heard by anyone other than his father.

'We'll get used to; we have to,' whispered Edward in return.

* * *

Thirteen hours passed. Thirteen hours of back-breaking labour, carrying, hauling, lugging dozens of ninety-four-pound bags across a hold, up steps, then across a narrow wooden gangplank to one of many carts that were lined up ready to take cargo. The steps were the worst. On more than one occasion, either Austin or Edward nearly lost their foothold. Both knew that if they dropped a bag and it split, then that would be it. The cost would be docked from their wage, and they would be finished – not just for the day, but for any day working for Munroe. They had to be extra careful.

Sweat poured from each and every man as the day progressed. Time was allowed for drinking water from a ladle hanging by the side of a water barrel, but that was about it for breaks. And neither man had eaten. McCabe and some of the others gave Austin and Edward a bit of bread, but that was it for food – for the whole day!

At seven, Munroe called a halt and invited all to be paid at The Baltic Fleet.

'It's a mile away. Why so far when there are plenty of pubs around here?' asked Edward of McCabe, as discretely as he could.

'It's where he lives. A mile there and a mile back for most of the rest of us. That's just the way it is,' replied McCabe.

Like the rest of the gang, Edward and Austin were hurting with fatigue. The last thing they wanted was a long walk to be paid. But what choice had they?

'You'll get used to it. And there are benefits. The further up the Dock Road, the more dangerous it is, especially at night. But then you probably know that by now, living where you do. And where might that be?' enquired McCabe.

'Near St. Paul's,' answered Austin, without waiting for his father.

'Where exactly?' asked McCabe, probing further.

'I don't know the name of the street,' answered Edward.

'You have a roof, don't you?' asked McCabe, showing some concern.

'We do, but it's temporary. We need to find somewhere permanent,' replied Edward.

'You should come to Stockdale. It's no palace, but it's better than the street,' said McCabe, clearly concluding that Edward and Austin had not found proper shelter.

'Visit me on Friday. I doubt there will be work beyond Wednesday, Thursday at best. I'll sort something out with my landlord,' said McCabe.

'I will,' replied Edward, aware that their time squatting in their present accommodation would be limited.

'When you get paid, you'll have to buy a jug or two for the lads. It will be expected. They're a good bunch and will help where they can. You'll need their goodwill until you settle,' said McCabe.

Edward nodded. A jug each from the two of them would soon eat into their two shillings but it had to be, and besides, they were both as thirsty as hell.

Paid, and after an hour or so in the pub, Edward beckoned Austin to leave. Leaving with one and fourpence between them, they left for their temporary home.

* * *

'We were out looking for work,' announced Bridget, upon Austin and Edward's arrival.

'I had to pretend to be looking for Murphy. That he told us to come here. There were two men and a woman. I think one might be the owner. It was lucky we were not already inside when they visited. More so, in that he did not discover the belongings we had left upstairs. They mustn't have come up here,' added Bridget, further explaining the events of their day. The family had left their adopted house, and were out when their unexpected visitors arrived.

'We can't stay here much longer, but McCabe said he would help again,' suggested Edward.

'It will be Friday, though. You'll have to carry everything out each day till Thursday. If it's empty at night, we'll return. If not... then it's the street for us. It won't be the first time we've been under the stars. As for tonight, it will be some food and then straight to bed for us.' he added.

'I can smell the beer, Edward. You've not drunk your wage, have you?' asked Bridget.

'We've drunk what we had to, woman. It's the way it's done around here. There's a shilling between us after keeping a bit back for food. We had none to eat today,' said Edward.

'That's not enough, Edward. There's chlann to feed,' replied Bridget, stating the obvious.

'English!' said Edward. There was no-one to hear their conversation, but speaking any Irish at all was illegal. It was not worth the risk of a lapse.

Bridget expressed some mild dismay, then nodded as Edward continued.

'I know about the children's food, Bridget. I may be a culchie, but I'm no fool. We have to do what we are told, and if that means going for a drink in the pub after work, then that's what we'll have to do. We have to work with them. There'll be more money tomorrow, and more the day after that,' added Edward.

'If you say so. Can you work every day?' asked Bridget, already calculating what food she might buy with what Edward and Austin gave her.

'The work's paid daily, and this week there will be three, possibly four days. We can only work on the days we get it,' replied Edward.

'Ma, that's the way it is. It's hard, and we don't know when the ships will come. Some days there are many, and others too few. The lumper, Munroe, will only pay us for the days we work. As I said, that's just the way the world is in Liverpool. It can't be helped,' interjected Austin.

'But what about America?' asked Bridget.

'It will be Liverpool for now. We'll have to pay for lodgings and food from next week. America will have to wait. It might be quite a long time,' added Edward.

He provided more clarity to his earlier comment about McCabe's help.

'McCabe said he could help us find somewhere to live. He doesn't know of our present situation, but he said he would have a word with his landlord,' said Edward.

Bridget nodded.

'I'll find what food I can with the money you gave me. Our savings, what there was of them, are almost gone. Edward, if you and Austin don't work, there won't be food on the table for long,' she replied, repeating her earlier concern.

'We know it, Bridget. The children will not starve, not if we can help it,' said Edward, avoiding his wife's lapse into their native tongue.

* * *

Their first week's work lasted until noon on Thursday. Munroe agreed to give each man sixpence, believing he was being generous at that. After all, it was only six hours work. Uncharacteristically, Munroe paid them dockside; there was no trip to the 'Baltic' that day. After receiving his pay, Edward and Austin joined McCabe on the walk back to their respective lodgings.

'Mikey, what now? Is there any chance of work tomorrow?' asked Edward.

'We're all in the same boat, Edward. It depends on when ships arrive. You know that. No ship arrivals mean no work. Munroe is pretty good, though. There's rarely a week when he doesn't get a job from a captain, merchant, or shipowner. He knows many. What I will say is that you impressed him, the both of you. He said you can come back again. He'll hire you. It looks like you and Austin are in. If you are really short, you could try one or two of the other pubs on the Dock Road. But you know how it is. You were lucky I could vouch for you with Munroe. It might be a lot harder with the other lumpers; unless you know someone that is,' replied McCabe.

Edward gave him a rather dejected look.

'Oh, and it will likely cost you in beer. With no guarantees. Better stick with Munroe, if I were you. It's not been bad for me,' added McCabe.

'There's not a lot left, Mikey. We might have to do without. Today's pay will not go far,' said Edward.

Their walk proceeded up Chapel Street past St. Nicholas, its lantern spire looming above their heads. A burial was taking place, clearly of a child, adding a sombre note to Edward's increasingly anxious state. No work, little money to buy food, and the risk of being forcefully removed from their accommodation were all thoughts now racing through his mind.

'Where was it you said you were living, Edward?' asked McCabe.

'I didn't. We don't have anywhere, Mikey,' replied Edward.

'You're on the street? Why didn't you say so earlier?' said McCabe.

'Well... no. We have a roof, just no landlord,' replied Edward.

'Illegal? Don't let 'em catch you, Edward. They'll have you all in Liverpool Gaol. And you don't want to go in there. Not everyone comes out,' said McCabe, repeating an earlier warning from their baggage thieves.

'What can we do? We've barely enough for food, let alone rent,' replied Edward.

'Go back. Get your family out, belongings, and bring them up to Stockdale Street later. I'll sort something out with the landlord. I'll stand you a week's rent if needs be,' said McCabe.

'I don't know what to say,' said Edward.

'Do as I say. Later today. Don't stay another night, wherever it is. Keep your nose clean, Edward. We're all only a step away from starving,' replied McCabe.

As the Exchange part of the road became Tithe Barn Steet, they parted company. McCabe headed up towards Vauxhall Road, with Edward and Austin veering left in the direction of St. Paul's.

'I'm ashamed to have to rely on the charity of others, Austin. I—' started Edward.

'It can't be helped, Da. We'll get back on our feet. I think Ma has more than she's letting on. I'm sure we'll have enough for food this week,' interrupted Austin.

'We'll see. But not enough for rent. We'll owe McCabe,' said Edward.

'That we will. But as he said, you helped his father that time back in Mayo,' replied Austin.

'That I did. Still, it hurts,' said Edward.

'I just hope no-one has returned to the house,' replied Austin.

Edward glanced at his son, a grimace on his face.

* * *

By three, the family were standing next to what they later learned was George Forrester's Iron Foundry on Midghall Street, at its junction with Vauxhall Road.

'Now what do we do?' asked Austin.

'You don't know the street? Is this it?' interjected Bridget.

Edward returned a blank stare. Neither he, nor Austin knew exactly where Stockdale Street was. Some had names on them, not that it would have done them any good. They asked the first person they saw.

'No, this is not Stockdale, it's Midghall. Stockdale's up there, then left. The first one on the right.'

That was helpful. At least the streets now had names. Within a couple of minutes, the family were standing at the bottom Stockdale Street. It was not an inviting sight. A third of its narrow access was paved in rough stone flagging, while the other part was covered in mud, dirt, and general detritus abandoned by dozens of families. A vague stench of rotting material, and likely human shit, pervaded the air. They knew by now that some preferred to defecate in the street, or over gratings, rather than use the facilities provided. This was the price the community paid for being poor: filth and stench. The street's housing comprised of both two-storey terraced and several blocks of courtyard houses – 'courts' as they had learned to call them in Liverpool.

'Now what?' questioned Bridget.

'We wait,' replied Edward.

Half an hour later the younger children were getting restless.

'We could try knocking on the doors,' suggested Austin.

As he asked the question, a woman appeared from one of the courts abutting the street.

'Do you know of Michael McCabe?' asked Bridget, seizing the initiative.

'I do. What of him?' replied the woman, with an unmistakably Irish accent.

'We are to meet him. Do you know which one?' questioned Bridget.

'That one.' The woman pointed at the entrance to the second court. 'Second door. Now I must be on my way,' she added.

Edward led the family into the second courtyard and then to the second door. The court itself was narrow, perhaps seven or eight feet separated one side from the other. Built of red brick, and not long ago, surmised Edward, there were several entrance doors on both sides of the stone-flagged court. Above each door there appeared to be two other storeys; each residence apparently consisting of three floors. Against the far wall, an iron water pump stood next to what Edward assumed was a shared closet built over a cesspit. Adjacent to that, two chickens could be seen, boxed in with a small ramshackle wooden fence. Despite the animal life, the space felt dark and oppressive, as its height and three walls occluded most of the little daylight a grey overcast day offered.

'It's dark, Ma. I don't like it,' said John.

Bridget winced a little. Her son had simply expressed her own thought.

'We need a house, John. We had to leave the other one. Look, see, there are some chickens. Just like home,' replied Bridget, anticipating her son's next question and trying to deflect his anxiety.

Edward knocked, loudly.

Fortuitously, McCabe answered a few seconds later.

'You found me then. Plainly you did. Come in,' he said.

The family trooped in behind Edward.

Once inside, the family filled the small room. Stone-flagged like the outside, it had little to offer in the way of furniture – a poorly constructed wooden table and two chairs. An unlit fireplace provided a centrepiece, and its walls were bare, showing clear signs of damp. A single window provided the room's only light. Several partially burned candles sat on the mantlepiece alongside a teapot and some mugs. A coal bucket stood by the fireplace, and next to that a box that seemed to contain some earthenware and other kitchen utensils. An unused washing line hung across the room. The impression was that of more like a cave than a house.

'We did indeed. I never introduced the family the last time...' started Edward.

'I know you all. John, you were not much more than a babe the last time I saw you,' answered McCabe, who was addressing the youngest member of the family.

John held back, hiding a little behind his mother. Though nearly eight, he was still shy of strangers.

'You can stay here, Bridget. We can share the rent. It's not much for these parts, but it's better to share the cost with the work not being regular. The Rileys are moving across the way on Saturday. It will work out quite well, as it happens. There'll only be twelve, and we're not all in at the same time. I'll tell you who else is in here. There's John Duffy, James and Honor Fleming, and Mary Reid. All the men work at the docks. We're all from the old country,' added McCabe, addressing Bridget rather than Edward.

'What of the rent, Mikey?' asked Edward.

'Ahh. We'll sort that out later, Edward. No need to pay for this week. I'll lend you for next if there's no work,' replied McCabe.

'I'll be grateful for that, but it's work we both need, Mikey. You know that,' said Edward.

'I do. If there's work, you'll have it, Edward. You can be sure of that,' replied McCabe.

Bridget shivered. It was summer but the house felt cold.

'Should I light a fire? Have you any coal?' she asked.

'We'll get some tonight. The cost, you know. We don't usually have it on during the day, unless it's very cold. We share the cost of that as well. Ask Honor or Mary. They'll sort something out with you. Explain to you how things work around here. Let me show you upstairs. Edward, you can have the top floor. There's only Mary up there. I'm sure you'll get on,' replied McCabe.

The stairs led to two other rooms, both the same dimensions as the ground floor. Sheets hanging on lines across each room served as simple partitions, with hay-stuffed mattresses laid on a wooden frame serving as beds.

'This will be your room. Mary sleeps in that corner, by the window,' added McCabe, pointing at the lightest part of the room.

Bridget, Austin, and Edward surveyed the room. There was even less space than back in Mayo, but it would have to do. They thanked McCabe, though for exactly what they were not sure. He left them to return to the ground floor, apparently repairing an old boot.

'It's horrible,' said Bridget, once McCabe was out of earshot.

'I know, but at least it's a roof, Bridget. If Austin and I can get more regular work, we'll be able to do better,' replied Edward.

Bridget cast him a dubious look. There was little point saying more. Their circumstances were as they were. This was the family's home now. They would simply have to get used to it.

* * *

'We should be going,' announced Bridget.

The children ignored their mother's announcement, remaining hidden under their shared blanket. Edward and Austin were already up, used to rising early whatever day of the week it was. Sunday was no different. Not that Sunday was always a work-free day, but both men had generally acceded to Bridget's need to go to Mass on Sunday mornings. The challenges of earth-bound living were many, and had to be met, but there was always Heaven to look forward to if she went to church. That is what the priests had told her, and that was what she believed.

Marine traffic was unpredictable, and if Edward or Austin were not already working, they would wait until Sunday evening before trying to seek some more. McCabe had also been as good as his word. After all, it was now in his interests as well. If Edward and Austin were working, their share of the rent would be paid. Both men knew this, and knew that if McCabe had work, they would now be at the top of his list.

Austin returned from the court, having finished his 'business' and having brought a pail of water and filled a kettle. Honor had also risen early, had lit a fire and boiled a kettle to make some tea. As Honor removed hers, Austin replaced it with his own. Tea was something the family had only recently started drinking. The regularity of the tea clippers bringing increasing volumes of tea into Liverpool had reduced its price, so much so that what would have been considered a luxury back in Mayo was now daily fare. Bridget had become addicted to the substance in the short time they had been in England, and now always had it at the top of any shopping list.

She appeared moments after Austin had placed the kettle on the open fire.

'Good morning to you, Honor. Is it ready yet, Austin?' asked Bridget.

'No, Ma. It's only just on,' replied Austin.

'Where's your father?' asked Bridget.

'Out. He said he would get some bread,' replied Austin.

Bridget turned to face Honor.

'They're still in bed. I'll have to tell them no breakfast again. Not that they'll get any before Mass,' said Bridget.

Honor chuckled. It was not practice to eat before Mass.

'Edward went out with Mary,' replied Honor.

Bridget looked surprised. She did not see Mary behind the screen and just assumed she was still in bed.

'She was to show him where to buy it,' explained Honor. It was usually Bridget's job to buy food, and Honor knew it. She did not want Bridget to think there was any funny business between Mary and Edward. With so many sharing a small space, trouble was the last thing anyone wanted.

'I know him well enough,' said Bridget. She had read Honor's thoughts.

'Austin, get the children up, will you? It's time for church. Tell them there will be no breakfast today if they don't come down soon.'

On most Sundays, almost the entire house went to Mass. All except McCabe. He always seemed to have something else to do. Most of the time it was to 'meet someone' or other about work. Sometimes the work did appear, but on other occasions it did not. And no-one was ever certain whether the excuses he gave were genuine or not. Not that Austin or Edward cared. His relationship with God was his own business.

Half an hour later, the family were ready. As clean as they could be, and wearing their best, or recently washed, the household left the court as a group. Honor and Mary accompanied Edward and his family, with only Michael McCabe and James Fleming missing. McCabe never went, but James Fleming... well that was new.

'James not with us today?' asked Mary.

'I don't know. He didn't come home last night after he went out with Michael,' replied Honor.

She appeared distressed. 'I didn't see McCabe either this morning. I am a sight worried about him, both of them,' she added.

'They will be alright. Probably blind drunk on some floor or other,' interjected Bridget.

An unexpected shower encouraged the party to increase their pace towards Edmund Street. St. Mary's was the oldest Catholic parish in Liverpool. The original building had been built over a century earlier, but had been destroyed by an anti-Catholic mob only twenty years later. Its replacement had been built a little further up, almost on Bixteth Street. Originally designed to look like a warehouse, there was now a strong movement to replace it with something more appropriate. The Irish Catholics were now a force to be reckoned with in Liverpool; the days of anti-Catholic mobs getting away with vandalism and destruction were rapidly drawing to a close.

The eastern side of the church looked to most to be a warehouse. Two large doors had been constructed on the upper floor, above which was fixed a rope and pulley, the latter capped against the rain; a usual practice in Liverpool. But the door was false. Behind it were solid walls, an architectural caprice designed to fool the uninformed. Getting into the church was a little unorthodox. Worship took place on an upper floor, which could only be accessed via a broad staircase on each side of the lower storey. To assist with the deception, in the last century the lower storey had been used for lumber – a means of disguising the building's true purpose.

By the time the Mass started, the church was standing room only. As the priest commenced his Latin introduction, Bridget's gaze lifted towards the large leaded windows which overlooked the courtyard end of the building. The rain had stopped and the sun had appeared, projecting elongated window-shaped beams of light onto the cleric, chapel floor, and congregation. It was one of the very few times in the week that she felt her worries about the family melt. She could not understand the priest's well practised ritual Latin soliloquy, but his voice felt good. Here at least she felt safe. Here she felt closer to God, her maker and saviour.

'Ma. Ma,' repeated Nancy in a whispered tone, suddenly tugging against her mother's hand.

Bridget drew herself out of a reflection. Everyone else was standing, and getting ready to sing a hymn. She quickly stood up. Temporarily mesmerised by the interaction of the sun and the church's windows, she had lost track of the progress of the Mass.

Everyone began to sing:

'Agnus Dei, qui tollis peccata mundi, miserere nobis...'

Life had resumed.

* * *

Months passed.

Summer transformed into autumn, and autumn into winter. Life on Stockdale Street settled into its daily and weekly rhythm. Some weeks the men worked almost every day, while others were barren. It was hardly possible to save. The rent and cost of food precluded putting much in the tin – the tin that Bridget believed represented the hope of something better. A hope that one day they might all get to travel to a new life in America. But the harsh reality of putting food on the table always seemed to thwart her ambition. If Bridget was lucky, there would be enough money left to feed the family for another week. But that was in summer. In winter, the economics of the household changed. The house was colder, darker, and even damper. The fire had to be kept lit most of the time, and that meant buying more coal. Every adult in the house had to contribute, and usually everyone did. Even so, the small amounts that Bridget had managed to save in summer were simply not an option.

When the distant bells of St. Nicholas rang on the first day of 1841, Bridget felt a little more hope. Spring was still months away, but she yearned for the better weather, and perhaps the prospect of more regular work, more income, and lower costs. Perhaps they could start to properly save. There was no obvious relationship between the seasons and ship arrivals that she could see, but in her mind the better weather ought to bring in more trade, and thus more money into the house.

January and February 1841 were particularly cold months. After the dry summer of 1840, the winter had been a harsh shock. No-one stayed on the streets for longer than they had to. It was simply too cold. Another change of season brought another sharp change in the weather. Warmer temperatures brought rain; rain almost every day. Their fire had managed to fight back some of the damp during the chill, but a spell of almost perpetual rain in March beat the meagre heating that a single coal fire could provide. In every room the walls felt damp to the touch. The kind of damp that permeated into the bedding, clothing, and the blankets used for dividing rooms and sleeping under. There was something of a competition to sit by the fireside. The closer you managed to get to the flame, the warmer you felt. No-one was in a rush to go to bed – not adults, not children.

And yet, despite the squalid life they now seemed to have, the family were settling in.

Bridy, the eldest of the children, had caught the eye of Michael, a fellow resident of Stockdale Street. Like her father and brother, Michael Tynan worked as a labourer in the docks.

Encouraged by her mother to try and do better, Bridy ignored her advice, already anxious to move on and have her own family. Although still a minor, seventeen years of age, she had fallen in love and would have none of it. What was good enough for her mother was good enough for her. Marrying a labourer held no fears. Michael, after all, seemed to be able to get regular work. He was six years older and better connected than even her own father, and Bridy was astute enough to realise that a life with him might actually be an improvement. She also reasoned that it would be one less mouth to feed for her father; it might even improve the lives of her younger siblings. As for America, well, for her that was already a pipedream. She knew about the difficulties her mother had in putting money to one side, and was realistic enough to think that it would never happen. Not that she would say; it would not do to remove the platform of hope her mother still rested on. But for the younger Bridget, the future would be Michael and Liverpool.

Liverpool was her city now, and for her at least, her parents' plans for a journey to America would have to change.

Chapter 3

AUSTIN & CATHERINE

Down at the docks, trouble had been brewing for months. A rift had developed between the Irish Catholic immigrants, mostly labourers like Austin and Edward, and their Orange Order counterparts. Both Austin and Edward had tried to avoid trouble, but it became impossible. Politics could not be avoided when it represented a choice between eating or not. Many of their new Irish friends had informed them that the Corn Laws were the reason that prices were so high. Protests against them increased as the less clement weather abated. The Corn Laws, they said, had forced the Irish from their lands and pushed up the price of food. Whether they believed it or not did not matter, Edward and Austin were still strongly encouraged to join the protests, preferably armed with bludgeons to defend themselves from the police and Orange Order troublemakers.

'But they are labourers like us, are they not?' asked Austin of Farrell, a protest organiser.

'They are not our brothers. Our Irish kin, the ones without work, are our brothers. The Orange, well, they get food and help at the parish. Not us. They're as bad as the masters. They're to blame,' replied Farrell.

Austin shrugged, unsure and not knowing who to believe. He did not want trouble any more than his father, but if they did not show support? Well, McCabe was a strong follower of Farrell. What could they do but help the cause?

With riots and havoc in Liverpool the order of the day, strangers – especially English officials of any kind – were not a welcome sight in the Irish quarter.

Sunday, June 6th, 1841, arrived like any other Sunday. It was Mass for the family in the morning and perhaps a drink or two in a beerhouse later in the day, always justified as a necessary means of getting work. But this day was different. A rumour had been doing the rounds that the police were taking names with the intention to prosecute those responsible for the riots.

'It's not true,' said Austin.

'I heard it was. They are writing down everyone's name, age, and where you work. Mary said so,' replied Bridget.

'Yes, they are, but they are not police. They are counting people. Everyone, not just the Irish. And in every city in the country,' said Austin with an air of authority.

'What do we do? Should we hide?' asked Bridget.

'Go out and find out more, Austin. Try the pubs on the docks. See what they say,' suggested Edward.

'I'll need some money for a keg. I've not much left,' announced Austin.

'Fourpence. That's all there is,' replied Bridget.

Austin took the money and disappeared into the June air.

Two hours later, he was back. A little less steady on his feet but still coherent.

'It's alright. It's for the government. They need to know how many people are in the country. Everyone is to be counted; even the Orangemen and children. I'm told there is nothing to fear. We are not to be paid, nor must we pay. We have to wait for him to knock. That's it. That's all there is,' said Austin.

Less than a half hour later, the visit they had been waiting for manifested itself in the form of a sharp rap on the door. Edward was closest. He took a couple of steps and opened it. A wiry dark-haired man with a pen and paper in hand announced himself.

'I'm John Smith, enumerator for this area. I'm obliged to take a count of the people inside. I'll need to come in,' announced Smith. It was more of a demand than a request.

Ignorant of the word 'enumerator', Edward stood aside to allow the smaller man entrance. He did not want any trouble or attention brought on the family.

'I won't be here long. I just need to know your name, age, where you were born, employment, and relationship to the head of the household,' added Smith, seconds after entering the room. He had already deduced that the occupants were Irish and in employment. They were just like all the others in this district. He tried to hide his disdain so that he could exit the stinking rathole as soon as was possible.

'I'll need to sit.'

Bridget, who had commandeered the best seat next to the fire, and to the table, stood up. She wanted him out as much as he wanted to get out.

'Who is the head?' asked Smith, pen in hand and paper ready.

Edward was unsure what to say. McCabe was upstairs, so he replied.

'I am he.'

'Name?' questioned Smith.

'Melia,' answered Edward.

'Is that Meeley, Meeliah. Melly, Malley? Say it again,' said Smith.

'Melia,' replied Edward.

Smith looked as puzzled as before, but attempted to repeat Edward. 'Mallia it is then.'

He wrote down 'Malley', his best interpretation of Melia. He had come across a lot of Malleys that night. This one was unintelligible. Malley would do. The Irish idiot would be none the wiser, nor would Smith's supervisor.

There were hundreds of them, mused Smith, as he recorded the occupants of the house one by one. Why do they keep coming? It's not as if the work is here for them. Then again, it was just as well. We needed a few for the docks. But not too many, mind.

Smith finished his scribbling in less than twenty minutes. No-one in the house could read what he had written. They had to trust that it would not be passed to Orangemen or the police. They had no idea whether Smith was trustworthy or not. It was a relief to see him go; a relief for everyone in the house.

'What about the protests? He has our names, Da,' said Austin, after Smith had departed.

'I know. But we have to do what we have to do. There are Corn Law protests organised for next week. We still have to go,' replied Edward.

'Why?' asked Bridget.

'You know why, woman. I've said before. We have to help our kin. If this is what is expected of us, then this is what we'll do. Besides, we can't be seen to be supporting the Orangemen. We are Irish and have to work with other Irish. McCabe. Well, you know McCabe's stand on this,' replied Edward.

'I don't like it, Edward. It never happened in Mayo,' said Bridget.

'We're not in Mayo, and there are many of us here. There's strength in numbers,' replied Edward.

Bridget was not happy. The children were listening and silently mirroring her concern.

'We should be away to bed. We're promised work tomorrow, but we have to be early,' added Edward, seemingly closing the discussion.

Bridget returned to her night-time tasks, mostly preparing the children for bed. As if worrying about the children and food on the table was not enough. Now there were the protests to think about. Life in Mayo was hard, but seemed easier than what they had in England. She knew that they had had to leave but nonetheless still longed for a lost world. And yet she consoled herself with the thought that perhaps things would eventually get better.

* * *

Alas, matters were destined to deteriorate further before they got better.

At the national level, the government was in disarray. Another national election was expected. Not that it mattered much to Austin and his father; they were not allowed a vote. Their concern was not about whether the Chartists managed to get a seat or two, or whether Daniel O'Connell managed to get some headway with repealing the Ireland and Great Britain Acts of Union passed over forty years earlier. Yes, they had heard talk of it by some of the more politically informed, but it was remote and irrelevant to their lives. It mattered little to them whether Melbourne or Peel was Prime Minister. Whigs or Tories? They were all masters; different names but the same old faces.

What did matter was what McCabe thought. They shared a house with him, and he was regarded as a friend, but what would be the reaction if either or both men declined to join the protests? They had to, both for their livelihoods and, to a degree, their protection. Tension with the Orangemen was rife; they needed their own people.

'There's another protest today,' said Austin to Edward.

'Not again. I heard you were nearly coshed yesterday, Austin,' interjected Bridget.

'It wasn't like that, Ma. You know we have to do it,' answered Austin.

'What about work?' asked Bridget.

'Mikey says not to worry. It's all taken care of,' replied Edward.

'What does that mean?' questioned Bridget.

Edward shrugged his shoulders.

'Look, we must be off. I told him we would be there when the clock strikes seven. Austin, let's go,' he said, determined to close the discussion.

Shortly after half past six, both Austin and Edward were down by the Graving Docks, one of the oldest in Liverpool and usually used to maintain ships.

'There are hundreds here!' shouted Austin. The noise level was such that it was difficult to hear the man beside you.

'Thousands,' replied Edward.

'Now what? I can't see Mikey, Can you?' asked Austin.

Edward shook his head.

'We should wait,' he replied.

'The carpenters are joining us,' shouted a man a couple of yards away. He pointed at a mass of two or three hundred Irish carpenters marching towards them.

As the two groups merged into one, Head Constable Whitty, the recently appointed chief of police, mounted a fire brigade horse and began to address the crowd.

'You must disperse. This is not the way to solve a grievance. Put down your weapons and leave. That is my order,' shouted Whitty to a jeering crowd. His accent was unmistakeably Irish, but the message was certainly that of his English masters.

The jeers became shouts. Some of the crowd began to throw objects at the policeman, forcing him to duck. His horse became restless and threatened to throw its rider. That was enough for him. He would not be giving them another chance. The constable and his horse rode off in the direction of a division of his men who had just arrived from Seel Street Station. Within minutes he had joined them on James Street and ordered them to stand across it, each man brandishing a cutlass and holding it in a threatening manner.

The crowd, many of whom had cheered thinking they had won the day, were suddenly caught off guard. They were not prepared for a mounted and armed charge, and most were already considering their options.

'Cutlasses, Da. We've got to leave!' shouted Edward.

Edward needed little persuasion. The two of them joined many others in seeking an escape from their central position.

'Forward!'

The Head Constable had ordered the police line forward. It was not quite a charge, but it was enough to strike fear into the formerly confident protest. Many men began to run in all directions. But this just encouraged the Head Constable. He ordered a faster pace. A small group still stood their ground and even started throwing stones at him. One had a pistol and started firing at the men with cutlasses. This was too much for the Head Constable. He raised his own cutlass and, somewhat unwisely, started a personal charge. Alas, his horse, unprepared for the sudden move, lost its footing in chasing a rioter. Head Constable Whitty fell, crashing to the stone floor and only narrowly avoiding a serious injury. Half a dozen of his men rushed to his aid, cutlasses raised, ready to help and defend their chief.

'That was a close thing,' said Austin.

They had both witnessed what had happened but were fortunate enough to have got far enough away to avoid attracting the attention of the police line. Edward sat down, exhausted, nervous, and shaking with fear. The adrenaline rush had been too much for a man in the later years of his life.

'Let's go for a drink,' added Austin, thinking that it would relax his father.

'Yes,' replied Edward. It was all he could manage.

'Not too close to the Dock Road. There might be police about,' said Austin.

Edward nodded in agreement.

'Don't tell your ma how close we were,' was all he could muster.

'She'll hear most, but she doesn't need to hear it all,' agreed Austin.

Austin had to help his father walk up Chapel Street. It was a first for him. He had never seen his father in such a state. And it was better his mother did not either. Better that she should think he was the worse for wear with drink.

* * *

After the close encounter on the docks, even the vague threat of a McCabe work boycott could not persuade Edward or Austin to return to the protests. Fortunate for them, they were not alone. The same discussions must have taken place in nearly every Irish household across the city, given that the appetite for mass protests seemed to have dissipated as the month wore on. The talk was still there, but the willingness to arm and revolt against the police had almost melted away. Though the Orangemen remained another matter.

With local politics set to one side, Austin soon turned his interest elsewhere.

Darby Cunningham had become a good friend of both Edward and Austin. He and his family lived in the courts on Stockdale Street, and Darby frequently joined McCabe's gang as a fellow labourer. The families had a lot in common. Both were fairly recent arrivals from Ireland, both families were similar in size, and most of the male members of working age were employed on dock work. When times were good, food was on the table, and when the work was not there, all suffered. As Irish, they would generally stick together. Antipathy towards 'Romanists' was fading, driven by the rapidly increasing size of the Irish population in Liverpool, but it was still there. So, the Irish tended not to mix outside of their community; the 'courts' became villages where everyone seemed to know everyone else, supporting each other but at the same time constantly seeking something better.

'Let's get some ale and celebrate with the women at home tonight. Bring them over to my house. Ann can make something to eat. There will be enough for all.'

It was Darby's idea. June and July had been particularly good, with Darby, Edward, and Austin working almost every day for over a month. They had money in their pocket; more than enough for food, and even some for the tin. Each man felt that they deserved a treat, a reward for their labours.

'Bridget will bring something,' replied Edward, economical in his answer. He had agreed to the suggestion and committed his wife to help in a single phrase.

Austin cast his father a quizzical look. It was not so much that he was against the idea, but he knew his mother wanted to save every penny they had. She might be less than enamoured at the idea of a 'party', and even less with the idea of spending savings on unnecessary food and drink. He knew she felt America was slipping away with every penny spent and not saved.

Edward read his son's expression; his unasked questions.

'It will be fine, Austin. She will understand. There's plenty to put away.'

Austin shrugged. His father had made his mind up.

An hour later, Austin and Edward were home. Bridget had overcome her initial reticence at the idea and was more supportive than Edward and Austin had hoped. She was curious. Darby she had met, but Ann, Darby's wife, and her daughters were still a bit of a mystery. Yes, she had seen them, and even spoken to Ann on more than one occasion, but only in passing. A polite nod in church, a morning, afternoon, or evening greeting. But that was about it. Perhaps a family gathering would not be such a bad idea. It would be a chance to get to know her.

Oblivious to Bridget's thought processes, Edward and Austin were simply relieved that the idea had not become an argument. Bridget had kept her thoughts to herself, but made it known to Edward that he 'owed her one', and that she 'would not forget.' Edward did not care. One way or another they were going to have some fun that evening.

Darby's house was of a similar size and state to Edward's. Perhaps the fireplace was a little larger, as was the mantlepiece, but the reception room's dimensions were no different. With both families in the same room there were would be few places to sit inside, so it was agreed that they would use the yard outside as well. After all, it was now August. The weather was generally warm and dry, though starting to cool in the evening rather faster than it had been a few weeks earlier. A fire had been lit at the edge of the flagged part of the court. They were not supposed to, the risk of uncontrolled fire always being high in the densely packed courts, but nobody cared. They wanted a fire. Not so much for the warmth but for what it represented – a throwback to the old country, to a time when each family would gather outside around an open hearth. The fire was the focus of a social occasion, its primeval glow perhaps helping sponsor a bonding.

The makeshift fire was ablaze by the time Edward and his family arrived. The journey had been only minutes, but the party was nonetheless in another part of the Irish quarter. Unfamiliar, and yet still familiar. Upon arrival, they found that they were not the only ones invited. The Cunninghams had opened their home to close neighbours, some of whom were already sitting on rickety furniture by the open fire. Many of the menfolk had already been drinking, which had affected the volume of discussion. Jokes were being told, with laughing and shouting on the increase. It already felt like an outside beerhouse.

'We have some catching up to do,' said Edward to his son.

Austin laughed. It looked like it was going to be a long, fun-filled night.

'Don't you be drinking too much,' said Bridget, addressing the two men, both of whom were still smiling at the prospect of a good party.

Edward simply smiled back at her.

'Yes, Ma,' replied Austin, somewhat wiser than his father when it came to conversation with his mother. It was usually easier to agree with her.

Aware of the limitations of their hosts, Bridget had brought some food with her, and had the foresight to bring mugs for the ale. Within minutes both Austin and Edward had joined Darby and the other men around the fire. Their evening had begun.

'Welcome, Bridget,' said Ann Cunningham, addressing her guest.

'I'm pleased to meet you at last. There never seems to have been the time to have a proper talk,' replied Bridget.

'Well, here's my family. You know Darby, of course. And these are my daughters: Catherine, Ann, Sisley, and Bridget,' replied Ann, pointing to each of her children as she introduced them.

'And here's mine. This is Bridget – we call her Bridy – Cecilia, Nancy, and John,' said Bridget.

'Three Bridgets in the room. That's going to get confusing!' laughed Ann.

'Oh, we'll manage. Just call her Bridy,' replied Bridget, looking at her daughter.

'We will. It must be nice to have two boys, though. We've always been blessed with girls. Not that I'm complaining. There are benefits, as I'm sure you know. Would you like some ale? We can't let the men have all the fun,' said Ann.

Bridget nodded.

'Just a little. I'll have to make sure we all get home in one piece,' she replied.

Drinks were poured and conversation started. Both Ann and Bridget found they had much in common. Both families had aspirations to do much better, and both had found themselves stuck in Liverpool through circumstances largely beyond their control. But that was in the past. In the present the two women expressed grave misgivings about the recent protests, the cost and availability of food, and the hostility of the Orangemen. As for the future, like all mothers they wanted better for their children. The challenge was in how to achieve it. Neither had clear answers, only vague ideas.

'I hear you are seeing Michael Tynan,' said Ann, addressing Bridy.

Bridget's mother took a breath. Discussions with her daughter about the blossoming relationship had not always been cordial. Michael Tynan had yet to prove himself. But tonight was not a time to raise any concerns. Indeed, perhaps she could learn a thing or two from her new friend. She let her daughter answer.

'I am. He's a good man. I'm very fond of him. Perhaps I'll marry him one day,' replied Bridy, giving the impression that their relationship was much further ahead than her mother realised.

Now that had not been discussed at all, mused Bridget.

'Ay. He's been a bit of a wild one in the past, but he seems to have settled down now. You must have been a mellowing influence,' replied Ann.

That was enough for Bridget. The comment called for a question or two.

'Ann, what do you mean wild one?' asked Bridget.

'Well, I don't want to talk out of turn, but he has been one for the fists. He's banned from more than one beerhouse. Even now,' replied Ann.

'He doesn't do that any more. He's promised me,' replied Bridy.

Bridget's mother made a mental note. She would catch Ann in private at some point, either later that evening or the following day. But not now. It was time to ask about Ann's children.

'And what of yours, Ann? Any weddings?'

'They're still young, Bridget. My own Bridget will be first, I'm sure, and then Catherine. But you never know. Bridget's thirteen or fourteen, and Catherine's not much different.

Twelve or thirteen, I think. I can't remember exactly. I suppose
they're both old enough to wed but I still think of them as
young ones,' replied Ann.

'I know what you mean. It doesn't seem five minutes since
Austin was—'

'Are you coming outside?' said Austin, bursting into the room
just as his mother was about to reminisce about him and
Mayo.

'We are, Austin. Just as soon as we have finished. We're just
getting to know each other,' replied Bridget, replying for
them all.

Austin disappeared from the doorway as quickly as he had
appeared, anxious to return to the merrymaking.

'Who's that?' asked Catherine.

'That'll be Austin, my son. He works with my husband,
Edward, and your da in the docks.'

Catherine nodded. The intervention of an unpaired, youthful,
and strong looking Irishman had not gone unnoticed.
She would have to learn a little more about him. Bridget led
Ann's, and her own daughters, out into the now very noisy
courtyard. The party was in full swing with songs from the
old country already being sung. Whether their close neighbours
had been invited or not, they would be part of it. No-one
would sleep that night until the last of the noisy bunch
had left, or collapsed in a drunken heap on the ground. Bridget
sighed with relief. At least she would get some sleep that night.
Perhaps she should ask Ann if she would like to stay over
at hers. One way or another they would find some room.

They just needed blankets. Bridget resolved to ask Ann later, if indeed it felt right and appropriate. She would wait for now.

'I feel sick,' said Bridy to her mother.

'Again? You've been sick every morning for the last few days,' replied Bridget. She already had her suspicions and had decided to confront her daughter as soon as she had a quiet moment.

Bridy vomited, yards away from the party around the fire. The darkness, noise, and freely flowing alcohol had dulled the senses of most in attendance.

But not Bridget's mother.

'That's it. Let's get you home,' commanded Bridget.

Addressing Ann, she made her apologies and excuses, and took her younger son and daughters home.

'She's not at all well. I'll call in during the week and we can talk some more. I'll leave the men with you. Not that I will have much choice tonight. I've enjoyed what time I had with you,' said Bridget as they parted.

'I'll look out for you,' replied Ann.

* * *

'You're with child.'

Her mother had waited until the men had left, and their downstairs room had emptied, before engaging with her daughter.

It was not a question, nor an accusation; it was simply a statement of fact. Bridy gave her mother a sheepish look. There was no point denying the obvious. The surprise was how long she had got away without her mother noticing. The sickness had only just started the previous week, but she already knew that it would not be possible to hide her predicament for more than a few days. She had just wanted a little time to think about what to do next. Not even Michael knew just yet.

'Is it Michael's?'

Her mother's question tore Bridy away from momentary reflection. She was bound to ask that question, although Bridy's wish would have been that her mother asked after her health before the 'whose is it?' challenge. Alas, it was not to be. She needed her mother's support, so an answer was called for.

'Of course, it is. Who else could it be?'

Her mother's expression gave away her thoughts. A look of concern softened into a more relaxed mien. Bridy felt a little shocked at the thought her mother might think she was seeing more than one man, but there was only Michael.

'Have you told him?'

Another obvious question. Bridy was not really prepared for this, but what could she do? She would have to answer.

'No. I wanted to be sure. I... I... I think I probably am with child. I'll tell him today.'

'You'll have to marry him. We can't afford to feed another. The sooner you do so, the better. Your father will have to know soon enough. He'll expect you to wed in the church. You know that, don't you?'

It was a question, but Bridy knew it was rhetorical. She knew her mother would not want a debate and what she had said was true. While the last few weeks had been kind to the family purse, she knew that bad times could be just around the corner. It would be expected that she would marry. Her mother had an expectation and so would her father, but Bridy's real concern was Michael's reaction to the news. Would he be awkward about it or agree to marry straight away? She was sure he was as much in love with her as she was with him. But there was still that nagging doubt of uncertainty, now amplified by the dawning reality that she was about to be a mother. If indeed she survived childbirth. There were too many emotions at play. Excitement and anticipation competed with fear, anxiety, and uncertainty for domination of her mind. She dearly wanted to feel joy and love, but every positive wave of warmth and happiness was almost instantly undermined by the fear of what might happen. The immediate fear of Michael's reaction to her news, and the more visceral fear of giving birth and the responsibilities of motherhood.

'Bridy?'

Her mother required an answer. But what was there to say? The facts of the situation had already been exchanged. What else should she add?

'I know everything you say is true. I don't want to be a burden. Michael will help look after me and the babe even if we don't marry.'

'You will have to marry,' commanded her mother.

'He'll have to ask me, won't he?' replied Bridy.

'No, he won't. If it's his child, and you tell me it is, he will marry you. Your father and brother will see to that.'

There was no point arguing with her mother.

'I'm sure it will be alright,' replied Bridy, desperately attempting to hide any doubt that Michael would not do what her parents regarded as 'the right thing'. Poor they might be, and they might be in England, but the son or daughter of a Catholic would not be expected to have a child out of wedlock – at least not for long, if there was an alternative. And with Michael there was.

'Good. You should see him tonight. I'll tell your father after you've spoken to him.'

'Yes, Ma.'

That was it. The die had been cast. She would see him today.

* * *

August 9th had been set for the day of the wedding, merely a week after the party at the Cunningham's court house, and only six days after she had shared the news with Michael.

It had happened so quickly.

Bridy's apprehension at Michael's reaction to her news had been needless. The moment she had shared her situation, Michael had asked her to marry. There was no doubt, no misgivings, no accusations; only love. The rumours of his wilder days could only have been that. The man she knew had not only shown no hesitation but had been positively enthusiastic about having a 'son' – he had already decided that.

'We can wed in the autumn. You'll probably be showing by then.'

It was not quite what her mother and father would expect, thought Bridy, as Michael floated his suggestion. She had to add a greater sense of urgency before the two of them faced her father and mother.

'I think my ma and da will call for it sooner.'

'That's alright. Whatever you want; whatever is right for you and the baby.'

Michael had proved to be malleable. It was a relief to Bridy, and a good sign that something could be worked out that met the requirements of all parties.

And so there they were, standing in front of a priest in St. Mary's, ready to make their vows. Pat Waldron, a friend of Michael's, and Catherine Donnelly, her own dear friend from the court, had agreed to witness the ritual. But it was a family occasion for both sides. Patrick, Michael's father, and his mother both attended, as did the entirety of her own family. A situation that could have become a disaster had been transformed into a celebration. While still in fear of the birth, Bridy had become hopeful of the future. With Michael by her side, and both her own and his mother offering to help when the baby arrived, she could perhaps relax a little.

Her mother had also stopped talking about America. Whether she had played a part in that, or whether the difficulties of saving for an overseas adventure had finally become too much for her mother, Bridy was unsure. Perhaps it was both, but she hoped that her mother, father, and brothers and sisters would never leave Liverpool. While her life was now with Michael, she had no appetite for losing the support of her family. But that would have to wait. For now, there was the baby to think of.

* * *

Ann Cunningham had taken an almost instant liking to Bridget Melia. It was not usually that way with most women she met, but with Bridget she felt she had much in common.

'I think I'll go round and invite Bridget Melia for a talk. I like her, and we didn't have much chance to speak a couple of weeks ago. She had to go home, and it was so busy and noisy.'

'I'll do it for you, Ma,' interjected Catherine. Her mother had been addressing the whole family, but it was Catherine who replied. Providence had provided her with an opportunity to see Austin. For reasons only her hormones could explain, she had been thinking of him ever since he entered her life. Those few brief moments had changed everything for her; she had to know more about him.

'Would you, dear?'

'Of course, I will. I'll go round after finishing the washing,' replied Catherine. She knew that there was no point going until the men had returned from their day at the docks. Her own father arriving home would be the signal for her to visit.

'Alright. But don't leave it too late.'

Catherine, wisely in her mind, left it until her father arrived home before undertaking her short excursion. She had already eaten with her siblings – a practice not unusual for the Cunningham family. Ann, her mother, usually waited until

Darby arrived so that she could have a few moments with him without the chattering of the younger members. It seemed to work. The younger children would often be playing in the court or outside on the street after their meal. They would greet their father on sight, but knew enough to know he would be hungry, and that it was always better to talk with him after eating. It had always been that way.

It was only minutes to the Melia court on Stockdale Street. But in those minutes Catherine's heart began to beat a little faster. She could not help it, nor could she understand it. Her brain seemed to have lost some of its control over her body. How she had felt ten minutes earlier, confident and at ease, had melted into a quivering and nervous disposition.

'Stop it,' she told herself. But it was to no avail.

She knocked on the door. This in itself was unusual. Her practice was usually to open a door and shout on entering if no-one could be seen, but today it had to be something different. She was annoyed with herself. Why did she knock? She was after all thirteen or fourteen years, and old enough to marry at that. It was a silly, juvenile thing to do, to wait behind the door of someone she knew.

Surprised, and no less alarmed by an unexpected knock on the door when they were eating, the older members of the family looked at each other with a tinge of fear.

'Who can that be?' said Edward.

'Orangemen, Police? It can't be, surely? What would they want with us?' replied Austin.

'I'll answer it,' declared Bridget, before putting down her spoon and leaving the table to open the door.

She laughed, immediately signalling an easing of the momentary tension.

'It's Catherine Cunningham, is it not?' said Bridget, addressing her visitor.

Catherine nodded, unable to speak for a second or two.

'Come in. Have you eaten?' asked Bridget, instantly resorting to being a hostess.

'I have. I have a message from my mother,' declared Catherine.

'Come in. Sit with us for a few minutes. Would you like some ale?' asked Bridget.

'Thank you. I will,' replied Catherine. She thought it might help with her nervousness.

'You know Cecilia, Nancy, and John. And of course, Edward, my husband, and Austin,' said Bridget, introducing each member of the family again.

It was the last introduction that had an effect on her. She blushed and looked down at the table as Bridget gesticulated towards Austin. He noticed her reaction but remained silent. She was grateful for that. When she did feel able to look towards him, what she saw was a tall, muscular Irishman. He had short brown hair, a complexion not yet weathered by years of dock work, and mongrel eyes – a fusion of brown and green which seemed to change with the light. Unlike his general complexion, his hands and forearms had already taken on a leathery appearance, and his fingernails were broken and serrated in places – signs of heavy labour. She had seen that in her own father. Despite the flaws, Catherine had become smitten, even before he began to speak.

Austin examined the girl who had entered the room. Was she a girl or a woman? He was not too sure. Her apparent girlish shyness was obvious to all, but her physical appearance suggested someone older. Coal black centre-parted hair down below her shoulders contrasted with a starkly white complexion, seemingly a shade lighter than his own sisters'. He found what he could see of her face attractive. A smiling mouth, slightly upturned nose, and eyes; well, he could not properly see her eyes as her head still faced the floor. It was as if she was avoiding eye contact. Her dress was much the same as his mother's and sisters'. A dark grey woollen gown and petticoat showing signs of excessive wear, and a charcoal shawl hung around her shoulders and small breasts. It was all typically practical, but then everyone had to be. The greys, blacks, and brown garments showed less of the dirt and grime of city life. But there was no bonnet. A surprise indeed. It facilitated an uninterrupted view of her unevenly combed hair, but offered no protection against the dirt, and one of the scourges of living so closely together – head lice.

He wanted to see her face in full.

'I'm Austin.' It was unnecessary and something of a surprise to the other family members present.

Catherine looked up, stared at him for an instant, and then immediately looked away towards Bridget. She blushed again, quite obviously at a loss for words.

But it was enough for Austin. For that momentary interval, no more than two or three seconds, their eyes converged. He was mesmerised. Catherine's eyes were green. Her apparent innate shyness had effectively hidden what might be her most attractive feature – green eyes. A fabled legacy of Icelandic Vikings mixing with Celts centuries ago, black hair and light green eyes were not uncommon within the Irish diaspora, but they were nonetheless not an everyday occurrence. It more than piqued his interest in her.

It was time to strike up a conversation.

'Do you work, Catherine?'

'Austin, leave Catherine alone. Let her give her message,' interrupted Bridget, as she handed their visitor a cup of ale.

Catherine took the cup and gulped down about a third of its contents, giving her a few seconds to think.

'Thank you. I can't stay for long. Mother would like you to come visit her on Friday. She wants to talk to you some more. You left early after the party,' replied Catherine.

'I did. I would like to come and visit. Perhaps after supper, and when the men have gone to the ale house. Was there anything else?' said Bridget.

'No. That was all,' replied Catherine, continuing to avoid eye contact with Austin. She desperately wanted to speak to him, but it just felt so awkward.

There would have to be another time.

Austin watched as Catherine consumed a second third of the mug. It was difficult to interrupt the discourse taking place between her and his mother. Should he perhaps suggest walking back with her? But that seemed silly, given the proximity of the Cunningham household, and way too premature. Even the suggestion might open the door to ridicule.

There would have to be another time.

Having completed her task and finished her ale, Catherine made her excuses and readied to leave.

'I'll have to go now. Mother will be expecting me back.'

'That's all right, my dear. Tell her I'll see her on Friday. I'll look forward to it,' replied Bridget, pleased at receiving a rather rare invitation to a house outside their own court.

And with that Catherine stood up and left. As she did, she cast an evanescent glance in Austin's direction, attempting as much concealment as she was able. It was over in the blink of an eye, and he missed it, leaving him to wonder whether there might have been some mutual attraction transmitted in that vanishingly short moment of eye contact they had experienced only minutes earlier. Her visit could not have lasted more than ten minutes, but in those fleeting moments both sensed that the paths of their lives were about to cross. Oblivious to either, these were the concurrent thoughts running through the minds of both Austin and Catherine as they parted.

* * *

Bridget visited her new friend, Ann, the following Friday as planned. It took very little time for the subject of each woman's family to arise, with members of both households receiving a fair share of what each considered worthy of telling.

And Catherine was no exception.

'Catherine's a pretty girl, though a bit shy. How old did you say she was?' asked Bridget, echoing the subject of an earlier conversation.

'Not at home she's not; she's always got something to say. Twelve, thirteen, or fourteen years. I can't be too sure of the

GED MELIA

exact date she was born, but I think she was about ten or eleven on *Oíche na Gaoithe Móire*. That was more than two years ago,' replied Ann, lapsing into a bit of Irish.

'Ahhh, the Night of the Big Wind. We were all terrified that night. We still talk of it from time to time,' said Bridget.

'It was terrible. We lost our roof and a cousin to a falling tree. It was a bad night for all, especially them at sea,' added Ann.

'She's of age to wed then. Is she courting anyone?' asked Bridget, more interested in the present than the past.

'No. She's shown no interest in men. I'll give her some time. I want to see her married to an honest and kind man. Darby's been good for me and the young ones. I want the same for her. There's no point rushing these things. I'll know when I see the right one come along. What about your eldest, Austin?' replied Ann.

'He's brought a girl back once or twice, but he's never really settled on one. He's now of an age when he should be wed and in a home of his own. But what can you do? It's up to him, and I must say that the money he brings to our door helps a lot. I've managed to save a little from time to time, not that I think we will ever get to America. The longer we are in Liverpool, the better the chance we will be here forever. I'm starting to get used to the idea that we might never leave,' said Bridget.

'It's not so bad, Bridget. We never really planned to go any further, though we often talked about it. Darby wanted to find some regular work here in England, and Liverpool offers it. They say the city is now the richest in the kingdom. I just wish a bit more would drop into my hands,' replied Ann.

106

Conversation strayed into the difficulties of feeding a young and growing family, given the challenges of an insecure income. Each woman had a similar story to tell, and each seemed to approach their lot in the same way, with wit, pragmatism, and with the odd white lie or two when it came to money. The men were notorious for spending what they had in their pocket; it was a woman's job to make sure that they took enough for food and rent. They were the ones who had to budget and who had the worry. The men would work hard, and might feel deserving of a night in the ale house, but priorities were priorities. If the family needed to eat, then an occasional untruth was required. Ann and Bridget both laughed at the thought of them having so much in common.

'And Catherine is getting quite good at helping out. She's also got some daily work with a fish seller on the market. She'll make a good wife for someone one day,' said Ann, returning to the subject of her daughter.

'Perhaps I should get Austin to ask her out,' suggested Bridget, giggling at the thought.

'Perhaps you should,' replied Ann, participating in the humour.

Both women laughed at the idea, sure in the knowledge that it would never come to be.

* * *

Oblivious to the conversation between his mother and Catherine's, Austin's thoughts had become peppered with ideas about how he might get to know her. But providence was about to make an ironic intervention. In the weeks after their short meeting, Austin had seen very little of her; his own commitments, and hers, ensuring that their paths would not cross. And yet circumstance was already weaving an eccentric path towards another meeting.

One of the few occasions where Austin had managed to catch a glimpse of Catherine was at Sunday Mass. Surrounded by family, it was difficult to talk, least of all have a private conversation, but by now the two households were no longer strangers. After Mass, Bridget would catch up with Ann, and Darby, Edward, and Austin would always have something to say, sometimes to share a joke, but more often to talk about the prospects for work in the following days. Within weeks they were sharing a pew in church, and soon after that had started a habit of walking back as a group from church to the courts on Stockdale Street. A bonding established, it had become much easier for Austin to strike up a conversation with Catherine.

One Sunday in October, he held back a little from his parents' conversation, expecting to be unnoticed in his efforts. His parents fully engrossed, and siblings sharing excitable conversation about their plans for the afternoon, Austin saw his opportunity. Unsure about what to talk about, he resorted to a comment about what he saw as Catherine's most striking feature.

'You have lovely green eyes. I always notice them.'

Surprised and flattered by the attention, Catherine declined to comment and simply smiled at him. She did not know what to say. Austin tried again.

'I hear you work in the market. A fish dealer?'

'I just help. One day I will be a dealer; once I have enough money. Yes, I work at St. John's,' replied Catherine.

Austin was familiar with St. John's. It was an enormous building, appropriate in size and design to Liverpool's growing status as a centre of trade and commerce. He had visited it on many occasions and was a little confounded as to why he had not seen her there. But then again, in between its brick walls, iron columns, and two acres of floor space, stood well over one hundred and fifty provision stalls, innumerable stands and nearly sixty shops. Despite the supplemental light its gas lamps provided, the sheer volume of people on market days perhaps ensured an inconspicuous presence.

'I've never seen you in there,' said Austin.

'Sometimes we sell in St. Martin over by Great Horner Street,' replied Catherine, feeling a little challenged. The fresh fish market was near to the capacious St. John's, rather than inside. She thought it not worth bothering to clarify.

'I know where it is. Does it pay well?' asked Austin.

'Not much. But it's better than Gibraltar Row,' replied Catherine, making a vague reference to prostitution. Everyone in Liverpool knew Gibraltar Row, the area running from Great Howard Street to the Prince's Dock. That particular quarter was notorious for its vice and crime.

Austin was taken aback at Catherine's comment. He had seen her as a rather shy young woman and did not expect such a worldly reply. Nor did he wish to be drawn into a discussion on the subject, lest he give way more than he wanted to. And it was a Sunday, and they had just been to Mass.

'So, what will you do this afternoon?'

'I've got a bit of time to myself. Ma always lets me do what I want for a few hours on Sundays after we have had breakfast,' replied Catherine, hinting that she might be willing to receive an invitation.

'I've not much to do either. Da and me will need to go to the beerhouse later. That is if we don't see Mikey today. We have to see about work next week,' said Austin.

'I know about that. Da always does the same. Ma would like to go as well, but he always says it's a man's business. It's not about having fun,' replied Catherine.

Austin smiled. They had similar conversations in the Melia household. He then searched for the right question.

'Would you like to walk with me today?'

Catherine looked at him. Yes, of course she would, but then she was not going to answer straight away.

'Where would you be walking, Austin?' It was the first time she had actually used his name. And yet it felt familiar.

Again, Austin had been caught out. He had not thought that far ahead. He hesitated, desperately searching for some interesting place to take her.

'What about...?'

Catherine returned an expectant glance.

'What about the Zoological Gardens?'

It was the first thought it his mind. He had heard some of his fellow dockers talk about its strange wonders, the animals, but really had no idea what was there.

'The Zoological Gardens. What are they?' asked Catherine.

'They have strange creatures, but I won't say any more. I don't want to spoil it for you,' said Austin, seeking an excuse for providing the minimum of detail.

Intrigued, Catherine agreed to the prospect of an afternoon walk.

'Don't tell anyone about it just yet. And we should meet away from the house,' replied Catherine.

'I won't. Meet me at one on the first strike of the clock. Can you be at the top of Dale Street and Shaw's Brow? Do you know the place?' asked Austin.

'I can, and I do,' replied Catherine, heart now pounding with excitement. She had been asked out for the first time.

Austin winked at her, then quickened his pace to catch up with the men, leaving Catherine to turn her attention towards her younger siblings.

* * *

The walk to the Zoological Gardens was a long one. Up through Islington, Brunswick Road, and then along the Derby Road. It was still quite a walk, almost to the city boundary, before the Gardens were within sight. They eventually reached their destination, which was not far from the West Derby Workhouse, and only a little beyond the Necropolis, Low-Hill Cemetery.

Unfamiliar animal noises could be heard as they walked up to the payment booth. Austin paid the entrance fees, and then they nervously entered the ten acres of irregular, but spacious and prepared ground. Two shillings. He hoped that the experience would be worth it. He had worked hard for that.

'It's lovely,' sighed Catherine, unused to the fresh air and open spaces.

Though the season had long since changed to Autumn, there was still a magnificent display of flowers, trees, and shrubs of untold variety and quantity. At least it seemed that way.

'What is that?' asked Catherine, pointing towards a large animal standing upright in a circular pit.

The gardens were situated in what was a natural amphitheatre. A circular menagerie had been constructed adjacent to a lake. Cages and enclosures for lions, tigers, monkeys, and elephants, and houses for various species of birds were spread throughout the park. Antelopes roamed nearby on a fenced field. The effect of the whole adventure, it's almost supernatural animal cacophony counterbalanced with the picturesque display of natural wonder, took Austin's breath away.

'I think it's a bear,' replied Austin. He had never seen one but had heard talk about bear fights in 'old times.' The descriptions seemed to match these creatures.

'You know, there's a story of someone being mauled by a bear. It was only three years ago. A bear had escaped into the lane and went for a man with a basket of nuts. When he saw the bear, he dropped the nuts and ran off. The bear then started eating the nuts. A boy then appeared to buy some nuts. But before he got close to the bear, another man grabbed him and whisked him to what he thought was safety. But the bear was distracted and went for the man rescuing the boy. It sank its teeth into his arm. He was lucky he wasn't killed and eaten.

It was an age before the keepers got to the bear and pulled it off, but not before it caused serious injury. They say the man's still alive but has gone mad with it all. Dangerous, them bears are. Keep away from the edge.'

Catherine stepped back, now very nervous of her proximity to the bear enclosure, and for that matter all the other animals behind cages. The story had put her off getting anywhere close to the wild animals.

'Can we walk some more in the gardens? There are lots of people near the cages,' said Catherine, looking for a way to put some distance between her and the more threatening creatures, whether they were behind bars or not.

'Yes, of course,' replied Austin, somewhat disappointed.

They walked to a quieter part of the grounds but could not escape the menagerie entirely. Smaller and less alarming creatures populated the area they had entered, interesting but not so distracting. It gave them time to talk.

'What will you say to your mother?' asked Austin, alluding to their afternoon excursion.

'She won't hear of this. I'll just say I've been walking to get some air. I've done it before. I won't say anything about you,' replied Catherine.

'Would you like to walk with me again?' said Austin.

Catherine turned to face him. She leaned her head slightly to one side, causing some of her hair to fall forward, thus covering part of her face. Her confidence had grown during the afternoon, and she felt far more at ease with Austin than at the start of their outing, but there was still a shy girl inside.

She hesitated for a few seconds. Of course, she wanted to say 'yes', and yet she still doubted that the invitation was genuine.

Austin examined her face as he waited for an answer. His own expression quickly faded from one expecting an affirmation to a look of discomfort. Was she about to reject his interest?

Noticing the subtle change in Austin's expression, Catherine realised that she needed to seize the initiative, or she might lose what she clearly wanted. She had to respond.

'Yes. I would very much like to.'

With both seemingly having reached a mutual understanding, their conversation became far more relaxed. Talk of the animals and gardens gave way to a discussion of family members and matters closer to home. Plans for the future were exchanged and interests explored. Neither could read or write but both wished they could. There was talk of children, church matters, and some of the 'goings on' at the docks. Catherine had heard some of the stories from her own father, but elected to keep her own counsel. Austin was good to listen to; she did not want to distract him when she was enjoying herself.

They retraced their steps and were back in Stockdale Street by five. On the journey home, they plotted how they might see each other. Neither wanted to share their interest in each other with other family members until they were sure what each wanted. In time they would have to, but not just yet.

* * *

1841 surrendered to the ineluctable march of the calendar. By early spring, Austin and Catherine had established themselves as a couple. The difference in ages mattered little to either; it was not uncommon in the courts for partners of significantly different years to live together. It was often a matter of survival. Industrial accidents would happen, diseases would snatch away family members, and formerly strong bonds would be broken by the temptations of the ale houses and by what they offered. A man needed a wife, and a woman needed a husband, more so when there were younger mouths to feed. Pragmatic choices were made on a daily basis.

It was Catherine's mother who noticed first. Ann knew her daughter and soon observed a change in her daughter's demeanour. Though she fought to hide her romantic interest, the girl had little control over those subtle, subconscious, signals radiating from someone falling in love. Ann might not be expert in semiotics, but she could read the signs. She also noticed the physical manifestations of her daughter's behaviour; the increasingly frequent 'disappearances'. There was always a sound explanation for an individual absence, and that was fine of itself, but the totality suggested something else was going on.

Within weeks she had worked out that her daughter was seeing Austin. Ann had met the family and, for want of a better way of describing their somewhat illicit entanglement, she 'did not mind'. In fact, Ann rather approved. Austin was a worker; he would probably be good for her daughter. Not wishing to disturb the attachment, she decided to avoid confronting Catherine. It would be their secret, only Catherine would not be aware of her mother's knowledge. Nor would her new friend, Bridget. Without Catherine or Austin admitting to the courtship, she could maintain a position of credible ignorance. Ann thought it better that way, at least for now.

Bridget remained unaware of Austin's interest in Catherine. Austin was simply Austin. He gave little away, and she was used to him being frequently absent from the home, typically in the ale houses. It was the nature of their work. The men had to go and find it, each day, each week, each month; all the time. A romantic liaison with a woman was far from her mind. Where would he find the time?

* * *

The first time was a clumsy affair. He was sure she did not enjoy it. Rushed, cold, dark, and in the open air; it was unromantic. She wanted to and so did he, but it just did not satisfy either of them. The act might have been completed but it left both feeling sheepish and a little embarrassed. This time would be different, vowed Austin. They had agreed that they should take a room in one of the ale houses on the Dock Road. It mattered little which. All they both wanted was a warm room and a bed, and perhaps a little ale to lubricate the mood.

The venue Austin chose was further away than the usual focus of the dockside melee. The building was nondescript, as was the room, but it would serve their purpose. An oil lamp had been left on a table in the hallway, together with the means to light it. He finished the task and led her into its rather dark and gloomy interior. Paint was peeling in one corner, and what furniture there was scuffed; it had clearly seen better days. The bed was cast iron, much better than the sleeping arrangements either of them had at home, and there was what looked like fresh bedding and down, and feather pillows. Austin surveyed their situation. It felt like luxury compared to what either were used to. He hoped she would approve.

'I want to wash,' said Catherine, heading over to a dresser by the window. A jug of water and bowl had been left for guest use.

Austin watched her for a minute, but then turned his back and began to undress. He would wash after she had finished, naked; she would soon get used to it. He poured two mugs of ale, leaving both on a simple table set beside the wall next to the bed.

Finishing her ablutions, Catherine walked to the other side of the bed and started to undress. Austin took this as a signal to wash and walked over to the bowl Catherine had just finished using. She noticed his nakedness, flushing with a mix of anticipation and arousal at the sight. It was a very unfamiliar situation, and yet she felt both comfortable and nervous at the same time. Dissonant emotions raged for a minute or two until something elemental in her appeared to take control.

Austin returned to the bed, unashamed in his nakedness, and climbed in next to Catherine, who had already wrapped herself in sheets and blankets. Now she felt apprehensive again. What was she supposed to do? But then Austin took the initiative. He leant over and kissed her on the lips. It was soft and gentle rather than passionate, but it felt right.

'Lay on my chest,' he suggested, in an attempt at helping her relax.

Catherine shifted her position and laid her head on his chest.

'We can just lie here for a while. There is no rush.'

It was what she wanted, needed even. Catherine started to breathe more deeply, and within a few minutes was in danger of falling asleep. Heat radiating from their bodies, skin to skin, warmed the bed while diffusing into the fingers and toes of each.

More minutes passed. Austin shifted to his side, encouraging Catherine to remove her face from his chest and to face him, head resting on her hand and arm. He leant over again and began a more passionate embrace. Catherine fell back on her pillow, already coupled to Austin's concupiscent lips. Her uneasiness yielded to something primitive. She put her arms around his back and pulled him towards her.

'You're too heavy,' said Catherine, soon realising her mistake.

Sweat now starting to seep from his pores, Austin withdrew to his side and began to slowly feel her breasts. She allowed herself to become aroused, her earlier more distracting thoughts now giving way to something more prurient and instinctive. Her confidence increasing, Catherine stroked and caressed Austin's arms and back, occasionally opening her eyes in between kisses to peer into Austin's. She could tell he was ready, but she was not. She gently pinched both his arms, hoping he would understand the message. Though she did not want to destroy the passion, she spoke.

'Slowly.'

Austin held back; he seemed to understand.

'Shall I stop?'

'No.'

He resumed his caress, moving a hand beyond her breasts.

Catherine was ready. Spreading her thighs, she coaxed Austin into a position where she could receive him. Firm in anticipation, he entered her and began to push forward. Catherine opened her eyes and stared directly into his.

'I love your eyes, Catherine.'

She knew he did. The sight of them seemed to increase his ardour, encouraging her own libido even more. She closed her eyes and soon sank into a sensual inferno of visceral pleasure.

After finishing, both lay on their backs for a few minutes of recovery.

'Do you want a drink?' asked Austin, leaning over to collect the two mugs of ale from the adjacent table.

Wet and flushed with the satisfaction of what they had both shared, Catherine answered with an affirmative nod. She was thirsty but was reluctant for the moment to end. Her muscles and emotions were floating in a sea of mental and physical exhaustion. The joyful type, not the senses experienced at the end of a hard day on the markets. But he was offering a drink and so she took it.

'I love you, Austin.'

There, she had said it.

Austin kissed her. 'I love you, too.'

The room had been hired for a few hours, not for the night. There would be a knock on the door half an hour before they were expecting to leave, but until then they could sit and talk. Half an hour would be more than enough for each to dress.

'What if I have a child?'

She needed reassurance, thought Austin.

'You won't be having one. Not with only two times. It took my mother months to become with child. I know. She told me when John was planned.'

It was not the answer she was looking for, but she did not want to press him. After all, he was probably right; he knew more of the world than she did.

An hour later, they were walking back to Stockdale Street, the memories of what they had both experienced already fading into more basic thoughts of family, food, and work.

'We should do this again,' suggested Austin.

Catherine smiled, reaching for his hand. Yes, of course they would.

* * *

Austin and Catherine's liaisons increased in frequency in the weeks after their encounter on the Dock Road. Both seemed happy with the arrangement, albeit their later trysts could not compare with that time. And nature was about to make a predictable intervention, as it often does in these situations.

'I think I'm with child. Ma noticed straight away, what with the morning sickness. It started a few days ago.'

Catherine had not seen Austin for four or five days, but in that time her world had totally changed. She was about to become a mother, and there was nothing she or Austin could do about that. It was May, and the warmer months were coming, but that was of little comfort to Catherine. She needed to know Austin's intentions, and so did her mother, given the significant change in situation.

It took Austin a few seconds to process what he had just been told. Catherine was looking at him and expecting an answer, or at least a comment, but he was temporarily at a loss. His first thought was that Catherine had probably known for days, weeks even. She must have become used to the idea. But he had only just been told; he needed some time to think.

They were out walking in the northern reaches of the Dock Road, Regent Road, near the old windmill. A light breeze was blowing, which helped turn its bright white sails in a clockwise direction. It was one of those spring days when the weather oscillated between a light shower and a warming sun occasionally peering from behind snowy cumulus and grey cumulonimbus cloud formations. A bit of everything.

It was a little cowardly, but he sought momentary distraction in examining the centuries-old engineering in the mill. He turned away from facing her and watched the mill's fantail guiding its cap into a position where it could take full advantage of the direction of the wind. The rotating windshaft, which had previously slowed, began to speed up as the sails drove its gear. Austin thought of a clock as he watched it. But then thoughts of the baby returned. He knew he had to take a position. As a Catholic, he could not countenance trying to abort the baby, and as a human being and a family man, it would not be his nature to run away.

'When will the baby come?'

'Ma thinks it will be December,' replied Catherine.

Austin reflected on the timeline. It would be months away. Perhaps it would be time to get organised. Still anxious about Austin's commitment, Catherine decided to be more direct.

'Will you help?'

Austin thought it an odd question. What did she mean 'help'? It was not a direct challenge, but then it might be. It demanded some sort of answer.

'Yes. The baby is mine. I will help wherever I can.'

'We'll have to tell people about it. It will be obvious by the summer,' said Catherine.

'I know,' replied Austin, uncertain how his own father and mother would react. And how would it affect his relationship with Darby, and Catherine's mother?

'I'll have to save more. Ma will understand. I won't be able to give her as much as I used to. And I think it will end the America dream she has. Not that I think we would be much better over there,' added Austin.

Thoughts and plans raced through his mind. Should they marry? How much money would he need to find a place of their own? What if the work dried up? What if his own father became injured, or his mother sick? And what of Catherine? Would the baby be well? And the birth. Would she survive it? It was that last thought that worried him most. Childbirth was often associated with death, often of the child, and not infrequently of the mother. Catherine was not even of majority. Young and healthy, yes, but in their circumstance, in the damp and dark courts, it was all too often a question of survival. An existence.

'Ma says we should tell them soon. By that she means by midsummer. She'll cover for me until then, though I don't know how I can work with the sickness. She said she's known about us for weeks. She guessed there was something going on. Ma likes you, which helps,' said Catherine.

'I'll tell my own ma before then. She'll need to know. And with her seeing yours so often, it would only be right,' replied Austin.

Catherine nodded in agreement. It was better out, and both mothers could help with the news.

After the exchange, there was little more to be said. Arm-in-arm, they started the walk back to Stockdale Street, less cautious than they had been. 'What must be, must be,' ran through Austin's mind as they neared home. What did it matter now if his father and family found out? He would do what all would say was 'the right thing'.

* * *

The Chartists' 'Great Strike' dominated gossip in Liverpool during the summer, but there was not the appetite to join it. Affecting over thirty counties, including many of the towns in South Lancashire, work almost stopped in the cotton mills. But the ships still arrived in Liverpool and their goods had to be unloaded. The dock warehouses filled for a time, and some of the better-known Chartists, William Jones and Robert Gammage, came to the city and spoke, but they failed to muster enough support. By July, it was over with, and in August a number of its leaders were arrested and put on trial in Lancaster. The uprising had failed to achieve much, and the Irish dockers seemed relieved that they had played little part in it. They had worked and fed their families, unlike the striking cotton operatives, many of whom had been forced to the brink of starvation before returning to work.

Autumn arrived and departed, and Catherine's bump grew larger. Austin had shared the news with his mother, who then coordinated with Ann in telling their respective spouses. It worked. Neither Edward nor Darby seemed surprised, or alarmed, by the prospect of a grandchild, though the promise of an extra mouth to feed was always a concern. Children might be a joyful fact of human existence, and yet the commitment they required was not always welcome. But then, in Edward and Darby's eyes, a grandchild was not a child they would have to feed themselves. It would be Austin's responsibility. They might help along the way, but he would have to find his own means of providing.

November and December were remarkably mild months. The weather stayed relatively warm, unusually so. As the city counted down the days to Christmas, Austin and Catherine began to wonder whether their child might not arrive until January. By Christmas Eve, they had both come to expect it.

But their son had other ideas.

Christmas Eve had fallen on a Saturday – one of the two main market days; the other being Wednesday. It had been a busy day for Catherine. Up several hours before dawn, she had already worked for twelve when her waters broke. With some assistance from one of her fellow market workers, she made it back home about an hour before her father was due to return. Upon seeing her daughter in some distress, and quickly realising what was happening, Ann had sent her own Bridget to bring the midwife, having already warned her the previous week. The midwife arrived, clutching a traditional birthing stool, and immediately took control of the situation. With the women of the household gathering round and being allocated tasks, young Ann was then sent around to the Melia household to tell Austin that the baby was on its way.

An hour later, Austin and Bridget Melia arrived at the Cunningham household. By then Catherine was already in full labour, a shriek, a cry, or an occasional shout punctuating the generally silent ambience of the dwelling. There was both fear and expectation competing for dominance, as concern for the welfare of Catherine and her as yet unborn child, vacillated with speculation about the sex of the baby. Most present hoped and expressed a preference for a boy, except for Ann who was adamant that it did not matter. All that mattered was that mother and baby would come through the experience alive and well.

Hours passed. As the evening wore on, Ann spent most of her time with her daughter, her other daughter, Bridget, being sent down to provide an update to the rest of the household and Austin. Edward called in a little later but did not stay. There was nothing he could do, and he had Austin's younger siblings to attend to.

Shortly after a distant church clock chimed ten, the baby arrived. Bearing down on the midwife's birthing stool, an exhausted Catherine gave a final push, allowing gravity to do the rest. She had produced a boy. The midwife quickly cut the cord and handed the baby to Ann, who immediately wrapped him tight in some old bed sheets. The child was already crying and apparently needed no encouragement. As the midwife dealt with the placenta, Catherine flopped backwards, seemingly unable to speak. Ann and the midwife helped her lie on the bed before showing her the baby. Holding her new son, she could only summon up a single sentence before handing him back to her mother and seeking the solace of sleep.

'Tell Austin that Edward has arrived,' whispered Catherine, clearly exhausted by the experience.

'Edward...' repeated Ann. '...I'll take him downstairs to meet his father and the rest of the family.'

Downstairs, Austin greeted Anne's presentation of his new son with both a wide grin and a look of concern.

'Is she well?' He also wanted news of Catherine.

'She's sleeping. The birth went well. I think she will be alright. The midwife will stay a while,' replied Ann.

Austin nodded. 'He'll be named Edward after my father.'

'I thought as much. We all thought as much. The old ways are how it should be,' interjected Darby, who had remained uncharacteristically silent for most of the evening.

'I'll take him back upstairs to be with his mother. You can see her, but she should be left to sleep. Go and get some rest yourself. It will soon be Christmas Day and we'll have Mass to go to.'

'I'm a father, Ma,' said Austin to his mother on the way home.

Bridget smiled. Today was a day for joy, and at Christmas as well. As for the future, well that was for another day.

* * *

Edward was baptised on January 8th, two weeks after his birth. Soon after the parish priest recognised the incongruous nature of Austin and Catherine's living arrangements, clerical pressure to formalise their partnership emerged. While both families understood the need for Austin to try and build some sort of savings, their parish priest was a little less patient. He started to ask when Austin and Catherine would be married, reminding the families that if the pair were to receive the grace of God, then they should be formally married in the Church. By spring the pressure to conform had become too great. Four months to the day after Edward was baptised, Austin and Catherine were married. It was a simple ceremony with only their parents and a couple of friends present to act as witnesses.

Catherine had moved in with Austin and his parents shortly after Edward's arrival. They had to share a bedroom, which was not ideal, but it was necessary. In time they might afford a room of their own, but for now Austin had to make the pragmatic decision to take what help was on offer. Whether that would be months or years away remained to be seen.

Chapter 4

1846

'No Irish Need Apply.'

Catherine had tried to find some employment as a domestic servant, in the belief that the work might be a little less hard and better paid than the street markets. As with the rest of her family, friends, and almost all within the Stockdale Street community, she could not read. Few Irish could, anywhere in Liverpool. But she now knew enough to recognise the depressingly familiar pattern of the letters proclaiming a prospective employer's employment criteria.

A few months after Edward's birth, Catherine had been told about some opportunities springing up a mile or so away from their own part of Liverpool. Quite a number of dwellings had been constructed in a newer part of the city, to the west of Rodney Street. Having made some arrangements with both Bridget and Ann for childcare, she told Austin of her plans, determined to see for herself. Austin seemed uncertain about the idea, but with work becoming less predictable, he agreed to it. They needed any extra money Catherine could earn.

After asking for directions, she duly arrived at the junction of the streets she now knew as Falkner Street and Bedford Street.

Already she felt out of place. The finely dressed women, and for that matter men, going about their business soon noticed her. Although wearing her Sunday best, they were nothing but rags to the occupants of the fine houses in front of her. People were staring and giving clear looks of disapproval. To add to the feeling of being underdressed, she now felt most unwelcome as well. Unsure of what to do next, she anxiously searched for some help. Everyone knew that the front entrance of these grand houses was out of bounds, so she resolved to find a back street. It was in Back Bride Street where the help, or 'guidance', was eventually provided.

Spotting a woman dressed in less imposing garments, perhaps a housekeeper she thought, Catherine summoned the courage to ask a question.

'I hear there's domestic work hereabouts. Can you tell me where that might be?'

She was as polite as she could be but was met with a stony face. It was as if the woman was insulted that Catherine had the temerity to ask her a question.

'Be away with you. Can't you read? There's no work for Irish here. Begone before I fetch a policeman,' said the older woman in an attenuated Lancashire dialect.

Taken aback by the repulse, Catherine hesitated. What had she said that was so wrong?

'I just—' started Catherine.

'I'll go back in the house and fetch the master. He'll deal with you, here and now. It'll be a whipping. Go back to where you came from!' interrupted the woman. She seemed unwilling to hear any more.

Crestfallen, and more than a little alarmed, Catherine began to retrace her steps, attempting to put as much distance between her and the woman as she could.

It was a lesson she would not, and could not, forget. The rich did not really want the Irish in Liverpool. They would tolerate them, use them to build the docks and undertake the heavy labour required to make the city function, but they seemed unwilling to accept them into their homes. Catherine knew then that she would never get any domestic work; she could not read, and her accent gave her home country away as soon as she opened her mouth. After that experience she thought once or twice about having another go, but underneath she knew that her life had already been mapped out. Her only chance to improve their lot would be to continue to work in the markets; the life of a fish dealer called out. It was not a pleasant or easy occupation, but was a step up from the alternatives – untwisting oakum, crushing sandstone or hawking broken boxes. And it was certainly better than working the streets like some she knew or, worse, starvation.

* * *

Some of the money Austin and Catherine had managed to save had been applied to acquiring a hand cart, not unlike the one Austin and his family had used in their trek across Ireland six years earlier. With the purchase of a cart, Catherine could now break free of servitude and deal in fish herself. The transition was almost overnight. On Wednesday she was taking orders, but by the following Saturday she was in direct competition with her former employer. New dealers were not welcome, with dirty tricks often being played to discourage them from trading. But these tactics did not last. Once it was clear that a trader was here to stay, the 'mob', as she called them, would move on to something or someone else. It was just the way it was.

Life in the fish market was hard. Catherine would have to wake so early that she often wondered why she had bothered going to bed in the first place. She would rise even before Austin, and would try to carefully ready herself without waking anyone else in the house. The rhythmic squeak of the hand cart would sometimes undermine her efforts as she wheeled it out of the court. Then, hours before many were on the street, she would push the cart down to the docks, usually starting with the relatively new Coburg Dock, which had become popular with a number of small fishing boats. She would not buy much in variety, typically shrimp and cod. Nothing too fancy. And she would have to be careful about buying too much. Anything not sold would have to be either eaten or thrown away, if not fresh. And the family could not afford the latter.

She would occasionally try and barter a few fish for some meat, but the nearby meat dealers were generally not too enthusiastic. More often than not it would be another fish supper. It was food on the table but not always as welcome at home as it ought to be. Nonetheless, it always got eaten when the choice was to eat or not to eat.

About six weeks after starting as a dealer, a haughty woman appeared in front of her cart to inspect what was on offer.

'I'll have four cod; only the best, mind,' demanded the woman.

Catherine recognised her immediately, although it was clear from her demeanour that the woman did not recognise her.

'Would you like some shrimp as well? It won't cost you a lot. Cheaper than most around here,' asked Catherine.

'No. I would have asked if I wanted shrimp. Do as you are told, girl,' replied the woman.

Irritated by the woman's 'girl' comment, and now reminded of how upset she had been after their first meeting, Catherine resolved to get her own back.

'I'll wrap them up for you, ma'am,' said Catherine, as she furtively replaced one of the fresh fish with one from under the cart – a fish now off and destined for disposal.

Handing over payment, the woman still had another complaint.

'You're not the cheapest, are you?'

'But I am the freshest. All caught last night. You can't get fresher than that,' replied Catherine, knowing fully that she had supplied something far from that.

The woman took the fish off Catherine and walked away without the hint of any politeness. Catherine was fully aware of the reputational risk associated with supplying bad fish, but on this occasion, she had decided to make an exception. 'No Irish Need Apply' indeed. She smirked at the thought of the woman's reaction once she returned home and realised what had happened.

* * *

'That doesn't look right to me,' said Austin, who had been removing some potatoes from a basket Catherine had brought home.

'It looks blighted, black spots all over some of them,' he added.

'There were lots of them like that. I tried to pick out the best, but...' replied Catherine.

'They shouldn't be selling them like that. I remember back in Mayo, if there were any like that, we threw them away. We didn't even want to give them to the dogs. I know how to plant potatoes. Plant them in a breezy spot; there was never any problem with that in Uggool. And pull any out that show the signs. You know, black spots on the tips of the leaves. We all knew that,' said Austin, stretching the truth a little.

'I know as much, Austin. We grew potatoes as well. But that's what we have. They're Irish potatoes, usually the best, but not any more,' replied Catherine.

'I'll see if I can get some better ones,' said Austin.

'I doubt you will. It's everywhere. And people are starting to talk. Haven't you noticed there's more people on the ships?' asked Catherine.

'There's always more Irish coming in. There were thousands more last year, many more than the year before. It will pass, I'm sure,' said Austin.

'We'll see,' replied Catherine.

The first hints of problems with potatoes had appeared a year earlier, but now the stories had started. Gossip in the market was that the blight of 1845 had returned in 1846, and that food was starting to become in short supply in the home country. Still, it was just gossip, and gossip was often wrong. They both chose to ignore the stories.

The quality of their potatoes improved somewhat in the ensuing weeks, so both Catherine and Austin dismissed the incident as an aberration, unlikely to be repeated. Prices had gone up, but not to the extent of causing any more of a problem for the family budget. Whatever the cause, it was not something that they thought they should have to worry about. At least, not yet.

* * *

Unlike his father, who had already accepted the capricious nature of the allocation of work and its gang-like tribalism and politics, Austin felt that he had to seek income that was more dependable. With a wife and young son to support, he felt he had to. It was also no use that the two of them had to rely on the same source. When times were good, and ship arrivals were plentiful, they would eat, but if they did not arrive there was simply not enough money in the household to feed everyone. As Catherine sought domestic work amongst the wealthy, he started to ask in the beerhouses, and explore other ideas for improving their financial position.

'We could open this room and sell ale and whiskey,' suggested Austin, after supper one night.

'Over my dead body, we will,' replied his mother. With Catherine working so much, Bridget had taken to helping nurse the baby who was now almost a year old.

'There's money to be made. We need more, Ma; you know we do,' said Austin.

'I've seen them. A few square yards with tables attached to each of the walls. Drunk, foulmouthed men, and striapach, prostitutes, shouting obscenities and crudities at each other. And in front of the children as well. I'll not have that under my roof. I'd rather starve,' replied Bridget.

'Ma, I just want to provide. Earn enough to move out,' said Austin.

'What's the point of that? You'll just move away from us into another court, and with strangers. It makes no sense. We're family. We help each other. It's the Irish way,' replied Bridget.

'I know that. But the porter work, it's so chancy. You never know when it will be there. McCabe has been good to us, but when the ships don't come, well, he always seems to find something for himself when we don't. And what if Da gets ill?' said Austin.

'Don't remind me of that. It's a worry every day, but we have to live our life. We survive. Ask around for something else. There must be other work. What about navvying?' asked Bridget.

'There's no work nearby that I know of, and the money is no better than the docks,' replied Austin.

'Have you asked? said Bridget.

Austin hesitated. He knew he hadn't. It was true that he knew of no work, but then again, he had not made any enquiries. His mother was right, although he remained reluctant to admit the fact.

'I'll keep my ears open, Ma.'

'See that you do that,' replied Bridget. She knew he had not asked but decided not to make an issue of it.

'What are these navvies?' asked John, who had been listening to the conversation between his eldest brother and mother.

Catherine had managed to get him some occasional work on the markets, but now he was getting older, and bigger, he wanted to learn more about man's work and 'proper' wages.

'Most of them used to work on the navigations, so they called them navvies. Hard work digging them canals. Now they call anyone working on building the docks navvies as well,' replied Austin.

'Can I get work as a navvy, or on the docks?' asked John.

'You're still too young and too small, John. When the time comes, we'll find some work for you. Meantimes, stick with your Aunt Catherine. Any money you bring home helps,' replied Austin. Catherine and Bridget nodded their heads in agreement. Dock work of any type was dangerous and not for the very young.

'Perhaps when you are sixteen, another three or four years, John,' suggested Bridget.

Disappointed, John returned to listening.

'I'll start asking around. There must be something going, what with all the dock building work going on,' said Austin, closing the discussion.

* * *

In the following months, Austin made it his business to ask around on a regular basis. As luck would have it, in late 1843 he had been asked by a friend, William Dolan, to help track down his daughter who he claimed had been abducted.

'Aye, she came in, she did. She said she was a washerwoman and that if our Margaret went with her, she would be sure of getting her regular work. Mary and me, we encouraged Margaret. We never thought that we would never see or hear of her again. That was two weeks ago. I need to find her,

Austin. She's a good girl. Only twelve, and at Mass every Sunday. We are both worried sick,' said William.

Austin had heard of these situations before. It was all too common in Liverpool. One day they were an innocent girl helping round the house, and the next they were in a brothel. It was impossible to know who to trust these days.

'Did anyone see where they went? Did she say where they might go? What was she wearing?' asked Austin.

William failed to give much clarity on any front. What he did say was not helpful, nor particularly useful.

'Do you think she might be in a beerhouse?' asked Austin.

William looked embarrassed, ashamed that he had been a prime mover in his daughter's disappearance. Austin seized the moment with a suggestion.

'We'll have to check the beerhouses. There are dozens, hundreds even, but what choice do we have?'

'I know. But I have to find her,' replied William.

And so, they started checking the beerhouses, one by one. Sometimes they would have a drink, but most of the time it was a case of going in and asking. At first, they asked about a 'fair-haired girl, about fourteen, goes by the name of Margaret'. But then they realised it was best to simply ask whether they had 'any young girls, thirteen or fourteen for service'?

Weeks passed by with little luck. But that situation changed, along with their style of investigation. Austin took the opportunity to ask about navvy work on the docks, before asking about entertainment services. It seemed to put his hosts at ease, willing to talk more about other things. One night was particularly fruitful. As usual, he asked the beerhouse keeper about dock work while the man supplied some ale.

'Aye. I hear there is some coming. There's an idiot that's been building small warehouses and burning them down again. He's been doing it for years now. He pays people to build them! There's many a fool. They say he's building the finest new dock in Liverpool soon. He needs hundreds to do it. I say he's an idiot with too much money and too much stupidity.'

Austin took the ale jug and split its contents with William. It was beginning to look like his good turn would be of help to his own needs.

Their search for Margaret had also extended to many of the grog shops and pennyale cellars, as well as the specialists in whiskey and beer. After nearly four weeks of almost constant searching, they heard about a beerhouse that they had missed the first time they checked. Leeds Street was only a short walk away from William's court, which was off Great Crosshall Street. Neither of them thought that Margaret would be so close, but they were about to be proved wrong.

They had decided to explore Scotland Road, close to St Anthony's and St. Martin's Church. It was far away from the Dock Road, but having spent weeks around Vauxhall and the Dock Road area, it seemed like a good idea to try it. Passing the pipe-smoking and noisy gangs of young lads, they paused for a moment or two to listen to the street singers who were entertaining audiences with bawdy tales and songs about death and destruction. It was here that William's ears started to burn with the tale of a drowning man, and a young girl who had become involved in the accident.

'Did you know about one right next to the canal, Austin?' asked William.

'No, I did not. There's a lot of roughs down there, William. We did not go round the back, if you remember. There was a gang of them. Dangerous around there,' replied Austin.

'I have to know, Austin. You know I do. Will you come?' asked William.

'We can try, but maybe we should bring a couple of the lads. You know, just in case there is trouble. Them shorties are evil,' replied Austin, referring to the short, stocky appearance of a typical 'rough', as they were called.

'Tomorrow then. I'll see if John Goff and Paddy Malone will come along. I've got a feeling about this one, Austin,' said William.

'I know. Of course, I'll come,' replied Austin.

Just after seven the following evening, as agreed between them, the four men met at the junction of Leeds Street and Vauxhall Road. Feeling safer in numbers, they marched down Leeds Street to the point where it intersected with the canal. In between the canal and the last property before it, lay a small unpaved path, probably leading to an entrance not immediately within sight. It seemed to be well trodden, with both men and women walking backwards and forwards.

'It has to be a beerhouse. Let's see,' said William, ever anxious for an answer to his missing daughter question.

They started to walk by the canal. As they did so, two white trousered roughs appeared, heading towards them. Spotting Austin's group, they suddenly turned and started back to wherever they had just come from.

'Trouble?' asked Paddy. He was known to be always ready for a fight.

'I dunno. We'll see,' answered Austin.

The group turned the corner and were confronted by three sullen looking males, thick necks, plain featureless faces, and heads which seemed disproportionate to their bodies.

'Beerhouse? Girls?' shouted Austin.

The three men ignored their comment, but made no threatening moves as Austin, William, Paddy, and John entered the beerhouse. They were, after all, outnumbered.

The room inside was much larger than the usual beerhouse; about three times the size. It was dark, filled with quite an unpleasant aroma of tobacco smoke and sweat, and already full of a large number of men shouting and leering. Women and girls were carrying ale, and either already entertaining men or trying to catch their attention. Younger children added to the social melee, adding their own distraction. It was still cold outside, but in here it was warm; hot even. A fire had been lit but was unnecessary – a curse even, given the heat of the room. The atmosphere was jovial, but not in the way you might celebrate a family event, more commerce than community.

Leading his companions, Austin walked towards a table set in front of a small door wedged in the corner of the room. Empty jugs lay across its surface. Seconds after he arrived in front of the table, a balding, squat, red-cheeked man appeared. His face had pockmarks, suggesting an encounter with some unnamed disease in his past, and he filled most of the available space on the other side.

'Two jugs of fourpenny,' said Austin.

The beerhouse keeper turned his back and started to fill the jugs. As he did so, Austin asked about dock work, as was now his habit.

'Eightpence. I don't know of any,' replied the beerhouse keeper, more curt than polite.

'Do you have rooms and entertainment?' asked Paddy.

'We do. What do you want? We have men, women, girls, and boys to suit any taste. If you've got the money, that is,' replied the beerhouse keeper, eyeing the group with a look of wistful disdain.

'What about young girls? Enough for one each for the four of us?' asked Paddy.

'We've got two good ones. Both young. You could have them in turns,' suggested the beerhouse keeper, his interest now piqued with the prospect of a more lucrative service.

'Let's see them then,' said William.

The beerhouse keeper disappeared into the doorway behind his serving table. He returned minutes later with two sorry-looking girls, both showing signs of having been recently beaten. The girls were looking towards the floor as they walked in for inspection.

There was instant recognition.

'Margaret!' shouted William.

A girl looked up.

Shouting 'Da!' she instantly burst into tears as William rushed past the beerhouse keeper to grab her.

'I'll be taking her home. She's mine!' shouted William at the beerhouse keeper.

'Like hell you will!' The beerhouse keeper was not about to let one of his prize earners loose.

'Stand back!' Paddy intervened. In response, the beerhouse keeper lunged at him. But Paddy's patience had already been tested to its limit. In seconds, his fist struck the beerhouse keeper to the ground.

And then pandemonium broke loose.

The three roughs who had been standing at the door rushed in to help the beerhouse keeper. Two other men stood up and threw their empty jugs at Austin and John. John caught one on his back, but Austin jumped to one side, allowing the jug aimed at him to hit a sitting drunken woman, who had seemed oblivious to the commotion. She screamed, which seemed to exacerbate the panic that had by now engulfed the room. Women, children, and most of the men rushed towards the exit, unwilling to be caught up in the fracas.

Paddy hit whoever came near him. He was good with his fists, well-practised in the art of street fighting. He had floored one of the roughs already, and was heading for a second. Austin had been caught in the stomach by another rough. He was smaller than Austin, but had got the better of him by his speed. Usually fairly placid in nature, Austin's adrenalin went into overdrive. As the rough tried to thump him on his back while he was still reeling from the stomach punch, Austin suddenly and deliberately stood up. He caught the rough's chin with the back of his head, and the man screamed in pain. He had not been expecting that. Austin's headbutt had the effect of causing the man to bite off the end of his own tongue.

As Austin straightened, he could see blood everywhere. The rough had spat the tip of his tongue out on the floor, together with more blood than the injury seemed to warrant. Holding his mouth, and continuing to scream in pain, he soon saw that Austin was readying himself for another punch. The rough had clearly had enough. He backed away and immediately ran for the door.

Austin was now angry. Angry at being caught off guard by the rough, and angrier still when he saw John being attacked by the other rough and another man. He leapt two yards to John's rescue, and decked the other rough with a single punch to the head. A couple of the drunken women, the only ones who had not exited the room as the commotion began, started laughing. One poured some ale on the rough's head, which had the effect of rousing him from his temporary stupor. He attempted to get up, but Austin put his foot on the man's back.

'Stay down or you'll get another. And I'll hit you hard next time.'

The rough stilled himself, apparently willing to be compliant.

Removing one of his attackers allowed John to deal with the other. Years of toil on the docks had its uses. It made you hard. With a couple of punches John had the other man on the floor, joining the two roughs, one of whom seemed to have lost consciousness; the one Paddy had floored. Only a single man remained in the ring. For a few seconds he did not realise his predicament. He had been threatening William, who was in no mood to let anyone near his daughter again.

'Shall I deal with him?' asked Paddy, more than willing to take on another.

That seemed to get the attention of the man. He turned round and saw Austin, Paddy, and John, and the men on the floor.

'No trouble from me. I'll be going.'

'He's not worth it, Paddy. Let him go. It's this one I want to talk to,' replied William, pointing at the beerhouse keeper also lying on the ground.

'Stand up!' demanded William.

The beerhouse keeper groaned but seemed unwilling to stand. William gave him a hefty kick in the groin.

'Up! Now!

Still groaning, the beerhouse keeper slowly raised his corpulent form to a standing position.

'Where is she?' William did not explain who he was referring to.

'Who?' replied the beerhouse keeper.

William punched him in the stomach, causing the beerhouse keeper to bend over coughing.

'She was called Harriet, Da. I heard it once. She's not here. I've not seen her since she brought me here,' interjected Margaret, who until moments ago had been cowering with the other girl behind William.

'What was your business with my girl?' demanded William.

'She sold me to him, Da. He kept me locked upstairs for two weeks at first,' said Margaret.

'Me as well,' added the other girl.

William grabbed hold of the beerhouse keeper under his chin and lifted his head to face him. Fearful of William's next move, the man attempted to plead ignorance.

'I didn't know. I thought she was off the streets, not respectable like.' He tried defending his actions.

But it was to no avail. William lifted his head and for a second stared at the ceiling. Still holding the beerhouse keeper's head by the chin with one of his hands, he then forcefully dropped his forehead onto the beerhouse keeper's nose. It was violent and conducted with all the force of a headbutt intentionally designed to cause injury. As contact was established, the beerhouse keeper's nose exuded an audible crack. William had broken it. The man collapsed onto the floor in pain, blood starting to ooze from both nostrils. He groaned in ignominious surrender.

'Margaret, and you, girl. Go and wait outside,' commanded William.

The two girls walked towards the doorway. With them both outside, William picked up a couple of jugs and faced Austin, John, and Paddy.

'Smash everything! This place is finished!'

'What about the Po...' said Austin, attempting to encourage discussion.

'Smash!' The entire collection of jugs on the serving table were in pieces before he finished. As William fragmented the jugs, Paddy picked up two stools. One went through the only window, and the other dismembered on the nearest wall.

Outnumbered, Austin joined them. Table legs were detached from walls and disassembled into fragments. Barrel taps in the anteroom were turned on, and anything that could be broken was. With four at work, the destruction lasted no more than five minutes. The room had become a disorderly scene of carnage, with blood, wood, beer, and pot fragments littering its floor.

'We should go now. It's done,' said Austin.

William nodded, Paddy smiled, and John looked relieved that it was now ended.

'Quickly, lest help has been called,' added Austin, leading the group out of the door.

'With me, girls,' shouted William towards Margaret.

It was dark outside, and the formerly noisy alcove had been reduced to silence. The four men and two girls soon melted into the side streets of Leeds Street, making a circuitous getaway in case they were followed. At the junction of Marybone and Great Crosshall Street, they parted, with William taking both girls home.

'We'll all have a tale to tell tonight,' he said, his anger now subsiding.

'That we will,' replied Austin, leaving Paddy and John smiling.

'I'll see you in the morning,' said William.

Heart still beating fast, Austin nodded to the other men and started making his way up Marybone to the top end of Stockdale. His injuries had been light, and he could not help feeling he had done some good that night.

* * *

Though it had now been months, Austin often thought about that night as he walked down Leeds Street, typically the most direct route to wherever he was working. At first, he had been a little nervous and would often seek a companion on his morning walk to work, but as the months passed his fear diminished. Whatever happened to the roughs and the beerhouse keeper was unknown; not that he cared. It was their own fault for being such fools.

The tip about dock labouring work had proven to be fruitful. In the weeks after the beerhouse incident, he started making enquiries at a flag yard close to the canal. A handful of stonemasons there got to know him by name, and when an announcement about the new docks needing more workers was made, Austin was high on the list of potential employees. As an unskilled worker, he was hired as a stonemason's labourer. It was hard and dangerous work, but it was more reliable than dock portering. He took the job as soon as it was offered.

Building the new dock required hundreds of navvies, mostly Irish, to dig out the cleared basin and erect its new stone river walls. Earlier docks had used sandstone – cheaper than granite, but less hardwearing and more prone to damage. By the time the dock basin had been started, the decision to use granite was a foregone conclusion. While the warehouses could use sandstone, the basin walls themselves would be of fine Scottish granite. The dockyard's trustees had acquired a quarry in Kirkcudbrightshire, and for several years the best granite the quarry could offer was hewn from the rockface and transported to Liverpool.

For two years Austin laboured under a succession of stonemasons, firstly working with the granite used in erecting the dock basin walls, and then carrying the red sandstone and bricks used in building the warehouses. During his work on the buildings, he saw the basin flooded some weeks after its completion. Shortly after that, he saw the first ships sail in. They could not use the partially completed warehouses, but the dockyard was now alive. By the spring of 1846, he had helped build what many were saying was one of the finest docks in Britain. It was achievement, but for Austin his main source of satisfaction was that he had worked every day, except Sundays, without interruption. There had been no stoppage due to the fickle nature of marine traffic; he had earned some good money and provided for his family.

* * *

The rumours had started in late spring. At first, they talked about the Queen, but then talk was of Prince Albert. They said he was coming to Liverpool for a visit and that he would open the new docks. Austin was no royalist, but having worked for so long around the docks, he felt them part of him, and the Prince seemed a little different to others of that class. For many in the city he was the respectable part of the wealthy and rich. He had already gained a reputation as a humanitarian reformist, against child labour and slavery, and seemed to be riding a popularity surge. By the middle of July, word had reached every part of Liverpool that the Prince would be arriving in the city to open the new docks. They were to be named in his honour, the Prince Albert Docks.

'The masons told me he will arrive at the end of the month. They all intend to try and see him if they can. He's coming on a work day, Thursday, but I don't think many will be working that day. I'm going to see if I can see him. They won't let the likes of us near, but we might get close enough to catch a glimpse,' suggested Austin.

'I want to go as well,' replied Catherine.

It was a Sunday evening, and most of the family had eaten and shared one or two jugs of ale.

'We'll all go. I want to see as well,' added Bridget, Austin's mother. It was not just the men who had heard of the impending visit; hearsay and chitchat in the courts and streets had already spread throughout. Everyone wanted to see the Prince, even those who professed to despise the monarchy.

'We'll all go,' said Edward, who had just walked into the discussion.

'Alright then. See what other people are doing. How will they catch sight of him?' said Austin.

After some short discussion, it was agreed that all would go and visit the docks on the day of the Prince's visit, and in the meantime they would each find out the best way to get the closest view.

* * *

Thursday, July 30th, arrived. It was a fine summer's day, the 'weather being everything to be desired', as the newspapers were later to report. The usual hurly burly of Liverpool life seemed to pause as wave after wave of all types of people descended on the docks. Hours before the Prince's arrival, the leading streets of the city were swarming with excited spectators, all apparently proceeding in different directions, and each hoping to secure a better position than others.

Unclear about when the Prince was due to arrive, Austin and Edward led their families towards the dock area a few minutes after eight in the morning. As expected, all the main access points were blocked. Liverpool's policemen were out in full force to ensure that only the city grandees could get anywhere near the Prince. Anyone not invited was robustly discouraged from hanging around.

'You knew that would happen,' said Bridget, seconds after a constable had almost threatened Edward and Austin if they did not return to where they came from.

'We had to try. It's still early. We might have got in,' replied Austin. He knew they had little chance, but he believed in Irish luck. Not so today.

'What about one of the boats? McCabe said they were allowing people to use them. But they wanted a penny,' suggested Edward.

'A penny!' repeated Bridget, unimpressed.

'What else are we to do. There's thousands here already. In a few hours there will likely be ten times that. And it will be only a half penny for children,' replied Edward.

'There's no money to be earned today, and we are supposed to pay to stand on a boat?' said Bridget, now clearly doubting the wisdom of the excursion.

'I know. But again, what else are we to do? Go home?' replied Edward. He knew Bridget was right. It would be a little harder this week, but there had been other times with almost no money coming in.

'It's not every day a Prince visits Liverpool. And I've never seen one. I want to see if he looks any different to the rest of us. They say he's German, you know,' added Edward.

'I'll help pay,' offered Austin. It was his idea, and he felt he ought to.

'It's settled then. We'll find McCabe. I know which boat he'll be on, and he's no fool. He's probably already found the best for a good view,' said Edward.

An hour later the whole family had located McCabe and obtained access to a small ship moored on the river. They were not alone. Dozens of others had the same idea, with everything that could float already crowded with spectators. Some were decked with bunting and flags of the Empire, while people on others were using scarves and hats as props for waving and welcoming the Prince.

'I'm hungry,' said John.

'You're always hungry,' replied Bridget. She had brought a little bread but that was about it. She turned to Edward and Austin.

'It's been hours. I heard the twelve o' clock chime not long ago. When do you think he will arrive?'

Edward and Austin shrugged, having no more idea than Bridget.

Less than a mile away, the Prince had already reached Liverpool. A special train had arrived in the city shortly before twelve o' clock. Even before Bridget had spoken, Prince Albert had already been received by the mayor and senior officials, and was well on his way to a reception at a judge's residence. Next on the itinerary was a visit to the Town Hall, where a speech would be made by the recorder, and a reply made by the Prince himself.

It was past one o' clock before he reached the pier, his arrival signalling commencement of the opening ceremony. As more caught sight of him, the crowds erupted in a wave of cheering and shouting goodwill. It was the same on the vessel Edward had chosen.

'I've never seen anything like this before!' shouted Austin. He was speaking for them all.

Dozens of ships of all types thronged the Mersey. Most were profusely decorated with colours and manned by sailors in their best dress. Royal salutes were being fired in all directions. The ceremony complete, the Prince drove down to the docks and proceeded to the Royal Yacht, *The Fairy*, accompanied by senior members of the dock committee and port naval officers. The Royal Yacht then rapidly headed to the Cheshire side of the Mersey before starting to steam upriver.

At last, they could see something. Hours and hours of waiting, time spent cheering at an unseen prince and distant ceremony, had eventually paid off. The yacht was not a large vessel. A more knowledgeable passenger had told Edward that she was 'about three hundred tons, less than a hundred and fifty feet, with a twenty-one-foot beam. She's a steamer and new.' That was about all he knew, but he shared what he had, much to the bemusement of Bridget and Catherine.

Their own boat was moored on the northern side of the Mersey, but they could see enough, probably more than those thronging the city streets.

'Look at her. She's fast,' opined Austin.

They cheered as the vessel passed by.

'Is that him?' asked John.

It was difficult to say from their position, but they knew that he must be one of the heads gently bobbing up and down on the deck.

'Yes,' replied Austin. He had no idea but did not want to disappoint anyone.

The *Fairy* swiftly sailed by. For a couple of minutes, they had a fairly clear view of the deck of the ship. It had a tall single chimney that exuded dark smoke, a wheelhouse, davit, and skylights along its side. It was difficult to count the people standing on deck and to tell one from the other, but they guessed at least twenty. Following the *Fairy*, about forty ships of all types steamed past.

'Where's he going?' asked John.

Austin and Edward shrugged. Neither knew.

But the question was soon to be answered. In the distance, the Royal Yacht crossed from the Cheshire side to the Liverpool side and headed back down river. The people riverside, and on vessels, cheered even louder as the flotilla passed them by. The Prince could at last be clearly seen. Artillery roared, flags were waved, and crowds shouted even more enthusiastically than earlier. It was a spectacle indeed.

As the Royal Yacht disappeared out of view, people on the riverside vessels began to disperse back into the city streets. Edward, Austin, and family joined them, knowing full well that they were unlikely to see much more of royalty that day.

'Let's go home. He's here for another day. I know that because the masons told me he is laying the foundation to the new sailors' home. There may be more work for me there. We'll have to see,' said Austin.

Unknown to the tens of thousands leaving their vantage points, at around half past two the Prince's Yacht had sailed into the new dock and around it to the cheers of those lining its sides. He later visited the Prince's Dock, South Corporation School, Blue Coat Hospital, St. George's Hall, and the Assize Courts, before returning to lodgings in St. Anne's Street.

* * *

A grand procession of local clergy, merchants, tradesman, Oddfellows, Rechabites, schools, and seamen, had been organised to precede the Prince on his short journey to the location of the new Sailors' Home. A handful of the stonemasons from Austin's yard had been asked to participate, though none of the labourers were deemed needed. The Prince followed this procession in an open carriage, again to thousands of cheers from many who had lined the streets for a second day. After the ceremonies, he departed Liverpool from Lime Street Station – now celebrating its tenth year – at around four o'clock. His visit was regarded as an outstanding success.

The flag yard did not have a full complement of masons present, but that mattered little. There was work to be done and pay to be earned. For Austin, Friday was a day like any day. He had seen the Prince and had little appetite to see him again. However, as the workers talked about the events of Thursday, he did hear a story which caused some amusement. Austin shared it with the rest of the family that evening over their meal.

'I heard a tale today. It caused some bemusement amongst the masters yesterday. A man in charge of organising the police and other officials caused the band to strike up *God Save the Queen* when the major arrived. He should have waited for the Prince, but no, they played the anthem for the mayor. A lot of people there were not very pleased with him; some were embarrassed.

Of course, the likes of us thought it funny and laughed at the bungle. I almost wish we had been there. It would have been worth it for that,' said Austin, doing his best to entertain.

'They're all fools, if you ask me,' said Bridget, more derisive than amused.

'Well, I thought it funny,' replied Austin.

Catherine smiled. It was a good little story but not as funny as many she had heard.

The protocols surrounding the use of the National Anthem had been explained to him earlier in the day. Alas, without this knowledge, the rest of the family simply did not see the same humour in the tale as Austin now did.

* * *

'He's a good lad, from Mayo like the rest of us,' said Austin to Catherine.

She had been asking about John Boylan, a man Austin's sister Ann had been seeing.

'I think they'll wed, Austin, before the year is out,' replied Catherine.

'She could do worse. He does labouring work like the rest of us. It always seems to be working either as a dock porter or general labourer for the likes of us. I said I would try and get him into the yard. I'm trusted there now,' claimed Austin.

'I'm sure you are, but he works with his brother, James. I think they carry bricks for the bricklayers. There's plenty of work there at the moment,' replied Catherine.

'That there is,' said Austin.

With Autumn's arrival came the predicted wedding. Ann married John Boylan in October, and moved out to live with her mother-in-law and new brother-in-law. Edward and Bridget's family were starting to move out to set up home elsewhere. They were usually not too far away, but moving even a few yards felt like progress. Austin, Catherine, and the baby decided to stay living with Austin's parents, despite earlier ambitions to move on. The advantages childcare provided remained too much of a benefit to contemplate shifting a couple of hundred yards. What would be the point?

1846 ended a little different than it had started. One of the mildest and wettest of winters was followed by one of the coldest on record. Severe frosts and below zero temperatures caused considerable havoc with the stonemasons' work, and a number of projects were periodically halted. For Austin this was a problem. When the work was halted so was his pay. There were times in the closing weeks of the old year, and in the opening weeks of the new, when he wondered whether he might be better off back working as a dock porter. He had little appetite for its uncertainties, but they needed the money.

After discussing it with Edward, who by now was already complaining of more aches and pains than he cared to remember, Austin decided to leave things be. He just hoped that the cold weather would soon yield to warm spring days. They might bring a bit of rain, but it was better than trying to work on ground the texture of granite, and with hands so cold they almost became glued to the stone he had to carry.

In the dark gloomy days of January when he could not work, and had no money for ale, he just hoped that 1847 would bring some better luck than the winter weeks had offered.

Chapter 5

'IRISH FEVER'

Austin was naturally worried about his own income and what the impact might be on the family during the closing weeks of 1846. But a greater disaster was already unfolding; a disaster which was already affecting thousands upon thousands of his countrymen. He had heard about the blight affecting the potato crop back in Ireland, and indeed had seen the evidence himself. Those black vegetables that seemed to appear from time to time often provoked comment at home, usually more critical than sympathetic. Alas, what those unsatisfactory products actually meant was only just becoming clear.

Increasing numbers were arriving from Ireland. Each one had the same story to tell; a story of catastrophe, famine, and death. By the end of November there was hardly a man, woman or child in Liverpool who was not aware of the plight of Ireland. The potato crop had failed again. Once was unlucky. Many still had the resources to make it through a bad season, but more than once meant starvation. Those that could afford passage, to anywhere, sought it, though that generally meant a short voyage to Liverpool. The message was also being carried by the voice of the Irish Catholics — the priests, both local and Irish.

Sunday Mass was a little different than usual on that first Sunday in December. A visiting priest, Father McEvoy – an Irish parish priest from Kells in County Meath – had been invited to address the congregation. What he had to say struck fear, pride, and empathy into the minds of those present.

'Last Monday I had the honour of giving a homily on the importance of charity and compassion to your fellow man. I spoke to your brethren at St. Joseph's Chapel on Grosvenor Street. Like yourselves, they are not of the wealthy class. Each must earn a wage to feed his family and keep a roof over their heads. Few have much to spare for any luxuries. But you and they are but rich as compared to your fellows back in Ireland. There is no food to fill the bellies of the children; the crop has failed. When a man can't feed his family, the children die. And dying they are. Everywhere I go I see death, parents selling everything they have, and offering what little they can to save their children. Even the clothes off their backs are sold. But it's still not enough. You've seen the thousands teeming into Liverpool Port every day. Half-naked, starving as they are, they are but the lucky ones.

'I appealed to those brave, compassionate Catholic men of Liverpool for help. Ordinary men; navvies they call them. That they may be, but they are but giants in the eyes of God. The men attending agreed to a man to give up a day's pay to help their fellows in the old country. A day's pay grafting, building a new railway to Bury. I have already received nearly fifty pounds. Fifty pounds! So, I ask of you, what can you do to help your less fortunate countrymen back in Ireland? What can you do to feed the starving children, whose parents are already lost to the scourge of the blight?'

The message was as clear as it could be. The emergency that had developed back in Ireland was cataclysmic and was already spilling over into Liverpool. Austin and Catherine had much to talk about on their walk back home.

'We should give something, Austin,' suggested Catherine.

'A day's pay? You know I've not been working every day recently. If we give what we have, how will we buy our own food?' replied Austin.

'We'll manage. So long as we have enough to buy fish, I'll be able to make a small profit. As Father McEvoy said, there are so many worse off than us. I've seen them in the markets these past weeks. They've asked me for fish. They'll even take the bad ones; such is their hunger. We have to do something, Austin,' said Catherine.

'What if your father or mine cannot work? Any spare we have will need to feed their families. There's more looking for employment as well now. The new arrivals are asking for work everywhere. Many have already been to the yard. They'll work for less as well. But for their state I'm sure I would have been replaced by now. The masons are not willing to take on a man who can't lift a stone, but who knows what will happen next year? I'm worried, Catherine,' replied Austin.

'I know all too well, Austin. It's me who makes the stew. But what are we to do? Nothing, while our fellow man starves? I just think of those poor children. No mother or father. I can't bear the thought. How will I be able to look at Edward without thinking of their plight? I'll find something to give,' said Catherine.

Austin shrugged. They were both right and each knew it. He decided that he had to trust that Catherine knew what she was doing.

* * *

The many thousands arriving had become an unmanageable flood by the middle of December. So much so that the Select

Vestry condemned ship captains for bringing over so many immigrants in so short a time. With tens of thousands clamouring to escape, the less scrupulous could pack their ships, charging a mere sixpence for passage. This simply encouraged more to seek escape.

By the end of the cold weeks of January, the streets were swarming with emaciated, hungry, and poorly clothed Irish immigrants all searching for hope. And still they came. Almost a thousand a day continued to enter the city from Irish ports, desperate for resolution to their wretched plight. The difficulties of these new arrivals were seen as an opportunity for some, and whether Austin, Edward, and their families wanted to help or not, they were about to be directly impacted by the misery that had descended on Liverpool.

Austin often worked in the flag yards, directly behind the new Northern Hospital on Great Howard Street that had opened two years earlier. It had been the site of the pig market, but a decision had been made that a far greater need had to be met: Liverpool's exploding need for some rudimentary healthcare. Of all the locations in Liverpool, this was one of least appeal to Austin. It was merely yards away from the beerhouse where he had helped his friend William to rescue Margaret, his daughter. Only the canal separated the perimeter of the flag yard and the path leading to the beerhouse. For weeks he remained wary of being seen, lest there were repercussions. Fortunately, as time wore on, signs of life returning to the establishment remained absent. In time he started to feel safe.

A fine mist, a drizzle, encompassed the city. The cold days of January had surrendered to slightly warmer but wetter February. The meagre increase in temperatures made Austin feel little better; the rain typically made him feel colder with its ability to penetrate his inadequate clothing. Working outside most of the time, he was almost always in a state of being wet and damp. For him February and March were the worst months of the year, and he always longed for them to end.

Leaving the yard after a hard day's labour, as was now usual, he passed by Liverpool's panopticon Borough Goal, which some still called the 'French Prison'. It was a place he never wanted to enter, after having been told tales of the abject misery of its unfortunate inhabitants. On a still day he would sometimes hear a demoniac scream, or a mystifying shout emerge from its characterless sinister walls, notable above the rhythmic pummelling of hammer and chisel against stone – the usual chime of the flag yard.

It was on these more misery inducing days of the year that he would think of an occasion, almost four years earlier, when he had witnessed an execution at another prison, Kirkdale. Encouraged by workmates at the docks, who thought it might be a good entertainment, he had been persuaded to join them. The case was somewhat unusual in that it was a woman, Betty Eccles of Bolton, who had been accused of murdering, by poisoning, ten people, including her husband and eight of her ten children. The case had caught the imagination of the people of Lancashire, with thousands turning up for the public hanging. There was little sympathy for the condemned as she was led to the scaffold. Women, horrified by Betty Eccles treatment of her children, spat at her and threw objects, some catching the guards. On the stroke of eight the executioner guided the rope around her neck. Recognising the finality of the act, the woman froze in fear, sure in the knowledge that these were her last moments on earth. And then the executioner pulled the bolt. The woman instantly dropped, and with the rope likely breaking her neck, with three or four flinches of movement she was obviously dead. Some in the crowd cheered, but most were more subdued. It was not really a cause for celebration.

Austin shuddered as he turned left onto Great Howard Street. He never wanted to see an execution again, or ever see the inside of a prison. Passing the hospital and several coal yards, he usually had a choice of whether to walk up Leeds Street, take Edmund Street, or if he really wanted to clear his mind, head towards the Exchange at the end of Old Hall Street. The Exchange stood behind the Town Hall. He had once entered in via the arcade, but it held little interest for him these days. It was a three-sided structure with one side consisting of Corinthian columns supporting caryatides, which in turn overlooked a monument to Nelson positioned in the centre of the piazza. Upon arrival in Liverpool Austin had been impressed, but not today. Familiarity had bred an attitude of indifference. It was just another of the fine buildings that Liverpool had to offer, and a sharp contrast to the dwelling he and Catherine shared with his parents and family. There was little justice in the world, and there was also little he could do to change things.

It was late and dark when he arrived back in his Stockdale Street court. As was now practice, Catherine would arrive home earlier and have a stew ready for both his and his father's arrival. Some days it would be Bridget, his mother, having charge of the cooking, but over time it had become more the responsibility of Catherine. Walking into the court towards his front door, he caught the usual whiff of stagnant air hanging in the enclosed space. It was worse than usual tonight, amplified by the still drizzly air; yet another day when the midden had not been cleared, allowing water delivered by recent rains to pool and stagnate. Feeling vaguely nauseous, he walked swiftly towards the front door and entered.

The room was even gloomier than usual, and there were no signs of cooking taking place. A single candle had been placed in the centre of the table, around which sat both his mother and Catherine.

'What—?' started Austin. He did not finish his question.

'Something's happened tonight, Austin,' replied Catherine.

It was only then, as his eyes adjusted, that he started to look around the room. There were strangers present, six of them. Two men, two women, and two children. None looked at all well.

'Who are these people?' asked Austin, slightly alarmed.

'The Fagans, Austin. They're from Galway. Arrived a few days ago. They've been sleeping on the streets for days. The landlord said we have to take them in. There's Henry Fagan and his wife Elizabeth, Brendan, Matilda, James, and Sarah,' replied Catherine, loosely pointing to each member of the family.

'You can't stay here. There isn't the room. We already have nearly twelve. There are not enough beds,' announced Austin.

'Austin!' Catherine sought to interrupt him.

'Henry paid the landlord the last of their savings. He said it wasn't enough, but they could stay a while,' Bridget explained.

'But we've paid the rent,' replied Austin.

'I know. Bridget knows. But what are we to do? We don't want any trouble. You know the difficulties we had in finding this place,' said Catherine.

'And he calls himself a Christian. Where's the charity in this? Packing us in with strangers. And taking our rent,' replied Austin.

'He told me it was his Christian duty to house them, and ours to live with them,' said Catherine, not totally clear on their landlord's motives.

'If he's a Christian he would have let them stay for free. But he took their money, didn't he?' replied Austin.

Catherine acknowledged the comment in the form of a shrug.

'That explains their presence, but why is there no food on the table?' asked Austin.

'They have not properly eaten for days, weeks even. Cabbages and turnips are all they've had. No fish. No meat for months. What am I to do? I can't feed them, Austin. Are they to watch us eat? Are we to watch them starve? I didn't know what to do,' said Catherine, clearly bewildered by the predicament their landlord had placed them in.

Henry Fagan, apparent head of his household, lifted himself to his feet. The family had been silent, simply listening to the discourse. He had little strength for argument.

'I'm sorry. I'm sorry for this. We'll have to go.'

Bridget then interjected. 'Where will you go? Back on the streets? What will you eat? What will you feed your children? You'll have to ask the Select Vestry, the Poor Law Guardians. But you can't do that tonight. Is your child well?'

Bridget pointed at the youngest, Sarah, who had started another bout of coughing. It was distracting and had the effect of promoting a feeling of guilt amongst the others present.

'It's our Catholic duty, Austin. We can't let them starve, can we?' said Catherine.

Austin could now read Catherine. He knew what she was going to say next and knew that he would have difficulty arguing against it.

'We'll have to share. We'll all have to have less tonight,' she added, looking for support from her mother-in-law.

Bridget nodded in agreement. 'It will have to be. I'll see if we can get any help from the parish as well. We can help for a few days, but we can't feed them forever. There just isn't enough.'

'Thank you,' said Henry.

'And may the grace of God be with you and yours,' added Elizabeth.

When Edward returned from working on the docks, he was less than pleased with the situation but could do little. A temporary solution had been found which momentarily alleviated the misery of their guests, but which already sowed the seeds of problems in the near future.

* * *

And still they came.

'It's getting worse. We had to take some in a few weeks ago,' said Austin.

He had been talking to one of the stonemasons, Andrew Murphy, an earlier migrant from Ireland. Older than Austin, he had left in more benign times and had been lucky to be taken on as an apprentice shortly after his arrival in Liverpool. Jobs had been easier to find in the thirties, and the Irish less numerous. Nonetheless, he admitted to his luck in not just being able to find work, but to achieve a skill that had remained in strong demand.

'Did the Vestry help?' he asked.

'They have, but it's not enough,' replied Austin.

'I've heard things are very bad in Marybone, Lace Street, Stockdale Street, Addison, Sawney Pope. Very bad,' emphasised Andrew.

Austin had never admitted to living in one of the streets his employer had mentioned, and winced when he listed them. He waited for Andrew to finish, always aware of his position and not wishing to jeopardise it.

'It's worse in the cellars. As many as forty have been found packed into a cellar. No air. No light. Rats, cockroaches, dirt, and damp. You wouldn't house a dog in it. And yet they expect people to live in such. There's too many coming in. It's got to stop. How, I don't know. But I do know it has to stop before there's riot on the streets,' added Andrew.

Austin agreed but had no solutions either.

'The authorities have to do more. They can't leave it all to the likes of Father Nugent,' he replied.

'Yes, I've heard of him. Even as far as Blackburn they are collecting money to help,' Andrew said.

'Austin, you have been a good worker for me, but I've got to tell you that times are getting harder,' he added, changing the subject.

Somewhat bemused, Austin had to seek some clarity on what was behind his employer's comment. It already had more than a hint of bad news in its tone.

'I'm having to take less from the builders. And that means I can't afford to keep paying you the wage you have. I'm sorry, but that's just the way it is. You know I've turned away many of the recent arrivals, but some are offering to work for less than a shilling a day; ninepence, sixpence even. I can't pay you a shilling if Samuel next door is paying sixpence. There will soon be no work for any of us. We have to accept the times,' said Andrew.

'I can't live on sixpence a day. What am I to do?' pleaded Austin.

'I didn't say sixpence, but I can't give you more than ninepence. That will have to do. You're a good worker but I can't do more. And I can't promise that I can keep it that high if things don't improve,' replied Andrew.

Austin felt sick to his stomach. Everything his employer had told him was true, but the knowledge of its truth did not help him. He still had rent to pay and food to put on the table.

What was he to say to Catherine?

* * *

The Fagans, McCabes, and Melias started to get on, though they had little choice. With the occasional help of the Vestry, alms from the parish, and what Edward and Austin had been bringing home, they just about managed. But as spring approached, conditions started to get worse. The Vestry, once the ultimate source of help, changed the basis upon which it gave assistance. Attitudes to the Irish had started to harden now that the financial cost of maintaining thousands of impoverished immigrants imposed a significant burden on the city. The less charitable officials started to blame the immigrants' plight on their proclivity towards drink, their willingness to send money back home, and general inability to budget.

It had always been difficult to have a private conversation at home, and with the Fagans and McCabes in the house it was now impossible. Austin felt he had to share the news about the threat to his pay as soon as he was able, though upon arriving at home his news had to wait. He was accosted by Henry Fagan with some news of his own.

'Austin, I have to tell you something. The Vestry are coming for us. I'm sure they want to send us back home. It'll be death for us if they send us back. Starvation for me, Elizabeth, and the children. I've seen it. I don't want to go back.'

Austin could see the fear in his eyes, but what he could not understand was why Fagan thought that way.

'Why would the Vestry send you back. They are there to help, are they not?' said Austin.

'It's not like that. The officials, they are complaining about the cost. Accusing many of fraudulent claims. Of stealing. We're honest people, but they just want to send us back, I'm sure. I've told Elizabeth that we shouldn't claim any more. I don't want the police knocking on our door and taking us,' replied Henry.

'They wouldn't do that. I'm sure they wouldn't,' said Austin.

'Last time we asked for help they told us that only people who have been here for five years can stay. You have been in Liverpool for years. They can't send you back,' replied Henry.

Austin had not for one minute considered that Liverpool officialdom could send him and his family back to Ireland.

Not for a minute. Like anyone who had been here for years, he was not happy with the hundreds arriving every day, but sending them back to starvation? Well, that was just un-Christian. Henry needed to know about his own situation.

'We won't be able to help you, Henry. I've been told today that my pay might drop by a quarter. The new arrivals will work for less, and my master told me he has to compete. I need more than ninepence a day for rent and food. I can't feed your family and my own. How will you pay your rent next week if there is nothing from the Vestry? What will you do?' asked Austin.

'I don't know. Trust in God's help, I suppose,' replied Henry.

Catherine, Bridget, Elizabeth, and their respective children heard everything. It was not how Austin wanted to deal with the problem, but Henry's report had forced the issue out into the open. Everyone now knew that they had the same problem as the thousands of other families in Liverpool – one that was not going to recede very quickly. They would have to work out how to bring in more money, or they might be the next Fagans.

* * *

Catherine was first with one or two ideas.

'We could take in more lodgers. One or two. Landlord need never know. They could sleep upstairs. If the landlord comes, we would just tell him they are visitors. And we could cut down on the leftover fish. I usually bring home the ones that are ready to go off, but perhaps I could try harder and sell them. And we hardly ever have meat. Now we won't have any, as we won't have as many fish to barter with. I could try selling on Sunday afternoon after Mass. If I can get some fish on Sundays, I can sell on the street. I don't want to, but times are hard. Perhaps I could ask Bridget to help with it, if she's willing.'

Austin listened to Catherine's notions but had little faith that any of them would make up for the money he would be losing. He was also none too keen on reducing their already meagre meals; he felt it was up to him to come up with something.

'There's night watchman jobs at the docks. They're having a big problem with theft. I could see if I could get a couple of nights a week there. I can't do more. I have to sleep sometime, or I'll lose my job at the yard.'

Catherine considered Austin's suggestion. It was a good one. Austin was still young, strong, and healthy, but even so, two full nights and six days work a week might be enough to kill any man, in time.

'I don't know. You'll never be home. It could kill you, Austin. I've seen what happens with other families when the man takes two jobs. They don't last.'

'But what choice do I have, Catherine? We don't have enough to pay the rent and eat. There will be nothing spare now. Nothing!' replied Austin, repeating the point to amplify it. He was tired enough already. The last thing he wanted to do would be to take on another job. But he had to provide. Perhaps they could ask his father, but he knew the realities of dock porter work. Though he was sure that Edward would help when he could, the stark reality was that those occasions would be infrequent at best. As had happened in the past, it was more likely that his mother would ask Austin for help rather than the other way round. After considering the situation, he felt that the decision was clear. He would have to see if he could get some watchman work, and sooner rather than later. Though with so many looking, there was no guarantee that there would actually be anything, even if he wanted it.

* * *

Austin was lucky. Lucky in the sense that a couple of recent watchmen had left due to the plague, Typhus – the latest scourge to hit Liverpool. The merchant who employed him was agreeable to Austin working two nights a week, and for ninepence a night. With both nights, it would make up the losses he now felt were certain to occur at the yard.

The first three weeks had been uneventful. For the first two, he had a companion, whose job it was to show Austin the routines and the areas they were employed to protect.

'Watch for the fire starters. We've had problems with them in the past. You'll get the blame if there's a fire,' advised his more experienced associate.

'What do I do if I see one? What if I get there after the fire has been lit?' asked Austin, already alarmed at the prospect of blame.

'You'll have to fetch the dock constables. They will decide what to do,' came the reply.

Austin had seen the dock constables walking around the docks, dressed in their distinctive but clunky black top hats, blue military style tunic, grey trousers, and sturdy boots. It was impossible to miss them. Indeed, on his second night as a goods watchman, he had been introduced to a couple of them to ensure that he would not be mistaken for a thief. Even as it was, the constables were none too sure about the wisdom of employing Irishmen as watchmen. When he met them, he more than had a feeling that they were going to watch him as much as the goods they were there to protect. He had also noted their fine watch huts – far better than the leaky, wind-prone, flimsy wooden pile he had been given.

He dropped the subject, sincerely hoping that he would not have to deal with anything as calamitous as a fire.

* * *

By early spring Austin had settled into a routine. On the days he was scheduled to work at night, he would head down to the docks to take instruction on his duties. It was not always in the same place. The work would move around, from dockside to dockside, depending on where the need was. Many parts of Liverpool's docks were already heavily protected by the dock constables, and had no need of people like him. But they could not cover everything. It was the transient and excess cargoes that were the problem. If a merchant could not get his goods into a warehouse, they would have to be left on the quayside. Without protection, these piles of vendibles were an open invitation for thieves. And with thousands starving, many more than in the past, people were not exactly unwilling to take their chances, with or without the threat of violence.

Catherine or Bridget would bring him some food, usually about six-thirty. He would not have much time to eat it, being expected to start half an hour later with an early evening tour of his protection duties. He had also been lucky in being able to arrange some cover with another man while he slept. No man can work for a full day without some sleep at least, and Austin was no exception. They each would sleep an hour, twice in the night, while the other covered. It was a risk, but a risk both men were prepared to take. Neither man had a choice.

For weeks the night watch had been relatively uneventful. Vagrants would try their hand now and then, but on most occasions, shouts and threatening moves would soon send them on their way. The sight of Austin and one or two other burly watchmen, sometimes a dock constable, would put the fear in most. Few wanted to be caught and risk an unwelcome stay in the Borough Gaol. But there were exceptions; not always the brazen, it was often the desperate.

The evenings were getting lighter, and Liverpool's winter rains were abating. In the cold and the wet, the risks of quayside fires were considerably reduced, but as the days grew longer, and drier, it seemed to encourage the fire starters and general law breakers. The opposite seemed true for the warehouses, where the winter nights facilitated criminal activities under the cover of extended darkness.

Austin thanked Catherine for his evening meal and breakfast food, and wished her farewell. He would not see her again until the following evening. His duties this particular night were to guard crates of tobacco which had been left near the tobacco warehouses on King's Dock. The warehouses were full that day, and their owner had no choice but to leave them in the open. They were amongst the most valuable goods, and very attractive to Liverpool's thieves. Austin knew it, and knew that of all the nights he had been working, this would be the one that would put him at most risk. He had an uncomfortable feeling that something was about to happen.

It was dark by seven. The moon was not yet full, and the wind was blowing westwards, bringing with it nebulous and doughy cumulous clouds. As the clouds passed, trailing a silver white-edged silhouette in their wake, the moon burst forth rendering the dockyards, its buildings, ships, and anyone one present almost daylight visible. For minutes Austin could see everything, before darkness returned with the next formation. Water gently lapped against the dock walls, and with this gentle movement, the abrasive creaks and groans of the wood and metal vessels moored for the night. He had become used to the noises and darkness, alert to the potential for something out of the ordinary.

Movement! He saw some movement from the corner of his eye.

Tightening his grip on the heavy wooden stick that had been given to him, he started to walk towards it. His heart started to thump. Not yet sweating, but already feeling warm and anxious, he was not sure what to do next. It was too early to call out; it might be a mistake, perhaps an animal or a trick of the light. He lifted the end of his pickaxe handle-shaped stick and started tapping it in his other hand. It was meant to appear like a threat, but he was on his own, and also knew that three or four could soon overpower him should they so desire.

Another cloud suddenly plunged the dock into darkness; the moon had disappeared. Austin looked upwards. It would be a good few minutes before moonlight would make a return appearance. He hesitated, reluctant to move further without sight of his way forwards. Perhaps he should have brought a candle lamp, but then that would have marked him out as a target.

Moonlight returned. Checking the sky, he concluded that he would have five to ten minutes before it again vanished into the elements. As he drew closer to the source of the earlier movement, he felt he heard some whispering above the ambient noise of the night-time docks. Then it stopped. Had they heard him, or had he imagined it? A few more yards, and Austin was standing at one side of a store of materials, piled eight or ten feet high, and perhaps as many in yards long. He edged around to the landside corner, attempting to be as quiet as he could.

He would see how many there were before deciding what to do next. If there was only one or two, the threat of a man with a big stick might be enough; more, and he would have to call out for help.

'What are you doing? Be off with you!' he shouted in a voice as masterful and threatening as he could command.

Both men turned, alarmed, at the interruption to their task. The cart they had with them was already almost full.

'Fagan! Uncle Patrick!' Austin was visibly both astonished and dismayed at the sight of two people he knew standing in front of him.

'Austin.' Both seemed relieved.

'Come and help us. There's much for all,' said Patrick.

Austin remained stunned. It had been years since he had last seen his Uncle Patrick, perhaps ten years. And yet here he was, standing right in front of him, attempting to steal his employer's goods. He was more than ever at a loss at what to do.

'I can't do that. I work here. You know that I do, Henry,' said Austin.

'You know him?' asked Patrick.

'I do. He lives in my court,' replied Austin.

'He's been working with me for weeks, Austin,' said Patrick.

Austin gave Henry Fagan a questioning look.

'It's true, Austin. I met Patrick weeks ago. Where do you think the money has come from recently?' said Henry.

'I assumed parish alms. I'm sure you told me,' replied Austin.

'I never said that. I would not lie to you. You must know that. I would not want to bring trouble on your head. That's why I never said a word,' said Patrick.

'Anyone who brings the police constables to our door will get us all thrown out. The landlord won't have it either. There's plenty who would have our roof,' replied Austin.

Henry's face tempered into one of guilt. He knew Austin was right but did not want to admit it.

'I-I had no choice, Austin. I have to feed my family. What would you have done?' said Henry.

'Not this. I'm sure not this. And you, Uncle Patrick. You've been here for weeks or months and not a word,' said Austin.

'I have the same problem as Henry here. No work. The Vestry will catch me and the family and send us back if they can. I can't ask for help. There's no work. You know that. We have no choice. Yes, it's a risk, but better that than starvation,' replied Patrick.

'Why didn't you look for us? You knew Da was in Liverpool,' asked Austin.

'I tried. I asked. I started to look. But we have to eat, Austin. And there are riches here on the docks,' replied Patrick.

'And dock constables. Some with weapons. You are not only risking gaol, but death. How will you family fare then?' asked Austin.

'It's hard, I know. But your circumstance is different to ours. What are you going to do now?' asked Patrick.

What was he going to do? It was the only question. A conundrum indeed. As every Irishman in Liverpool knew, times were hard, and starvation was real. It was not a vague and distant threat. It was happening to people every day. And if lack of food did not kill them, then disease surely would. What should he do?

'Leave now and I won't tell. Leave the cart. I'll say I caught you in the act and you ran off. They'll believe me,' suggested Austin.

'We've got a buyer already for this, Austin. We could give you a cut. You just need to forget you saw us,' replied Patrick. Henry nodded in agreement.

This was getting harder, thought Austin.

'I can't do that. You'll have me in chains like the two of you. I work hard for what I have. You just steal what's not yours. I don't want to ever go near a prison. I know enough about them to know better,' replied Austin.

As Austin remonstrated the rights and wrongs of the situation with Henry and Patrick, he was struck from behind. A third man had appeared, unseen and unheard, and hit him with some sort of blackjack. Falling to the floor, he lost consciousness before he hit it, hearing only 'tie him...' before blackness took control.

* * *

Dawn brought with it the usual hustle and bustle of activity. Gulls squawking overhead, shouts, and the clanging of machinery helped rouse him from his unplanned sojourn in wherever; he did not know. As he became aware of his surroundings, he soon realised that he had been tied and loosely gagged. He tried to shout but could not raise much of a voice. The wind had also changed direction which did not help. It was half an hour before someone noticed. It was a dock constable who saw Austin writhing on the pile of tobacco crates. At least he was not on the floor. Someone must have decided that he should spend the night on wood and tobacco rather than stone. He could smell it. Not entirely unpleasant.

On investigating Austin's predicament, the police constable released first Austin's gag, and then the rope tied around his arms and ankles.

'What happened?' Austin guessed that the constable could have guessed.

'I was jumped. Three of them. One got me from behind. I thought there were only two. My head. It hurts bad,' replied Austin.

The dock constable examined Austin's head. He could see the bruise that the blackjack had created. It was a big one.

'Can you walk?' asked the dock constable.

'I think so. What am I to say? I had no chance,' asked Austin.

'They usually sack people who lose their goods. Not your fault, but that's the way it is. The way it's always been,' replied the dock constable.

'You as well?' asked Austin.

'I don't work for them. I work for the City,' replied the dock constable.

'I have to work. Will you tell them what happened? That it wasn't my doing. Will you?' asked Austin.

'I'll tell them what I have seen,' replied the dock constable.

And with that the conversation closed. With a sore head, and a dizzy, slightly nauseous feeling, Austin started to make his way out of the docks and to the flag yard. It would be a long day, and with little certainty that he would be paid for the night. He also had Patrick and Henry Fagan to deal with. Austin needed to talk with his father, wife, and mother, before deciding what to do next. Problems everywhere he turned; nothing seemed to get any easier.

* * *

Austin thought he knew where his father was working in the docks that day. He had heard something about timber earlier in the week, and from the description he guessed that it was probably Brunswick, so he headed there to meet him rather than go straight home. They needed to decide what to do before any discussions with Catherine and Bridget. He felt that he needed to regain some control of a situation which risked getting out of hand. Edward usually finished a little later than Austin, so Austin was waiting for him opposite Queen Street by the time he appeared.

'Da!' Austin shouted to a group of men leaving for the city centre.

Edward looked towards the direction of his shout and waved. He left the group, and a couple of minutes later was standing next to Austin.

Edward coughed, a dry cough, wincing as he did so,

'It's been hard today. The wood. Heavy. I've got blisters, aching muscles. I don't feel at all well,' volunteered Edward.

Austin was not expecting this. His own issues started to recede as he realised his father was not his usual self.

'Are you...?' started Austin.

'I'm fine. Why are you here? Something wrong? Is somebody ill?' said Edward.

'Yes and no. Nobody is ill.'

Austin paused. What should he say?

'I've seen Uncle Patrick. He's here in Liverpool.'

'Where? When did you see him?' asked Edward.

'That's what I need to talk to you about. That's why I'm here,' replied Austin.

As they walked up Queens Street, Wapping, and past the Salthouse Docks, Austin started to relay the story of the previous night. Edward stopped walking in front of the Custom House.

'It's a fine building, is it not?' said Edward, before starting another bout of coughing.

Austin interrupted his tale. Had his father taken everything in?

'Yes, it is, but what about Uncle Patrick and Henry Fagan?' asked Austin.

'You know it's Liverpool's finest, besting Dublin I think,' said Edward.

Austin decided to humour his father by joining him in admiring the building. Perhaps he needed time to think.

In front of them stood a building in the form of a double cross: one side facing Castle Street, and the other Canning Place. Ionic in general design, and sitting on a rustic basement. Apparently, the old dock had once stood on the site, but that was long ago; long before the family's arrival in Liverpool. Built of freestone, its columns were fifty feet or more in height, and must have been five or so in diameter. When they walked its length, it was at least a hundred and fifty paces. A simple enough building, but majestic and quite suited for a city of Liverpool's growing status.

Austin needed an answer. They could not spend longer admiring Liverpool's architecture.

'Da, what shall we do about Uncle Patrick and Henry Fagan?' He needed to be direct.

Edward turned to face him. He was back with him in the conversation.

'Nothing. Do nothing. Patrick's family. And everyone has to eat.'

Austin was dumbstruck. This was not the advice he expected. 'But...' started Austin.

'Everyone has to eat. Even Henry Fagan. And don't tell the priest, in or out of confession. The less people know, the better,' added Edward.

'Is that your last word on it?' asked Austin.

'It is,' replied Edward.

They walked together up past the Custom House, then left on John Street towards Dale Street. It was not their usual or most direct route home, but then everything about the last couple of days had been strange. After a few minutes' silence, conversation shifted to what the meal might be that evening, a welcome diversion to the more difficult matters they had been discussing.

Edward coughed again, wincing in pain as he did so. Austin paid a little more attention than he had earlier. Sore though he was himself, it was beginning to look like his father was worse. He just hoped that whatever was ailing him would soon pass – not only for the good of his health, but also for the need of his father's income. If he lost his job, and his father could not work, what would they do? He put the thought to the back of his mind. It would keep until another day.

* * *

Henry Fagan successfully avoided Austin and Edward for several days, by which time Austin had calmed down somewhat. Unusually, Austin's employer had told him not to report the theft, and that if he did as he was told he would remain a night watchman on the same terms and conditions as before. It was a pleasant surprise in an otherwise unpleasant set of circumstances.

Six nights after the incident on the docks, Henry Fagan appeared with Patrick. It was brazen. Henry walked straight in, accompanied by Patrick. Their ground floor room was crammed with people. Almost everyone was there for once; nearly twenty people in a tiny, cramped space, some sitting, most standing around.

'We need to talk to you both,' said Patrick. He seemed to have assumed superior status to Henry.

'I heard you were here, Patrick. We have a lot to talk about,' replied Edward.

Catherine and Bridget accorded each of their husbands a bemused expression.

'Patrick. What are you doing here? Edward never said anything,' said Bridget, looking at her husband.

'Later, Bridget. I'll explain later,' replied Edward, as he led Austin, Henry, and Patrick outside.

The open air forced Edward into another, now all too regular, bout of coughing.

'That's a bad cough you have. Perhaps you should see a doctor,' suggested Patrick.

Edward saw it as a facile remark and replied accordingly.

'You know there's no money for doctors. You've got questions to answer, Patrick,' said Edward.

'You have. I could thump you myself, uncle or no uncle. And you, Henry Fagan,' added Austin.

'Not so fast. I said we would share. And I didn't know he would strike you. He's sorry for it,' said Patrick, referring to the third man on the dockside.

'I'm still sore with it,' replied Austin, unwilling to drop the matter so easily.

'Would three pounds make it better?' asked Patrick.

Austin was not too good at adding up, but it did not take a genius to calculate that at ninepence a day it was three months' pay. Three months. Another conundrum.

'And if we are caught? What will we say? And if you are caught, what will you say?' asked Edward.

'We'll say nothing,' replied Henry Fagan.

'Drink and gamble it away,' said Patrick.

'And a pound to you, Edward. By way of saying I am sorry for not calling. That'll be four pounds to the two of you. I can't say fairer than that,' added Patrick.

'You'll not say a word?' asked Austin of Henry Fagan.

'Not a word,' replied Henry Fagan.

'And is it to stop?' asked Austin.

'We're going to move out, Austin. There'll be no risks to you. I thank you for everything you've done. We won't be far away, but far away enough,' replied Henry Fagan.

Austin mused on the offer of money. It was temptation indeed, and it would help them through difficult times. He could always give some to charity if he felt guilt. Not that he thought he might. In a strange way, it seemed like natural justice. It was only the rich giving to the poor, and it was the poor who needed it more.

'I'll let it pass,' said Austin.

'We'll take the money. Tell no-one. No-one about this,' interjected Edward. He seemed to have made the decision for them both.

Edward started to cough again, almost uncontrollably.

'You could see a doctor now,' said Patrick, handing over a bag of coins.

Austin took the coins.

'I've got to go now. Henry will tell you where I'm lodging. Give my best to Bridget,' said Patrick, as he walked out of the court.

'Say nothing to Catherine or Bridget,' said Austin to Henry. 'I'll tell them when I'm ready. But nothing tonight. Let's eat now. I'm hungry,' he added.

Edward stopped coughing and followed the other two men inside. Perhaps he should see a doctor.

* * *

What was left of the pile of looted goods had been left covered, and untouched, since the night of the theft. Austin had worked several night shifts since then, and thoughts of the incident had started to recede from his mind. For goods to stay covered, and untouched, for so long was unusual, though Austin assumed that it had something to do with how his employer was dealing with the aftermath. He speculated for a moment or two, but soon decided that it was not worth the bother, and anyway, it was not any of his business.

More weeks passed, and it still remained sitting on the dockside, exactly where it had been left. Goods and materials around it had been moved several times, and yet this particular pile remained as if forgotten. Austin did not know much about tobacco, and started to wonder whether it might go off, or somehow lose its value. Still, as he had on several occasions in the past, he reminded himself that it was not his business, and really ought to be of no interest.

'Fire! Fire! Fire over here! Help! Fire! Call the—'

A cry emanated from the direction of the stored tobacco goods. Austin ran over to the scene as fast as he could. The neglected pile of tobacco was indeed on fire. An Albert Dock constable, standing next to his hut on the other side of Duke's Basin, was shouting and waving. When he saw Austin, the constable stopped raising the alarm, and shouted instructions to him from across the other side of the narrow basin.

'Go to Temple Court! Raise the alarm! Ring the fire bell!'

Austin had been advised to seek the aid of a dock constable in the event of a fire, but this was more than expected. Temple Court was not exactly close, and what about the rest of his duties? It was a conundrum. Would he get into trouble, or worse, lose his pay or job for leaving his post?

'Go now! There is no time to waste! Go now!' The dock constable was insistent; he had to follow instructions.

He raced past Canning Dock, stopping for a minute at the Dock Police Station to report the fire, then right up Brunswick Street and Cook Street to Temple Court. Seconds after arriving at the fire station, the Superintendent issued an instruction to ring the fire bell. Minutes after that, fire officers started to appear. Austin watched, fascinated by the procedures. Horses from the adjacent stable were quickly harnessed to a fire engine, and a water cart organised. From Austin's description, it was not deemed to be a large fire, but with any fire there were always risks to nearby warehouses and a greater conflagration. A third piece of equipment – a cart carrying loose bits of firefighting apparatus – had to be pushed by hand. Austin offered to help but he was instructed to join the fire fighters sitting on the engine. Less than five minutes after arriving they were on their way, with Austin providing directions.

They were at the scene of the fire five minutes after they left. Every corner of the stacked crates of tobacco was now ablaze, with fingers of flame threatening other goods that had been stored on the open dockside. Smouldering remnants thrown off from the main fire dropped in all directions, the wind blowing some pieces as far as the Albert Dock warehouses themselves. Austin could see that the dock constables, firemen, and other interested parties that had gathered, were getting nervous. A constable was directed by a more senior member of the group to disperse onlookers, including Austin. He was instructed to return to his duties, as they would 'take care of the fire'. He had clearly outlived his usefulness.

It was difficult to focus on any other duties that night. The dull orange light, noise, and general sense of frenzied excitement emanating from the fire-fighting activity were too much of a distraction. It went on for hours, and by dawn all that could be seen in place of the tobacco crates was a smouldering pile of dark mush, a fusion of water, tobacco remnants, and wood; a stale, pungent smell hung over the area. As far as the firemen were concerned, it was a success. Their efforts had contained the fire to the place where it started. But their tired eyes, and dirty and dishevelled uniforms told their own story. It had been a success that had taken its toll. Few in their company looked like they could take on another blaze any time soon.

More time passed, and Austin settled into his earlier routines. The fire incident receded further, until one night when he witnessed a conversation between two other watchmen. It was only then that he realised why he had been told to keep quiet about the earlier theft, and had not been sacked for 'allowing' it to happen. 'Say nothing,' he had been told, and in fear of losing his employment he had complied. Feeling like a criminal in the face of his later silence, his guilt was somewhat assuaged when he heard that his ultimate employer had claimed insurance money for everything lost in the fire. Their gossip speculated that this included the materials stolen a few weeks before the fire. Austin's guilty conscience ameliorated. If it were true, then in his eyes no-one would have lost; not even his master. All the same, he still felt it better to maintain some silence on the matter, including what he had heard. After all, if his master was accused of some sort of wrongdoing, then it would only be a small step to implicate him.

He was not angry at the thought of one of Liverpool's masters getting away with that sort of thing, but it did make him feel that whatever he and his fellow Irishmen did to feed their families paled into insignificance when compared to the profiteering undertaken by Liverpool's gentry. He resolved to stay on the path laid out by his Catholic faith wherever he could, but if feeding or housing his family was in jeopardy, then he would do whatever it took. He hoped it would never come to that.

* * *

Edward's condition seemed to improve for a few weeks during April and early May, but then suddenly turned for the worse. A day or two away from work was not a cause for alarm, but if it threatened to stretch into a week or more it would surely be a problem. They had some money to pay to see a doctor, but Edward remained reluctant. He saw it as a waste. Despite its questionable origins, he saw their small pot of money as security for when times really became bad; when there was no work to be had.

'I'll be fine. Just give me a day or two and I'll be back on my feet. It's just this aching head, sickness, and backache. I'm getting older, Bridget, and the work is not getting any easier,' said Edward.

His bed had been moved to the ground floor to be next to the fire. There was less space for the domestic chores of the kitchen, but most in the household understood the need for warmth and ministering the unwell.

'But what are we to do if you're not? We don't know what's wrong with you. Today it's the headache, sickness, and backache; yesterday it was the runs, coughing, and pains in all your joints. We should call a doctor. We really should. I'm worried about you,' replied Bridget.

'Don't worry, woman. I've been ill and recovered well before. And I will again. No doctor. I don't want him telling me I've probably got the "Irish Fever", as they're calling this plague now. I told you the Vestry have taken some of the warehouses for the sick, and I don't want them moving me there. Too many never come out. And I heard last week they're going to use some of the old prison hulks because the warehouses are bursting to capacity,' said Edward.

'Hulks?' asked Bridget.

'Old warships. It's what they seem to do with them, floating prisons. Well, they're now going to be floating hospitals, or floating cemeteries. I don't want to go on one of them either. I'll never come back again,' said Edward, emphasising his last sentiment.

Bridget examined her husband's expression. He did look fearful, but then she had to do something. But what?

* * *

By the end of May, Edward's condition had not improved. Indeed, it had deteriorated further. He had not worked for two weeks, and to make matters worse, other members of the household had started to succumb to whatever contagion had despatched him to bed. No work meant no money. Bridget had already been forced to resort to plundering their meagre savings.

'They say it's Typhus, Ma. Everyone is getting it. We're not the only ones. I can go to any house on Stockdale Street, and I'll bet there's few without it. Some are dying. It's the worst I've seen it. And every day people are arriving from Ireland with it. If it's not starvation, then it's Typhus. There's no justice,' said Austin.

Austin remained healthy, but was already wary of others in the household, court, and street who did have it. He was also aware that if he couldn't work, there was nobody who could earn enough to feed the family and keep a roof over their heads. There was still their 'little savings pot', yes. But that was for use as a last resort. He thought very much like his father.

'I know, Austin. I've heard the same and seen almost as much. Your father won't see a doctor because he doesn't want to be removed to a hospital. And he calls them hulks 'death ships'. He won't go anywhere near one. But without a doctor there is no medicine. You can see he's getting worse. He started with a fever this morning after you left,' replied Bridget.

Austin looked towards his father lying prostrate on a makeshift bed positioned near to the fire. Edward looked even worse than when he'd left him. Austin felt helpless.

'What about McCabe?' asked Austin.

'Oh, he's alright, but Mary Reid's unwell and John Duffy has been better. Our John looks poorly as well. It's spreading if it's Typhus. Bed rest, some soup; what else can I do?' replied Bridget.

'You're doing everything you can. I just hope Catherine is alright. We both need to keep working. We'll help you and Da as best we can. You know we will,' said Austin.

'But for how long, Austin? How long can we hold out like this? I can minister ours, but I'm worried sick. And Edward can't even keep awake long enough to speak to me,' replied Bridget.

'We just have to keep going, Ma. We have to, for the children. I'll see if I can buy some medicine from somewhere. I don't know where, but I'll do what I can,' said Austin.

There was little more to be said. Huddled together in a small room, barely kept warm by the open fire, it felt better to talk about the good times, spring, summer, the warmer days ahead. No-one felt like singing a song, a habit they had occasionally indulged in when money could be found for a few jugs of ale. And no-one felt like praying. Praying was for church and for the deathbed; no-one wanted to think about that.

* * *

Austin's efforts in finding an effective medicine proved fruitless. There were plenty willing to sell him some concoction or other, but few could provide much evidence of their efficaciousness. And he was not in the business of wasting their precious resources on some charlatan remedy.

As the fever progressed, a small, localised rash which had developed on his father's torso spread across his arms and legs. June's warmer and brighter days offered no solace. Edward began to experience unpredictable bouts of delirium, punctuated by short periods of coherence. He started to complain about the light when the front door was opened. By the middle of June, everyone in the family feared the worst. The pattern of Edward's decline was now familiar. Hundreds, if not thousands, had already succumbed, with many households already losing loved ones to the pernicious disease that was Typhus. Four weeks after complaining about aches and pains, Edward fell into a coma. He was clearly dying, and there was nothing anyone could do to help other than offer palliative care.

Edward died on June 22nd. Barely five weeks earlier he had been working and earning a living. His death struck both fear and grief into their house and court. Grief for the loss of a loved one, and fear for their own lives. Everyone seemed helpless to prevent the scourge of the fever, lacking understanding of where it originated and what to do if it struck. Even the doctors appeared limited in the tools they deployed to combat the epidemic.

It was now Austin's responsibility to look after his mother.

* * *

'He was nearly sixty years,' said Bridget.

Austin and Bridget stood near to the hollow where Edward was to be buried. It would not be a dignified internment, exacerbated by the odour of the dead which seemed to hang over the area. 'Miasma' some called it, blaming the noxious aroma for many of the ills of the still living; Typhus, Typhoid, Cholera, and whatever else that seemed to strike the unlucky. Unable to afford the best class burial ground, Edward's remains would be interred in what was effectively a deep pit – a hole in the ground shared with a dozen or more nameless others.

They both watched as the gravediggers almost threw the coffin into the hole. The poorly constructed thin pine casket collapsed into another, sinking through the few inches of soil that masked what was underneath. Bridget looked away, clearly shaken by the spectacle. It might not have been a full pauper's burial, but there was no dignity in what they saw.

'I can't watch this, Austin,' said Bridget as she began to walk away, holding a thin piece of loose cloth to her nose in an attempt to abate the smell. Austin followed, putting his arms around her when he caught up. He was glad he had spared the rest of his family the macabre performance of the necropolis workers.

'Let's go home. He's with God now, Ma. He's left his body. Whatever is left out there is no longer Da. You know that,' replied Austin. He was trying his best, but whatever he said, he knew that his father deserved better.

'I know. Life will go on, as they say. At least I hope it will,' said Bridget.

'We've got to think of the young ones. Do the best we can for them,' replied Austin.

Bridget gently nodded in agreement, though failing to hold back her tears.

'Yes, we do. Yes, we do. But I miss him already,' said Bridget.

'I know, Ma. So do I,' replied Austin.

The walk back to Stockdale Street was slow and reflective, with Bridget needing occasional stops to catch her breath and recover her composure. Liverpool, once a lighthouse of hope, had not been kind to her family. She longed for the fondly remembered warm days of summer, when a moderate breeze whipped up the surf on the familiar silvery shoreline of Uggool. Life was hard there as well, and yet somehow it seemed better.

'I'll be alright, Austin,' said Bridget, as she raised herself from a stone wall she had been resting upon.

Austin looked on. His mother was with him in the flesh, and yet she suddenly felt so distant. A cold shudder rippled through his body. He felt uneasy, unsure of whether it was the burial of his father, grief, or a sense of foreboding that had gripped him. Something was not right, but whatever it was, it was unknowable.

'Another ten minutes and we'll be home, Ma,' replied Austin.

Bridget acknowledged the fact and reached out for help. She wanted her son to hold her. Austin locked his mother's arm into his and supported her the rest of the way home.

'Don't say anything about what happened back there, Austin,' said Bridget.

'Of course not, Ma. It will be told as it should have been,' replied Austin.

'He was buried with the grace of God,' said Bridget.

'He was, Ma,' replied Austin.

* * *

In the weeks after Edward's death, they heard of at least two dozen from Stockdale Street alone surrendering to the fever. Some called it 'Irish Fever', but Austin objected to that characterisation. It was unfair, he would say, 'They are blaming us for something we have no mastery of. It's not our fault, even the gentry, merchants, lords, ladies, and all catch it. Who is to say that it was not they who started it?'

But life for him went on, harder than ever. He thought about asking for more night watchman work, but he knew he was already stretching himself to his limits. And he was no use dead like his father. He also considered asking his Uncle Patrick for help, but he knew where that would ultimately lead; he was no use in gaol either. Austin had no choice but to keep on doing what he was doing, keeping in work, and earning whatever he could.

For Bridget, life after Edward's death seemed unreal, almost as if it had become suspended in time. She increasingly resorted to reminiscing, divorcing herself from the demands of daily living. Some days she would not eat, saying that the 'children needed it more', and on others she seemed to forget. Listless and increasingly forgetful, her face took on a pallid, lacklustre appearance. Austin and Catherine did their best to bring her back, but it was obvious that her grief was getting the better of her.

And then it happened. When it did, it felt inevitable, the will of some unseen force pressing down on his mother's demeanour, bleeding into her physical state. Bridget had developed a rash similar to the one seen on Edward earlier in his decline. Her grief, her state of mind, had disguised other physical symptoms that had also developed. The headaches, aches and pains, had all been ignored, unmentioned. She just did not care about anything, including herself.

Both Austin and Catherine could see that she no longer had the will to live, to survive.

The slump in Bridget's health exceeded the speed of Edward's decline. By the last week of July, everyone in the household recognised Typhus rather than grief as the affliction. All knew what was to come. Austin chose not to challenge it; he knew even then that it would be futile. His mother had chosen death over life, even if she could have fought the disease. In the first week of August, delirium took hold. Not terrors, such as those experienced by Edward, but replays of happier times in Uggool. At least his mother had been spared that. Before leaving for work, early in the morning, Austin checked on his mother's condition. Each day he thought the same thought: would this be the last time he saw her alive?

Bridget's weakened frame yielded to the disease tormenting her emaciated form on the August 10th. He was working a night when the news arrived. McCabe had volunteered to go down to the docks and tell Austin. He thanked his former overlooker for passing on the news, but there was little he could do. He could not leave; he had to finish his work or there would be a loss of pay, and possibly even a job. Leaving his post would not be looked on kindly, whatever the reason.

After McCabe departed, he was left to his own thoughts. Losing both his father and mother in such a short space of time was a shock, and yet they were both older than most. They had each lived a long life. He thought about the times they had had together; the good times, the hard times. Perhaps he should be thankful for that. In some ways, it was a relief to lose his mother. The priest would say that she had joined

Edward in Heaven. Austin hoped so. But he had more temporal matters to deal with. He still had a family to look after, and hopefully, a better future than present adversity.

After a simple service at St. Anthony's, Bridget was buried at Low Hill, close to where his father had been interned. Austin wanted no-one else present. Despite paying a little extra, the treatment of his mother's remains was barely better. He would have liked to pay for improved burial ground, but they needed the money for more corporeal needs. They might need it to put food on the table. He felt a tinge of guilt, but then that was the way it was.

It had always been so, and perhaps always would be.

Chapter 6

'AN GORTA MÓR'

'I managed to buy some rabbit,' said Catherine.

It was Christmas Eve. She had been working on the markets all day Friday. Christmas Day was on Saturday this year, and was the only Saturday in the whole year when the markets were completely closed. Austin had just arrived home, exhausted from almost a full day of gruelling labour, as a watchman on the docks and labouring for the stonemasons in the flag yard.

'Are you making a stew?' asked Austin.

'I am. I have some fish as well. It will be a feast indeed tomorrow. I also got some jugs of ale. The others said we should eat together, share what we have,' said Catherine.

'Have they enough to share?' replied Austin.

'I think so. There'll be some bread, and I know they have some vegetables, carrots, onions, potatoes, and some cheese,' said Catherine.

'And meat?' replied Austin.

'I don't know. But we live with them, Austin...' started Catherine.

'I know we do. But we can barely afford meat ourselves. Two rabbits won't go far. You know they won't,' he replied.

'But we may have need of their help one day, Austin. We could go to church on St. Stephen's Day. You know they open the alms boxes. The rich always put more in them just before Christmas. And it's a Sunday. We should go to Mass anyway,' said Catherine.

'We have enough to feed ourselves. And we still have that other money. I don't want charity. We're poor, but not starving like them we see in the streets. It's just that I think everyone should try and bring some meat in the house if we are to share. Christmas is the only day I get off in the whole year. I want to celebrate in the best way we can; with food on the table,' replied Austin.

'We will. After Mass I'll make a stew, and we'll celebrate the rest of the day. You're lucky this year, Christmas Day being on a Saturday; you won't have to work the day afterwards,' said Catherine.

'Well. So long as there's enough,' replied Austin, slightly grudgingly.

* * *

'Mama. Mama. Mama. Maaaaaama. I'm hungry. I'm cold. Mama...'

Edward had been sleeping in a small wooden cot situated at the end of Austin and Catherine's bigger bed. A large thin blanket separated the three of them from Mary Reid, who still shared the same room, and of course John and Cecilia. It was effective in reducing the drafts and establishing some minimal privacy, but was a poor substitute for some heat in the room. There was a fireplace nearby, but no-one used it. The cost of coal rendered it no more than ornamental.

It was still dark outside, and even darker and colder inside. The air was damp and slightly fetid, with the stale smells of irriguous clothing and blankets, urine, and walls stained with small patches of black mould.

A child waking so early on Christmas Day was not particularly welcome.

'Edward's up early again. He'll wake everyone. You'll have to see to him,' said Austin.

He knew it was not very gallant, but then again, their son was Catherine's responsibility. One day he would guide Edward in the ways of the world, but certainly not today. He wanted to stay warm under the blankets and enjoy one of the few days of the year when he could stay in bed an hour or two longer than usual. And he had just worked for a day and a night. These were the arguments he had rehearsed should Catherine resist his direction.

As it happened, she had decided not to argue.

'I'll take him down and start a fire. You get some more sleep. I'll have some breakfast and tea ready in an hour or so,' replied Catherine.

Austin grunted, covered his head in a blanket, turned over on his side, and returned to his slumber.

An hour and a half later, Catherine roused Austin, who subsequently joined his wife and son downstairs. The rest of the household remained sleeping, so they had the main communal room in the house to themselves, at least for a time.

Breakfast was nothing special, some toasted bread and some eggs, though Catherine had also acquired some cheese in an attempt to make breakfast more memorable.

'You remember today, don't you? You must, Austin,' said Catherine.

'How could I not? It's Christmas Day,' replied Austin.

'And?' asked Catherine.

'And what?' replied Austin, now starting to feel uncomfortable.

'And Edward,' said Catherine.

'But it was Christmas Eve, was it not?' replied Austin.

'It was, but you know we started remembering it on Christmas Day. He was born only a few minutes before midnight,' said Catherine.

It had slipped his mind, but then he was still tired. And yes, they had decided to celebrate it on Christmas Day so that they always had the day together.

'I have something for him. Da carved it. I'll go and fetch it,' replied Austin.

Austin reappeared a few minutes later clutching a carved wooden horse. His father had made it for his grandson only a few months before his death. Austin knew that he had planned to give it to his namesake on Christmas Day. Alas, it was not to be. It was now down to Austin to gift it.

'Edward. Edward!' Austin tried to catch the attention of his now four-year-old son.

'Edward. This is for you. Granda made it,' said Austin, offering the wooden toy to him.

Edward took hold of the object for a minute, inspected it, and then dropped it on the floor, returning to the toast that he had been systematically demolishing before his father's interruption.

Austin looked disappointed at his son's lack of interest.

'He'll come back to it when he's eaten. It's what they do, Austin,' said Catherine.

Austin shrugged.

'Are we going to Mass?' he asked.

'You know we are. We always do. It's Christmas. There will be carols. You know I like to sing with them,' replied Catherine.

'But we've eaten,' said Austin, mischievously.

'Well, I won't tell if you don't. After we get back, I'll start cooking rabbit stew, the fish, and I'll sort out the rest of the food with the others. Everything will be good, Austin. Oh, my ma and da will be coming round as well. I should have told you. They will be bringing some meat. There will be plenty for all this year. You take Edward out for an hour or two while I cook. That's all you need to do today,' replied Catherine.

Austin acknowledged Catherine's planning efforts, and had no objections to Darby joining them. He had been a good friend to his family, and Austin knew that his in-laws would help out should he get into any difficulties with work.

'And there's something else as well. I wanted to wait until today to tell you,' added Catherine somewhat nonchalantly.

'And what's that?' replied Austin.

'I'm with child,' said Catherine. She had been waiting for over a week to tell him, but had decided that Christmas Day would be ideal. It had also given her even more time to be certain of her condition. She looked intently at her husband, attempting to gauge his reaction before he spoke.

Austin's mind raced with the implications. Yes, of course he was pleased, but it still meant another mouth to feed. He knew it would not be what she wanted to hear, so he walked over and gave her a tight hug.

'I'm happy, Catherine. Edward will have a brother, I'm sure.'

'It might be a girl,' replied Catherine.

'It doesn't matter. I just wish I could do better for you. It's so hard to get more pay,' said Austin.

'You do your best, Austin. I couldn't wish for more than that,' replied Catherine.

'How long have you known?' asked Austin.

'Two or three weeks. But I wanted to be sure before I said anything,' replied Catherine.

'I know. If only Ma and Da were still here. They would be overjoyed,' said Austin.

'I know, Austin. But the fever. Well, you know. What can I say? They're in Heaven, I'm sure of it. I've said prayers for them both. At least they met young Edward. Let's think of the future and today,' replied Catherine. She dearly wanted Austin to think of Christmas rather than dwell on the past. There had been a couple of occasions since the death of Edward and Bridget when her husband had taken to the bottle to drown his grief and miseries.

'You're right, Catherine. I'll think of today and the future, especially today, Christmas Day. And with the grace of God, we'll both see grandchildren before our graves,' replied Austin.

By the time they had finished breakfast, the rest of the household had stirred and appeared, each ready to cook their own. With Austin now informed, Catherine started to tell of her news. It seemed to lift the spirits of a house where there was already a sense of growing excitement. There were few extra luxuries on Christmas Day, and yet it was still a day that was out of step with others in the calendar. A day without work, and a day of Catholic celebration, family, and with a little bit of luck some extra food and drink on the table.

* * *

Christmas Day passed, as it had in previous years, as a day of congenial family celebration and Catholic observance, flavoured with more than a hint of Hibernian folklore and song. Austin had little reason to fear the rest of his household community. Three more rabbits appeared, and plums; plums enough to make a pudding. Where such out-of-season opulence had been obtained remained a question no-one cared to ask. More ale arrived, and Michael McCabe produced some gin. Lubricated by drink, boisterous songs from the old country were sung well into the evening, and tall tales told during the scarce moments of relative quiet. More candles were lit than was the norm, cost dismissed as a consideration. Each felt like a king or a queen, at least for a day.

St. Stephen's Day, or 'Boxing Day' as some now seemed to call it, dawned far too quickly. Groggy heads trooped downstairs at random intervals, memories of the previous day already receding. There were a few smiles at the breakfast table, but the stark realities of life were returning to thought. It was a Sunday, and there was no work to do, but everyone knew that on Monday, the need to venture outdoors would puncture the transient cocoon of relative joy and happiness that had enveloped the household. A fire might take the edge off the cold in the downstairs room, but there was little anyone could use to fight the cold outside. And there was no escaping the need to work.

Austin and Catherine went to Mass as they usually did on a Sunday. After Bridget died, Cecilia tended to look after Edward. They took it in turns. Sometimes Catherine would stay home, allowing her sister-in-law to attend church, and on other occasions it would be herself. They would also sometimes take him round to one of Austin's other sisters, his Aunt Bridy or Aunt Nan. Both were now married themselves and had started their own families, but there always seemed to be room for a nephew or a niece. It was the Irish way. Aunt Nan, or Ann as she now called herself, was a particular favourite of Edward's, perhaps because of the amount of attention she had given him before she left Stockdale Street. He always seemed pleased to see her.

Young children were welcomed at Mass, but Austin and Catherine had resisted; they considered him too young. But now he was five, and the parish priest had already started to ask questions. He was in no mind to lose one of the youngest members of his flock. Edward was baptised Catholic, and Catholic he would remain; at least as far as he was concerned. The priest's remarks were gentle at first, but then they became a little more incisive, the result being that both Austin and Catherine felt under some pressure. Not wishing to prolong the moratorium on attendance, and at the same time wanting to assuage the reservations of their father confessor, Edward attended his first Mass the day after Christmas. The priest noticed, and approved, with an almost imperceptible nod in the direction of Austin and Catherine moments before the service commenced. His overtures had been understood. He knew it and so did they.

The church was full to bursting with Liverpool's poorest. So full that many had to stand outside in a bitter wind that the weather had whipped up during the early hours. Everyone knew why they were there. It was the day when the alms boxes would be opened and its contents distributed to the unfortunate. The doors of the church were always open to the Irish poor, though many arrivals had already lost the faith, succumbing to the desperate misery of near starvation, and a sense of worthlessness. But St. Stephen's Day restored a tiny amount of hope. For a few days the ceaseless grinding search for food and shelter might be suspended. Gifts of money, and sometimes food bought with the alms boxes, would be given to the needy.

Austin looked around the church at the end of the service. More had managed to cram themselves around its rear, sides, and even into the centre aisle. He turned to Catherine and whispered, 'An Gorta Mór.'

Catherine acknowledged his comment with a nod. She knew exactly what he meant, 'The Great Hunger'. It had been with them for years now. All around them, everywhere. The priest called them mendicants, street beggars. People like themselves, Irish people, forced through no fault of their own onto the streets to beg for food and money. Whatever the cause of the blight, the way it had been managed back in Ireland had caused this. She felt a tinge of patriotic anger. These poor, desperate, wretched creatures deserved better than this.

Guilt rippled through Austin's thoughts. Only two days ago he had been questioning Catherine's generosity. Only yesterday they were feasting on rabbit and plum pudding, and drinking ale and gin. They had little, and yet the Irish diaspora patrolling and literally living in the streets of Liverpool, had even less. Forced to rely on the mercy and charity of an increasingly reluctant Vestry, and a progressively malnourished donor population. The poor giving to the desperate. It was no way to manage a crisis and quite obviously risked chaos. Austin could not read or write, but he was not stupid. He knew something was wrong but felt helpless to do anything about it. All he had was hope, hope that a solution would be found back in Ireland; that the potato crop would not fail yet again.

This was his prayer for 1848.

* * *

The more Austin saw of the dire state of recent immigrants into Liverpool, the more he started to think about his parents' dream, that of building a new life in America. Circumstances at the time had precluded travel, but he was now in a different position. They still had some money left over from his father's decision to forget about the fire incident on the docks. Austin had never been entirely comfortable with it, but that was more to do with the associated risks of losing his watchman job, and possibly even having to face the law. A lot of time had passed since then, and with it any concern and guilt about taking his uncle's money. Having something put to one side gave them choices, and a safety net should work become harder to obtain.

During the early months of 1848, the topic of America had become a recurrent conversational theme. Unfortunately, Catherine was less sanguine about the opportunities such a trip offered, and was not averse to being outright hostile. In response, Austin would seek support from other members of the household, especially Michael McCabe, who would frequently be disposed to tease Catherine – a trait he had developed over the now many years of cohabitation.

'Not again, Austin. You know that we've talked about this already. I don't want to do it. My ma and da are still in Liverpool. I've got family. So have you. Why would you want to leave them?' said Catherine.

'I don't want to leave them. They could come with us, everyone. We could start a new life together,' replied Austin.

'And what about payment for passage? We may have enough for us and one or two others; John perhaps. I don't know. I'm also pregnant. It makes no sense to me at this time. I want my ma to help with the birth. I've said it before,' said Catherine.

'There are ships bound for New York leaving nearly every day. I'm sure there are other pregnant women sailing on them. What do you think, Mikey?' replied Austin, turning towards Michael McCabe.

'If I had the money, I might. There's many who have done well there, so I hear. But I wouldn't want to come between you,' said McCabe, a twinkle in his eye.

'It's our business, Michael McCabe. I wouldn't tell you yours,' said Catherine, addressing his less than welcome opinion.

She then turned back to look at Austin.

'As for travelling passengers, that may be so, but they probably don't have a choice. We do. You know we do. And as for the ships, you know what they call them now, don't you? "Coffin Ships." They call them that for a reason. Too many who sail with them don't survive. I've heard about what happens. They just throw them over the side when they die. Is that what you would want for me?' asked Catherine.

'No. You know I would never want that. I know what they call them, but they can't all be like that. Most get to America whole,' replied Austin.

Austin knew much more about the ships that operated on the Liverpool to New York route than he cared to let on. He knew their owners' reputation for overloading, dismal passage accommodation, and inferior food and drink. And yet he still believed that the risk would be worth it. America's reputation as a land of hope and opportunity seemed to grow, even as Liverpool's offering appeared to sink.

'I'm not going, Austin. And I won't have Edward go either. We probably have as good a life here in Liverpool as we can have in America. I just don't see what it can offer,' said Catherine.

'It was always my parents' dream. It was mine too for a time. Bad luck kept us in Liverpool,' replied Austin.

'You met me in Liverpool. If you had gone to New York, we would not be married, and with a son, and another on the way. I still think we can improve our lot here. Besides, your ma and da are now gone. You don't have to go because they wanted to,' said Catherine.

'But look at Liverpool, Catherine. It's not the city it was when we arrived. Too many beggars; too many people looking for work. I'm sorry for the famine, but it's affecting my wages. There's talk of them being lowered again. Many of our fellow Irish still think sixpence a day is good pay. We can't live off that. There must be something better. What about Manchester then?' replied Austin.

'I want to stay here. Have they said they are going to cut your pay?' said Catherine.

'Not yet. But there's talk,' replied Austin.

'Well, we'll talk about what to do if it happens. I want my baby here. After it's born, we'll have to see how things are. We can always use some of the savings,' said Catherine.

'Passage money,' replied Austin. It was more of a statement than a question.

'Savings money,' replied Catherine.

Austin gave up. He had tried to persuade her several times already, and failed. Though abandoning the subject for today, he resolved to have another go in spring. If that still did not produce the desired result, then he would wait until after the baby was born. He was still working two jobs and could not work this way forever. Today they still had enough to live on, but tomorrow could be even harder. He felt frustrated. America seemed so much like a solution to their current survival lifestyle. As he kept reminding himself, they might not be on the streets but he felt he needed more. In the meantime, he thought that there might be some advantage in getting involved in English politics. Perhaps there was the prospect of change there.

What could he have to lose?

* * *

It was unusual for Austin to have breakfast at home on a working day. On most days he would take with him a piece of bread, some vegetables if there were any spare, and some tea. A couple of hours after starting work in the flag yard there would be a break. A kettle, or pan, for the tea would have been boiled by one of his fellow workers in time for their morning meal. Within the yard there was not much of a hierarchy. The masons would sit with their labourers to eat and talk.

Though they all sat together, there were some unwritten rules followed by the labourers. There was respect for the masons. Everyone knew they had served time to become qualified, and most could see the skills they deployed on a day-to-day basis. And if a mason required your assistance, a labourer would be expected to comply with a request or demand without questioning it. In that way the yard worked. The stone required by its customers was always supplied. As the stonemasons' labourers respected the masons, the masons respected their customer's demands. If stone, flags, or slate could be supplied to a customer's specifications, then it would be.

To Austin, the stonemasons' loyalties always seemed torn when it came to politics. On the one hand they were 'above' the labouring classes, apparently aspiring to leave their lower working-class roots. But on the other, most of them were well aware that Liverpool's middle and upper classes still had sneering opinion of any men who worked with their hands. And every man knew that they were no different than the next. Most had families to feed and to shelter.

The politics of Chartism competed with Irish nationalism for the attention of Liverpool's Irish. Austin had dabbled with Irish nationalism – not seriously like some in the city, but he had joined the St. Patrick's Day marches until they had been virtually banned a couple of years earlier. Parading Irishmen wearing shamrocks, carrying Hibernian flags and banners, and marching bands playing Irish nationalist music and ballads were not a welcome intrusion in the more gentile parts of Liverpool. And it was also not unusual for these marches to culminate in brawls with Orangemen, who continued to object to the increasing ascendency of the Irish enclave, at least in terms of population.

The Chartists were less prominent a movement in Liverpool than those based on Irish nationalism, but the objectives of the movement nonetheless attracted considerable sympathy. Who could argue with secret ballots, all men having a vote, regular elections, equal constituency sizes, and payment for members of parliament? And few working-class men would argue against removing the candidate eligibility requirement of owning property. Talk of supporting Chartism had spread across Lancashire, and indeed the country, during 1847 and early 1848. To many it had started to feel like an unstoppable movement. While wary of losing his work, Austin was always keen to learn and would listen attentively to any talk of politics, especially during those breaks in the flag yard.

'Will you join us on the Chartist march in London next month?' asked Donal of Austin. As was their usual practice, they were sitting on a bench in a rather crude shelter erected on the canal side of the yard. There were eight sitting, and standing, by an open fire that had been blazing in a round metal container. Sitting on top of the metal barrel was a makeshift grill upon which a large kettle had been placed. Several of the men had already emptied boiled water from the kettle into tea mugs. Donal, a fellow labourer, was known as being politically well informed, but also a bit of a troublemaker. How the stonemasons had tolerated him was a bit of a mystery to Austin, who would hardly have dared to utter some of the things he said.

'We'll have none of that talk here. We don't want any trouble in this yard. There's enough with our own Irish to get involved in any of that,' interjected Kevin, one of the older and more senior stonemasons. He rarely liked the men getting involved in any political talk during work time, or any time for that matter.

'Aye, Kevin's right. We've never had trouble here, and we don't want to see any started. Trouble with politics means trouble with business,' added Brendan, another stonemason.

Austin listened to both masons, unsure how to answer his friend. He did not want to cause his supervisors to lower their opinion of him, but at the same time he was interested in what Chartism represented. He had heard the term many times before, but had never really asked what they wanted. He decided to sidestep the question with another question. He knew a little more than his companions might infer from his query, but was sharp enough to play the middle ground.

'What do these Chartists want, Donal? I don't know much about it. Are they from the old country? How will it help us?' replied Austin.

Kevin and Brendan remained silent, clearly curious as to how Donal would answer.

'Free elections, votes for all good men. Secret ballots, and away with the need to own property to represent the people. They stand for working men like you and me, Kevin, and Brendan. They supported the Anti Corn Law League for a time as well. The Corn Laws helped starve our countrymen; you know that, don't you?' replied Donal.

'Aye they did,' said Kevin. It was an undeniable fact. Every Irishman knew that it wasn't just the blight, but the Corn Laws that had exacerbated 'The Great Hunger'.

'Well, there were bread riots in Manchester last month. Feargus O'Connor, he—' started Donal.

'He's not one of us, is he? Protestant, Orangeman no doubt,' said Brendan, interrupting Donal's reply.

'That maybe so. But he's for the working man and he's an Irish patriot. And we are all working men, are we not? He's for giving all men a smallholding. I would be for that, wouldn't you?' said Donal, looking in the eye of each man present.

It was hard to disagree with the sentiment. Even the masons could not resist responding with an 'Aye'.

'What would you have us do, Donal?' asked Brendan.

'There's a march in London on the tenth. We should all go there and support it,' replied Donal.

Brendan and Kevin laughed, as the other labourers looked on askance.

'And how would you propose we get there?' said Brendan.

'We can get to London by railway now. You all know that. We've cut the stone for part of it,' replied Donal.

'And where would the money come from for that? How would we feed our families?' asked Colin, a fellow labourer.

'It's a fair question, but I'm sure you could manage for a few days. It would be for a cause,' replied Donal.

'What about work? We've got customer orders to meet. Speaking of the railway, you know we have stone for the Southport Railway to cut,' said Kevin.

Austin just listened. He planned to go with the flow of the discussion.

'It's not possible. I know it's not trouble on our streets, but it's too far, too much money, and not our concern. If you go, Donal, just remember there's plenty out there would be pleased to have your job. We've got work to do, and that doesn't involve Chartist politics. A good cause it might be, but not one for us, or any of you. We won't stop any of you, but don't expect to have work when you return. Be warned,' added Brendan.

'If Brendan had not said this, then I would have. There are other yards in Liverpool who would be glad of the business. I might agree with the Chartists, and the Irish cause, but I can't afford to be seen to take sides against the masters. Maybe one day that will change, but not today. That's my last word on it. Now it's time to get back to work,' said Kevin, apparently satisfied he had closed the discussion.

Donal's face turned bright red and stony. He knew that if he pushed it further there would be repercussions. It looked like he had a decision to make. Would he risk his livelihood on a London excursion, or live with a loss of face with his fellow labourers? He was not at all happy with the outcome, but remained silent.

Austin and the other labourers avoided looking him in the eye. Each knew he had his heart and politics in the right place, but every man present had family to feed. Most might wish to support the cause, as Donal framed it, but they knew it was neither practical nor affordable. And not a single one would be prepared to lose his livelihood over a Chartist cause. They were even wary of being seen to overtly support Irish nationalism; even amongst fellow Irish. It was just the way it was.

* * *

'It just seems to rain all the time here. It was never as bad as this in Mayo; I'm sure it wasn't,' said Austin. He was commenting on what was turning out to be one of the wettest summers on record.

'Never mind the weather. Go see if my Uncle Patrick and Aunt Mary are ready,' replied Catherine.

It was July 30th, the day of John's baptism. John had made his entry into the world at least a week earlier than expected. It was a Monday, and as it wasn't a market day, Catherine had been out selling in the streets. Over recent weeks, working had started to become a little more difficult, so she had enlisted the help of Cecilia to help. On most days, Edward had been placed with one of his aunts and uncles, or grandparents, but there were occasions when he had to stay with them. These were the more difficult days. Even with Cecilia's help, trying to sell fish from a cart at the end of a street was difficult enough, but with a young son to keep a watchful eye on, it was almost impossible.

Catherine could not afford to take much time off. Her waters broke late afternoon, and by midnight John was with them – an apparently healthy and screaming baby. Both parents were pleased with their new arrival, but both also knew that if they did not work there would soon be no food on the table. Fortunately, their circumstances were slightly better than with Edward's birth. They had a small amount of savings, and could manage for some weeks before returning to work.

'If it's not for this sort of thing, then what is it for? I need the rest, Austin. I'm older than I was.' Catherine made a good case for rest and recovery. He knew she needed it and could find little good argument against spending some of their savings. A rested mother would also be good for the baby. Nonetheless, nine days later she was back on the markets selling her fish.

As was tradition in the Catholic Church, John's baptism would take place on a Sunday. They still attended St. Mary's, but in the new larger building on Edmund Street.

'Are you ready, Patrick?' asked Austin. Catherine's Uncle Patrick and Aunt Mary had called on her father's house, as agreed.

'We are that,' replied Patrick Cunningham.

'We wouldn't miss it. It's not every day I'm godmother. How's John? It will be John, won't it? You haven't changed your mind, have you, Austin?' asked Mary Cunningham.

'No, we have not. Catherine wanted to call him John after my youngest brother. Darby doesn't mind, do you, Darby?' Austin turned to face his father-in-law who was listening to the conversation.

'Of course not. John's a good Catholic name,' replied Darby.

There had been a little uncertainty at home. Edward had been named after Austin's father, as tradition expected. Austin expected to call his second son after Catherine's father, but over the time she had shared a house with Austin's family, she had got on particularly well with his brother, John. Sensitive to her father, she nonetheless had agreed to break with tradition; after all, John was not the only grandson he had.

'We'll have to walk in the rain. Nothing we can do about that. At least it's not winter,' said Austin to the Cunningham group. About ten would be joining them.

They collectively trooped back to Stockdale Street where Catherine was waiting, babe in arms. Around twenty people set off for the church shortly afterwards.

'It will be a gathering indeed, Catherine?' queried Mary Cunningham.

'Yes, maybe forty or more of us. I don't know how many,' replied Catherine.

'What about the Chartists, Austin? You talked a lot about them back in spring?' asked Darby, changing the subject.

'It was a nonsense. Austin talked about going on some march or other in London. It was just as well. You know they had to cancel it. The police refused permission,' interjected Catherine.

'Aye they did. But they still delivered a petition with six million signing, so they say,' replied Austin, a tad irritated with his wife's interjection. He gave her a look of disapproval, but this was not a day for an argument.

'You don't hear much now,' said Darby.

'I would never have gone. Too far and too much money,' said Austin, attempting to thwart any further comments Catherine might have offered.

'Well—' started Catherine.

'Well, we had better walk a little faster if we are to be at the church on the stroke of two. You know there will be others baptised today,' said Austin, cutting off Catherine's reply.

Catherine examined Austin's face but thought better of saying any more on the subject.

The summer rain eased just as the group arrived at the Church of St. Mary around five minutes before the hour. Waiting inside were Bridy and Nancy, Austin's sisters, and their families. Overall, the group totalled over thirty, not unusual for an Irish Catholic baptism. The church's main entry doors had been left wedged open to ensure that the air inside the building stayed as fresh as possible. A few minutes after arriving, the distant sound of bells striking the hour formed a vaguely undulating backdrop to the excited whispers that echoed through the almost empty sanctorum. As the sound of the final strike dissipated into the ether, the priest emerged from the sacristy wearing full vestments: cassock, surplice, and purple stole.

'*Cead mile failte.* A warm welcome to you all.' It was a surprisingly familiar greeting to those present, clearly intended to put all present at ease.

He then beckoned a smaller group – mother, father, baby, and godparents – over towards the altar, and wasted little time in starting the ritual. With a brief nod, he started.

'What are you asking of the Church of God?'

It was a strange question to ask of a child barely two weeks old, but was rooted in the ancient tradition of baptising adults. However, life expectancy had now become so short that over time the age at which people were baptised had become younger and younger. There was genuine fear amongst Liverpool's Irish Catholics that a baby might die well before reaching adulthood. Austin and Catherine were no different. As they had with Edward, they wanted John baptised into the mother church as soon as possible.

Darby and Mary responded, indicating that they wished the child to be baptised into the Catholic Church, and to receive the grace of God. Following the brief discourse, the priest blew three puffs of air from his mouth onto John, and then directed the unclean spirit within to give way to the Holy Spirit. After making the sign of the cross on the baby's forehead and chest, he addressed him once again before starting a prayer to God for John's present and future protection.

The ritual continued. The priest produced a small vessel of salt, addressed and exorcised the object, and then asked God to sanctify it. Acknowledging John by name, he then placed the 'salt of wisdom' on his tongue – an act intended to help strengthen the prospects of eternal life.

More prayers and exorcisms were offered, including speeches to both God and the unclean spirit. He then placed his hand on John's head, which startled the baby. For a second or two he looked like he might start to cry, but then he just settled down. The priest then laid part of his stole over John's head and led him, his parents, and godparents, towards the baptistry. Together they recited the Creed and Lord's Prayer, whereupon the priest licked his thumb and traced saliva on John's mouth, ears, and nose. Again, the baby stirred, but remained silent.

He then addressed John again.

'Open your ears and nostrils. Do you renounce Satan?'

As was expected, Darby and Mary responded on John's behalf.

'Yes. Yes.'

John was then anointed with the oil of catechumens, after which the priest wiped it off with some cotton.

He then exchanged his purple stole for a white one, and led the group towards the baptismal font.

'John, do you have faith in the Trinity?'

'Yes. Yes,' replied Darby and Mary in succession.

Cold baptismal water was poured over John's head, whereupon he erupted into a shock-driven scream. Away from the font, the rest of the family engaged in subdued, but amused, chatter. While that part of the ceremony was largely out of sight, everyone knew exactly what had just taken place.

'I baptise you in the name of the Father, and of the Son, and the Holy Ghost.'

As Mary held John, the priest dipped his thumb into the chrism oil and made the sign of the cross on the crown of John's head.

'I ask God to anoint John with the chrism of salvation.'

After wiping his thumb with a spare cloth, he placed another white cloth over John's head, and then made a request of the child.

'I ask you to carry this, John, unstained to the judgement seat of Christ.'

He then lit two candles and offered one each to Darby and Mary. They both took the candles.

'John, protect this baptism by keeping God's commands. Go in peace, and may the Lord be with you.'

With the ritual concluded, the priest led the baptismal group back to the rest of the family who had been waiting patiently in the first three rows of pews at the front of the church. As he did so, another family appeared at the church's entrance.

'I'm sorry. I have another baptism to perform at half past the hour. John is now baptised into the Catholic Church. May you help him to keep the laws of God. I'll see you all at Mass next week.'

It was clear he needed to see his next set of new parents; his concluding remark had clearly been a gentle encouragement for them to leave.

'Thank you, Father. We'll go now,' said Austin.

'Peace be with you,' replied the priest.

As they walked out of the entrance, Darby recognised the waiting parents.

'Good day, John, Sarah. And this must be Anne.'

'It is, Darby. I didn't know you were here today,' replied John O'Hara, a fellow dock worker.

'No. I didn't say. We had better be off. I'll see you in the morning,' said Darby.

His friend, John, nodded in agreement as they walked out in single file past the O'Hara group, who were already walking in the opposite direction.

The sun was still out as they left the church, already drying the previously shower-soaked streets. It suddenly felt warm and bright.

'See, John, the sun has come out for you,' said Catherine.

John momentarily opened his eyes, squinted in the sunlight, and then closed them, completely unaware of what had just taken place. One day he might be told that his catechumenate, his religious journey, had started that day. But today all that mattered to him was some food and the warmth of his mother.

'There's jugs of ale, food, and even some gin back home,' said Austin, as they headed back towards Stockdale Street.

Ensuring there was enough food and drink on the table was usually a struggle, but the arrival of a child was a special occasion to be celebrated properly. Though the famine still tormented much of Ireland and Liverpool, with the help of Darby and friends within the household, a small banquet had been prepared. The baptism of John would be celebrated in the old Irish way, with good food, song, and fun.

* * *

The brief interval of joy that John's birth had provided was shattered only weeks later with a confirmation of the news that most people in Liverpool had been fearing. The potato crop in Ireland had failed yet again; the blight had returned. Everyone knew what that meant. More starvation, more desperation, and more exodus from Ireland. As the summer progressed, the paddle steamers brought more Irish into Liverpool. As before, many hoped to continue a journey to America, but for others Liverpool itself was a destination. Every arrival saw hope in the great city, only to be dashed within days when the awful realities of its harsh environment set in. Desperate, many sought work wherever they could. On almost a daily basis, there was a queue of the forlorn and malnourished waiting at the gates of the flag yard. Austin felt threatened and uneasy. He wanted to help, but he had his own family to feed, and these new arrivals were prepared to undercut his wages and might even take his job. Guilt set in. His fear started to morph into a guarded hostility, a hostility shared by most of his fellow workers.

Catherine had her own problems. What Austin earned from his two jobs had never been adequate; she needed to make more money to supplement the family income. While selling on market days was permissible, encouraged even, what money she took there was not enough. She had to sell her fish directly on the streets, which often attracted the unwelcome attention of the constables. Her usual position was standing at the top of her own street, Stockdale Street, at its junction with busy Marybone.

'Fish, fresh fish! All caught early this morning! Best quality fish at a good price!'

Loud and unrelenting, she repeated an invitation to buy for hours on end.

The trade was unpredictable, but over the time she had been routinely standing there, it had become better. She had even managed to acquire one or two regular customers, for whom she would usually offer a slightly better price, and one that certainly undercut her nearest competitor. Shine or rain, Catherine would stand there; only on market days and Sundays would she be absent. And yet there was still competition everywhere. Over time, informal agreements had been made between those that got on well with each other, to recognise certain areas as places where a particular hawker stood. While many of her fellow hawkers recognised the place she used as 'her' spot, others were less sanguine and would try to better her pitch.

Opposite Stockdale Street, on the other side of Marybone, Sawney Pope Street, there would almost always be another also selling fish. A new girl had recently appeared, calling herself by the name of M'Tague. She had somehow managed to usurp the position opposite from its previous occupant. Catherine had taken an immediate dislike to her. The woman seemed to be a recent arrival and was more aggressive, or desperate, than other street sellers. She seemed unwilling to recognise the unwritten rules that the more established street vendors would follow. M'Tague simply did not care. She wanted money, and appeared willing to do almost anything to get it.

'Ara, Catherine. Two cod for me.' She was one of Catherine's best customers asking for what was apparently one of her favourite dishes. Catherine selected two of her best-looking examples and handed them over in some old paper wrapping.

'You'll get better over here! No question of it!' shouted M'Tague from the end of Sawney Pope Street, an unwelcome interruption to the transaction. Catherine's customer turned round to look at the source of the intrusion. For a second or two, she delayed handed over her payment to Catherine.

'Ignore her. She's a sleeveen if ever there was one,' said Catherine, controlling her anger.

Her customer turned back to face Catherine and finished handing over her money.

'I'll be seeing you, Catherine.'

Catherine waited for a few minutes before giving her Sawney Street competition a little more attention. Twenty minutes later, there was an opportunity to get her own back.

'You'll get better over here! No question of it!' shouted Catherine, just as what looked like a M'Tague customer was about to make a purchase. She had basically repeated M'Tague's earlier provocation.

M'Tague's customer turned towards Catherine and started making her way over. As she did so, M'Tague threw some salt at her, cursing as she did so.

'*Má ithis, nar chacair*! You won't with what she sells you.'

'Shut up, you sleeveen!' Catherine shouted back.

The customer they were both fighting over backed away, clearly wanting no part in the argument that was brewing.

As the customer briskly walked away from the scene, M'Tague crossed the road at a similar pace, carrying two quite obviously rotten fish, one in each hand. As she neared Catherine, she threw one, then the other, directly at her. They both caught Catherine by surprise – one on the face, and the other on the right shoulder. M'Tague laughed, turned, and started marching back to her own corner.

Catherine was furious. She abandoned her cart and ran across the road towards M'Tague. On reaching her own street corner, M'Tague turned just as Catherine caught up. Catherine whacked M'Tague across the face with one of her own cod, repeating her earlier insult.

'You sleeveen! Bitch! Don't you come near me or my customers, or else!' screamed Catherine.

M'Tague instantly saw red and grabbed hold of Catherine around the neck. Within seconds they were both on the ground landing light punches on each other, shouting insults, and pulling hair.

A hundred yards away, one of Liverpool's Irish Quarter constables was on his usual rounds on Marybone and its surrounding streets. He had just appeared from Naylor Street and was walking down Bush Road when he saw the commotion developing on the corner of Sawney Pope Street and Marybone. Recognising that it was women, he decided not to run but merely quickened his pace. It was, after all, a bit of entertainment, a diversion from chasing Liverpool's 'street arabs' – the Irish children who were adept at helping the unwary to part with their money. He caught up with the brawling hawkers about a minute later, just as they were already showing signs of tiring.

'Stop this! I'm ordering you to stop this!' he bellowed.

Catherine and M'Tague paused, recognising the constable's uniform, but still seemed willing to continue their dispute. M'Tague punched Catherine on her breast, with Catherine immediately responding in like manner.

'One more like that and I'll charge you with a breach of the peace,' said the constable.

Catherine and M'Tague stopped their aggressive behaviour and began to sidle away from each other.

'I can see that you've both got carts. I'm charging you with obstruction. You'll have a fine to pay. You're lucky I'm not charging you with something more serious,' added the constable. He knew it would be easier for him to prove, and less bureaucratic, than a street brawl.

He took both their names, addresses, and other details he needed for the charge.

'I know who you both are. If you don't appear before the magistrate tomorrow at eight o'clock, you'll be arrested and sentenced to gaol. Do you understand that?'

Catherine and M'Tague both indicated that they did.

'Now be off with you. And if I catch you here again today, it will be handcuffs.'

'Yes, constable,' replied Catherine. M'Tague just provided a disgruntled nod, clearly unhappy with the outcome.

Crossing back over to the top of Stockdale Street, Catherine collected her hand cart and considered what to do next. Continuing her trade here was not an option, at least not today, and yet she still needed to sell the rest of her fresh merchandise before it went off. Unsure of the limits of the constable's area, she headed towards the bottom of Naylor Street and Vauxhall Road, hoping that it would be far enough away. Fifty yards down Stockdale Street, Catherine turned. M'Tague was still there, shouting out as before. She waved and laughed at Catherine, apparently unconcerned by the threats of Liverpool's constables. Catherine seethed, but continued to follow her instinct.

'One day they'll have you, bitch. One day,' she mused, quietly resolving to get the better of M'Tague.

* * *

Each day appeared worse than the last.

1848 closed as it had started, cold and wet, hungry, sick and wretched. The Hunger continued through the winter months into the spring. Again, hopes were raised that the blight would end. That there would be a natural resolution to the human suffering that had devasted Ireland, and its tormented and destitute population. As nature's plague still ran rampant, wealthy landowners sought protection by sponsoring laws which did little but exacerbate the conditions of its suffering masses. News of these latest acts of intentional persecution soon found their way into Liverpool.

On almost every day a thousand distressed Irish immigrants entered the city, many bringing with them stories of the tribulations of their recent past. A growing awareness of the misfeasance of Ireland was starting to filter through, feeding the Irish nationalist cause, and fostering additional dissent amongst Liverpool's Irish diaspora.

As ever, Donal was the one to tell of the injustice at their usual place around the fire in the flag yard.

'Palmerston's been at it again. He's no good. I've said it before.'

'Palmerston? What's he done this time?' asked Kevin, one of the yard's members who was less interested in politics. Even he had heard of the man, but that was about all.

'He's no good. Made "The Hunger" worse,' replied Donal.

'How so?' asked Austin.

'He never sets foot in Ireland. Doesn't care about his tenants. I'll tell you what he's done. I've been told myself about it by good men. Men who had land in Ireland, until Palmerston threw them out,' replied Donal.

'Why would he do that with thousands hungry? It's not Christian. I can't believe it,' replied Kevin, somewhat incredulous that a person of Palmerston's note would cause any suffering.

'He has. Thousands thrown off his lands, so I'm told. Thousands!' Donal emphasised his last point.

'But I ask again. Why would he do that?' said Kevin.

The rest of the group stayed silent, giving Donal the opportunity to collectively address them.

'It's to save him money. If he throws the smallholder off his lands, he saves having to give them help. Only a quarter of an acre, that's all. You can't grow much in a quarter acre, and with the blight, it's starvation. Lucan is worse. He says the land cannot support the people, so what does he do? He brings in the crowbar brigades and hut tumblers. Throws thousands off the land. As if starvation were not enough. No roof over their heads as well. So, what do they do? They come here. They come for our jobs. I blame them not, but we also all have families to feed. It's the British aristocrats at fault. They're causing our kin to starve,' explained Donal, with increasing passion.

'Aye. You may be right, Donal. But what can we do? We all have to survive,' said Austin. Kevin nodded his head in agreement.

'We can take to the streets and protest. The Chartists did,' replied Donal.

'And much good it did them,' said Kevin.

'We've got to do something. This can't go on,' replied Donal.

'Maybe so. But what will they do? Bring soldiers, that's what they'll do. And that will be it for us all,' said Kevin.

'You're all...' Donal started to say something but remembered where he was. He paused before finishing.

'Just as well you stopped. As has been said, we don't want trouble brought to the doors of our yard. And if you want to eat tomorrow, you'll make sure it stays that way. Every one of you,' said Kevin, hinting at threats in his tone.

Austin, as usual, remained silent for most of the discussion. He, as did everyone else around the fire, knew that Donal had his heart in the right place. But Austin also knew that he needed his job more than ever. So long as the blight continued, everyone in the yard, stonemason or labourer, was under economic threat. They each felt that there was little choice but to protect their own interests; perhaps give a penny or two to the alms box now and again, but that was about all.

It was family first, at least for now.

* * *

M'Tague still irked Catherine weeks after the incident on Sawney Pope Street, but more pressing concerns emerged during the dark days of March and April. As if the 'Fever' had not been enough, another scourge had been billowing through the Vauxhall district. Mistaken at first for Typhus, something even more deadly had taken hold, Cholera. Rumours abounded at first, and the complaints of the Irish poor were not taken as seriously as should have befitted a plague of this magnitude. Though lacking a formal education, Catherine was sharp. She had listened to the stories other women told, of how a fellow immigrant by the name of Kitty Wilkinson had helped contain an earlier epidemic some ten or more years earlier. She knew exactly what to do and would be damned in hell if the Cholera were to take her sons in the same way the 'Fever' had taken Austin's parents a few years before.

'Take off your clothes, all of you,' said Catherine to Austin and her son Edward. She had already removed John's and replaced them with others.

'I'm wearing them. What am I to do, walk around naked?' replied Austin, somewhat mischievously.

'I've bought some more with our savings,' said Catherine.

Austin looked at his wife, a horrified expression on his face.

'They're not worn out. Why did you do that? We may need to eat with what's left. You know it. And America...' replied Austin.

Catherine sighed.

'It's the Cholera. It's here. There's hundreds dying. How can you not see it, Austin?' said Catherine.

'I see it, woman. But what has it to do with my clothes?' he replied.

'They need to be washed. Mine do as well. So do Edward's, John's, and everyone in this house should do the same,' said Catherine.

Austin returned an even more befuddled look.

'We also need to bathe at least twice a week from now on. I'll be washing with chloride of lime and boiling water to kill the Cholera. Kitty Wilkinson says that's the best way to keep as safe as you can. It might also help with the "Fever",' said Catherine.

'I suppose it will be a trip to Frederick Street. More expense,' replied Austin.

'If a trip to the baths twice a week will keep us alive, then that's what we shall do. Better a penny or two spent there than on a bed at the necropolis,' said Catherine.

'Cholera, the "Fever", and the "Hunger"; what more pestilence can there be? You must have heard about Ballinrobe? It's the talk everywhere. I'm sure something will be said a Mass on Sunday,' replied Austin, moving the discussion on.

'I have. They say nearly a hundred dead in the workhouse in a week. But the Cholera is taking more than that every week around here. There's dozens died already on Lace Street. There'll be no doctors for us, Austin. We have to do for ourselves. It's better that we don't catch it, if we can. Promise me you'll do as I say,' demanded Catherine.

'Aye,' replied Austin.

'What's that?' I need to hear it louder,' said Catherine.

'I'll wash every week, twice if I have to. And I won't complain if you wash my clothes. But don't buy any more,' replied Austin.

'I'll do what I need to do, Austin. Whatever is needed to get us through this, I'll do. The other women in the house are also of the same mind. If we can all wash and clean, we might live to see another year,' said Catherine.

Austin shrugged. 'As you wish. Now what are we to eat tonight?'

Edward giggled at his father's question, while Cecilia, Austin's sister, turned away. Out of sight, she smiled to herself, wondering what else she could learn about handling a husband from her sister-in-law. In time she would let her brother and Catherine know that she would be leaving Stockdale Street before long. They did not know about John Cunningham yet, but they would in time. Cholera, the 'Fever', and the 'Hunger' were all around, but life would go on. She fully intended to get through this and one day have her own family.

* * *

Liverpool had become a city of sharp contrasts over the famine years. The destitution and misery of the Irish immigrant population had been amplified by wages falling and abominable living conditions. And yet the metropolis prospered. Plagues raged and people protested, but the wheel of commerce inexorably turned. Buildings were erected, docks constructed, and railways built. The amalgamation of this growth created wealth, but it was a wealth bestowed only on the lucky few – the landlords, the ship owners, and merchants. Both serious and petty crime were a constant problem, more so with the exponential growth of the population that had taken place in just a few years. With the Irish no longer a minority, the city's culture had evolved to reflect the change. It became known as the 'capital of Ireland outside of Ireland'.

Like tens of thousands of other Irish immigrants, Austin, Catherine, and their families took only a subsistence share of Liverpool's accelerating prosperity. They had managed to elevate themselves from the starvation imposed by the blight, and yet they still existed more than lived. Austin was becoming politically aware, yet remained afraid of the consequences of being seen to take action. Faced with a choice between the loss of his livelihood and a 'cause', he would always choose to keep his work. It was a simple choice for him: to eat or not to eat. Without work there would be no food.

Cecilia's plans unfurled in the way she wanted. During the summer months she shared her news with Catherine – unsurprisingly in the bathhouse. They were to be married before the end of the year, with Cecilia becoming Cecilia Cunningham. A little later than expected, on November 11th, 1849, Cecilia and John were married, leaving Stockdale Street soon afterwards. And, at least for a time, the news appeared to get a little better. The Cholera epidemic seemed to burn itself out as the year drew to a close. Hope began to emerge on the streets of the city. Policing improved to help tackle both petty and serious crime, and the effects of Liverpool's sanitary inspectors were slowly starting to have an impact on conditions.

And Catherine also thought she had got one over on M'Tague. Together with some of the other hawkers, they had formed a club to save and pay the now regular fines for obstructing the streets. Policing had improved their safety, but it also had its consequences. As for M'Tague, there were very few of the street sellers who got on with her. She had not been invited to join their club, and if Catherine had anything to do with it, never would be.

As the city's bells tolled for the new year, Austin's thoughts were again of the future. He hoped that it would be better, that the plagues would end, and most of all, that the blight would not return next year. Catherine's thoughts were similar, but nuanced with a notion closer to home. She longed for the day when she saw M'Tague hauled away by a constable from her perch at the end of Sawney Pope Street. She might even tell of the woman to hasten the day when she could not pay her fine. It was not exactly a Christian thought, but then she did not know if M'Tague was even a Catholic. In this way she justified her actions.

Chapter 7

THE VISITOR

The priest was more ebullient than usual in giving his sermon. He had promised the congregation some news that would 'change the Catholic church in England' forever, and that he would tell of it at the end of the homily. Edward fidgeted on the hard unforgiving wooden pew as he listened to the unintelligible drone emanating from the front of the church. He could not see much, other than the backs of the adults sitting in front of him. From time to time, he would attempt to stand up on the seat, only to be reprimanded and told to 'hush' by Catherine. Meanwhile, Austin looked on, sitting at the other side of his son, barely more interested. A priest's sermon was always something of an endurance test, occasionally animated by the raising or lowering of tone as the cleric forced emphasis in an attempt to maintain the attention of his flock. And today seemed no different than any other Sunday sermon. Towards the end of a religious exhortation, the priest would often recall a parable. It was a sort of supplement to the main message, and usually indicated that the lesson was coming to an end. Austin's mind snapped back into focus as the parable of 'The Prodigal Son' was told. He was familiar with it, as it was often retold – an apparent favourite of their current parish priest.

'...and it is only by God's grace we are saved, not by works that we may boast of. That is the message I want you to take home.'

The sermon ended with the priest pausing for longer than was comfortable for most of his congregation. It was unclear to Austin whether the clergyman was simply gathering his thoughts, or whether he had created a deliberate hiatus for effect; perhaps to ensure rapt attention from his flock. Either way, it worked. There was an expectant though uncomfortable silence, as he stood facing them, still and silent. Apparently assured of an engrossed audience, he suddenly sprang back into speech.

'I have some news. The Pope has issued a Papal Bull – a decree, for those who do not know what that is. I am very pleased and happy to announce that he has issued the "Universalis Ecclesiae". Pope Pius has recreated the Catholic Church in England. New dioceses have been created, with bishops and parishes throughout the land. For nearly three hundred years England has been without the full grace of our mother church. But today, as our venerable Archbishop Wiseman has pronounced, "Catholic England has been restored to its orbit in the ecclesiastical firmament." Some will object to "Popery" as they call it. But fear them not. Go home in the knowledge that the true religion of God is again marching. Go home in the knowledge that one day perhaps the errors of Protestantism will be rectified. Our Father will perhaps one day accept his errant and repentant sinners back into the glory of the Catholic Church, just as in "The Prodigal Son". This is a good day for every English Catholic.'

The priest concluded his somewhat pompous message and resumed the Latin ritual of the Mass. A few whispers were heard within the pews, but for most the implications of what he had told them were not really appreciated. They understood it was good news, and that he was a happy man, which seemed enough for many of those present.

'Just wait until Donal hears of this. He's bound to have something to say. I think there could be trouble brewing. There's enough with the Orangemen without this happening. I worry about it,' said Austin to Catherine and his younger brother, John, who was still living with them.

They were standing outside the church, hoping to catch some gossip before their walk home. But they were soon disappointed, as every conversation centred on what this 'Papal Bull' actually meant. Few appeared able to work out what difference it would make to their lives.

'We should go, Austin. Most here don't seem any the wiser. It may mean something to the priest but not to the likes of us,' said Catherine.

'It could be trouble on the streets. It's happened before when anything Catholic is in the news. The Orangemen never like it. And they don't like that there are now a hundred thousand or more Irish in Liverpool. They can't tell us what to do any more,' replied Austin.

'But they still do; at least the masters do. It's still the rich who own the land, the big houses, the ships, the shops, and the stores. Who buys your stone? The rich. And if the masons don't sell it cheap enough, that will be the end of it. The rich don't care. You're only as good as the cheapest price. As for the Orangemen. Huh. Stupid men with stupid ideas. They're no better than us. In fact, they're worse. Puppets of the masters, I say,' said Catherine.

'You've got a lot to say for yourself today, Catherine,' said John.

'You learn plenty about how the world works selling on the street. There's much of life that I see,' replied Catherine.

'Well, let's hope it's the beginning of something good rather than the beginning of something bad,' said Austin.

'I'm sure we'll know soon enough,' said Catherine.

After a little badinage and pleasantries exchanged with some familiar faces also standing in the church grounds, they left for home, thoughts of the 'Papal Decree' already replaced with talk of plans for the following week.

* * *

In the following months there were reactions across the country to the Papal decree. Effigies were burned, protests organised, and even the Prime Minister raised a complaint. Parliamentary laws were passed, all attempting to hamper the establishment of a new Catholic diocese hierarchy, but they largely failed to gain much traction. In Liverpool, Orangemen also marched, vandalising known Catholic-owned premises, smashing church windows, and generally antagonising the Irish Quarter. But instead of success in fomenting sectarian discord, their effects were marginal. Instead of an explosive firework of religious dissonance, it was more a damp squib; low level, and generally subliminally racist and personal. That, of course, was nothing new.

Still bothered by M'Tague, for months now Catherine had been talking about moving to another part of Liverpool – a fresh start, perhaps even in better accommodation. With 'The Hunger' showing clear signs of abating, not least due to the fact that so many had already left Ireland, and the plague of Cholera and Typhus retreating, life seemed to be getting slightly better. Though wages remained depressed, there were fewer numbers entering into Liverpool than there had been. It seemed like as good a time as any for a move, but within Liverpool rather than further afield. As luck would have it, their current landlord was about to force the issue, with McCabe acting as messenger. He burst into the court one autumn evening, a little earlier than usual.

'I'll need a word when Austin's back home.'

'What would it concern?' asked Catherine. She was not one who cared to wait for any news.

'There's no need. I'll tell you when he's home, Catherine,' replied McCabe. His demeanour suggested something serious; he did not appear to want to tease her.

'I can pass on any news. There's no need for you to wait if you have to be somewhere else,' said Catherine.

McCabe sighed, appearing to think. 'Alright. It's the landlord. He's putting the rent up. We'll all have more to pay,' he replied.

'For this hovel of a place? He's done nothing to deserve that,' started Catherine.

'I know it. There's no need to tell me. But what are we to do? There's many that would still take it for a roof over their heads. I'm sure of that,' replied McCabe.

'It's no joke, then?' said Catherine.

'As God's my witness,' replied McCabe.

'We've been here for years, longer than I ever expected to be. I've never met the man. I don't expect us to be treated like this.

Where does he think the money will come from?' said Catherine.

'He will say it's not his concern where the money comes from. You either pay the rent or you are thrown out. You know that's as true as it's ever been. And I've got to pay him what he wants. So, if you are staying, you'll have to pay. We've known each other a long time, and Austin... well, I knew his father before him. Catherine, I don't want to fall out, but we have no choice. I have no choice. I'm sorry, but that's the way it is,' replied McCabe.

'If that's the way it is, I'll tell Austin. You can be on your way if you want,' said Catherine.

'I will. I'll need your answer tomorrow. He wants to charge from next week,' replied McCabe, standing at the door.

'I'll be sure to tell him,' said Catherine.

McCabe closed the door behind him, knowing full well the irritable state he had left Catherine in. In some ways he felt pleased that it would be Catherine who would have to tell Austin, and not him. He had known them both for years and considered them friends, but he also knew that he had not the means nor the willingness to subsidise other occupants' rents. There were more conversations to have, but perhaps Catherine would save him the trouble. If other members of the household also had problems paying, then that could be a bigger problem. He just hoped it would not lead to him ending up on the street as well.

A half hour or so later, Austin appeared. As ever, hungry, and not really in a mood to talk. Catherine waited until he had eaten before passing on McCabe's news. He was usually more amenable on a full stomach. She waited until the kitchen cleared of people and then launched into her plan.

'Austin, you know we've talked of moving.'

She waited for his response.

'I've always talked of America. Perhaps now is the time,' replied Austin.

'Not America, but across the city. I'd like to be closer to the markets. And you know about the M'Tague woman. She's at the top of our street almost every day. I don't like her at all,' said Catherine.

Austin smiled. He certainly remembered the story of Catherine's more physical brush with M'Tague.

'Well, if we are to move, it should be close to where we are now then, just far enough away from that woman of yours. I think the rents are higher nearer the markets,' replied Austin.

He knew it was not the time to talk about America again. In fact, it never seemed to be the time to talk about America. He did not really want to move, even if Catherine did have an ongoing problem with her local competition.

'About the rent. McCabe says we have to pay more. He says the landlord is putting it up,' said Catherine.

'Did he now? It's the first I've heard of it. Well, I can't work any more than I am doing, so we can't pay more in rent. That's it. Why did he not tell me himself? I've known the man forever,' replied Austin.

'He wanted to, but I said I would pass on the message. But what I say is that if the rent is going up here, then we might as well move to somewhere better. It makes sense to me,' said Catherine.

'There'll be less to eat if we have to pay more for a roof,' replied Austin.

'We'll work it out. We always do, Austin. Besides, if I sell on the streets closer to the markets, I'll sell more than up here. I'm thinking near the baths and St. Martins,' said Catherine.

'When will this rent go up?' asked Austin.

'McCabe says next week,' replied Catherine.

'Next week! Damn him. I mean the landlord. McCabe is a good man,' said Austin.

'Most of the time,' replied Catherine, more circumspect.

'I'll see what I can find, but I don't have much time,' said Austin.

'I'll find something. Leave it to me,' replied Catherine.

Disgruntled, Austin settled in for a snooze on a chair he had recently acquired. Second-hand, green, worn, and threadbare, but with a cushioned seat and armrests, it was a small luxury and a welcome alternative to the wooden seating he had traditionally used. They still shared a house, and yet the other members of the household respected his seat close to the open fire. No-one else would sit on it, not even McCabe – the man usually seen as head of the household. Within minutes Austin fell into a nap, the concerns of paying the rent receding into abstraction.

* * *

It took Catherine a matter of days to find somewhere new to live. Austin was right; the rents were slightly higher than in Stockdale Street, but there was hardly a difference after the increase. She looked up and down Scotland Road in the nearby streets – Lawrence Street, Horatio Street, Great Nelson Street, Virgil Street, Mile End and Bevington Hill – but eventually found an acceptable court on Collingwood Street. In truth, it was little better than Stockdale, but it was certainly more convenient for St. Martin's market. There were two families, the Kaynes and the Pecketts, and three other lodgers, and themselves. In all, there would be seventeen living in the house, including two infants. There were more people sharing a household than in Stockdale, but the rooms in the court were slightly larger. Timothy Kayne, the head of the household, had told her that the rent would have to be higher if there were less lodgers, so it made sense for him to share with as many people as they could reasonably cram into the space.

Austin was less impressed.

'There's more people than in our court in Stockdale. You said you would look for something better. It's further to walk as well.'

'We talked about it, Austin. I'll sell more to make up the rent. I might even make more selling on Scotland Road. It's an easy walk for you, down Burlington Street, over the Houghton Bridge, and a walk on the canal towpath. What could be easier?' replied Catherine.

'Well, somewhere nearer the Dock Road,' replied Austin.

'Huh. Over my dead body. *An té a luíonn le madaí, eiroidh sé le dearnaid.* He who lies down with dogs, gets up with fleas. I'm not living anywhere near them Dock Road women,' said Catherine.

'There's plenty of places nearby. And you would be closer to the docks for buying fish,' replied Austin.

'I've found somewhere, and Darby is looking to get somewhere there as well. We're moving Saturday afternoon,' said Catherine, attempting to close the discussion to her satisfaction.

Defeated again, Austin resigned himself to a weekend move and getting to know a new household of people. They did not have much, but one thing he would be taking would be his chair. He was going to have that whatever the circumstances. His new house companions would just have to get used to it.

As the dark and foggy November days set in, Austin and Catherine found themselves in 2,14 Court on Collingwood Street. They had soon settled in, apparently getting on quite well with the court's existing occupants. But then they had to; it was in nobody's interests to fall out. New routines were forming, with Catherine already establishing herself on a pitch on Scotland Road, close to the weighing machine near Virgil Street. It was an increasingly busy junction, with four or five streets intersecting. Somewhat surprisingly, given its proximity to the market and the presence of other hawkers, she was the only fish seller. Without the competition she could be as good as her ambitions. Sales increased and business got better. For a time, Catherine could not have wished for a better outcome.

* * *

Austin was tired.

Exhausted from years of trying to keep up with two jobs, it was obvious to Catherine that something had to change. Either that, or she would soon be without a husband. The move to Collingwood Street had gone better than she had expected. The street itself was situated towards the edge of the city, near to St. Martin's and St Anthony's churches. But it was a city rapidly expanding. New buildings were being thrown up on Scotland Road and Great Homer Street, the two roads bookending Collingwood Street. More buildings and housing meant more new customers for Catherine and the circle of fellow hawkers that shared Scotland Road with her. A little extra income provided some choices. At first, she began to save, but then she began to notice a deterioration in Austin's health. He had no disease to speak of, but it soon became obvious that he was no longer the man he was when they first married. Years of heavy toil on the docks, in the flag yard, and working two jobs, had clearly had an impact on his physical health.

Unknown to Austin, Catherine had been saving. She had admitted to 'doing well', but had not been too specific. Nine years earlier she had been very much a naïve young girl when she married Austin, but now she was a grown woman, world-wise, and more than capable of making her own decisions. Life without a man, a husband, was certainly harder, but not impossible; not that she wanted to lose him. In fact, it was very much the opposite. She wanted to keep him as fit and healthy as she could, even if that meant a drop in income.

Over the winter of 1850 and 1851, she managed to increase their savings. They could now survive for several months should they have to – not that either of them expected such a hardship. Unfortunately, during the early part of 1851, Austin began to complain of aches and pains, as well as general fatigue. He looked drained and began to act as if everything was an effort. Catherine noticed, as did others in the household. Some had only known him for a short time, but they had already seen a difference, a deterioration in Austin's physical state. Catherine knew that she had to act or Austin would just continue on the same path. She resolved to speak to him about leaving the night watchman job, when providence intervened, as it had many times in the past.

Austin waited until after Mass on Sunday before sharing his news. In truth, he was a little embarrassed and needed some time to work out what to say to Catherine and, more importantly, come to a decision about what to do about it. Since moving to Collingwood Street, they had moved parishes, and now attended St. Anthony's a short walk away. Although the area around St. Anthony's was rapidly being filled with housing, countryside was still accessible. On a fine day, Austin and Catherine would take a walk further out, up Scotland Road, or perhaps in the direction of Great Horner Street. It would be an opportunity to breathe some fresh air, and talk of the old country, Mayo, and Ireland.

'We could walk up to Kirkdale Road, Catherine. I've got something to tell you,' said Austin. They had just left Mass at St. Anthony's, and had finished exchanging pleasantries outside with some of the other attendees.

'We could. It's a good day,' replied Catherine, picking Edward up.

Leaving the church, they turned right and began the walk on Scotland Road. He decided to fill in some time with talk of the sermon.

'It was interesting about Daniel O'Connell. My da used to talk about him and the Catholic Association, and parliament. He never went to a rally, but he knew of them; everyone did. Donal knows more about him; he talks about him a lot. He says we won't be fully free until every man has the vote. We all laugh when he talks about us getting to vote. The masters will never let us; the Chartists didn't get far either. I knew very little about Daniel O'Connell's fight against slavery, the evil it is,' said Austin.

'Nor did I. America, the place you talk of going to. They still have it. How do we know we would not end up in chains ourselves?' replied Catherine.

'It's not like that. And there's no slavers in the north, so they say,' said Austin.

'I'm happy enough here. The grass is always greener somewhere else, Austin,' replied Catherine.

Austin stayed silent. He did not want an argument about America before divulging his news. At the stone quarry near Everton Valley, he summoned up the courage to tell Catherine that which he had been too ashamed to admit in the days before. He decided to just blurt it out.

'Catherine, I've been sent away from the watchman job. They don't want me any more.'

'And why is that?' asked Catherine.

Austin looked at her then looked away. 'I was caught sleeping. It was too much, Catherine. There was a time when I could work a day, a night, and then another day, but I can no longer,' replied Austin.

'And what will you do?' asked Catherine.

'Look for another, of course. Though it won't be nights. I had an arrangement with another at the docks. He would sleep while I kept watch, and then I would sleep while he kept a look out. We would both sleep a little. That's how I managed it; how we managed it. He lost his work as well, though it was me they caught,' replied Austin, now more willing to share details.

'Where will you look? There's still so many desperate,' said Catherine.

'I know it. I might try the docks, porting again,' replied Austin.

'Stay at the yard, Austin. Fish sales are good on Scotland Road, much better than the last place. I've saved a little as well,' said Catherine.

'How can that be?' replied Austin.

'Well, there's no M'Tague for one. In fact, no other fish sellers near Collingwood. Perhaps they think it's too far, and yet the market is so close. I don't understand it, but I will not complain about our good fortune,' said Catherine.

'It's a lot of money to lose, Catherine,' replied Austin, probing for more details.

'I make enough, some weeks as much as you brought home for night work,' said Catherine.

'In truth, I am tired, Catherine. One job is more than enough. I'm going to see if they will pay me a shilling again. There aren't the same numbers at the gate as there once were,' replied Austin.

'Maybe so. But don't offend any of the stonemasons. I make enough, but not enough for you to lose both jobs,' said Catherine.

'I won't, I promise. I'll ask quietly. I won't even tell the others,' replied Austin.

On reaching the top of Walton Road, they turned back, retracing their steps to the stone quarry. There they took the Netherfield Road fork to Hillside and Roscommon Street, the street leading towards Collingwood Street. They had been walking for over an hour, admiring what was left of Everton's diminishing unspoilt landscape. Few people were working on the Sabbath, but the signs of Liverpool's expansion were all around, partially constructed buildings and unfinished streets clawing their way into the open countryside. It remained unsaid, but it was obvious to both, that before long the area they had just walked in would soon just become another ward in Liverpool's gallop towards commercial pre-eminence.

* * *

Three-and-a-half thousand miles away, and six months earlier, the United States Congress passed a law which would eventually reach out and touch more than a few in Liverpool. The Fugitive Slave Act of 1850 required that all slaves, upon capture, be returned to the slaver, and that all citizens and officials of free states cooperate.

James Watkins, by his own admission, was in a state of 'great perplexity'. Having already escaped from slavery in Maryland, he had long thought he had found a place of permanent safety in a northern state, Connecticut. For six years, since his flight from the South, he had enjoyed comfort and prosperity, a wife and three children, and was surrounded by a wide circle of friends. But that all stopped on September 18th, 1850. On September 17th, 1850 he was living without fear; on September 19th, 1850, the old dread of capture and restoration to a detested existence returned. With the full weight of law imposing abominable requirements on all, he no longer knew who to trust, and who to fear. Close friends advised leaving Hartford as soon as possible; even his wife, in the full knowledge of the personal hardship it would cause, said that he should leave. 'Better be buried in the blue seas than be taken into slavery again.'

Unwilling to immediately deal with the distress of parting with his wife, children, friends, and life in Connecticut, it was some months before James reached a decision. Having eventually made arrangements to leave, on January 20th, 1851 James bade his final farewells to his family and friends, and started his journey to New York, and then on to England. He left with a heavy heart, unsure whether he would ever see them again. With the assistance of friends, and friends of friends, in New York he took lodgings for several days, staying indoors to avoid being seen. On the day of sailing, he was transported by closed carriage to a ship, and concealed again until well out to sea.

Safe in the hands of a sympathetic captain, James caught his first sight of free land three weeks later – Cape Clear, Ireland's southernmost inhabited island. As his temporary home entered the safety of the Mersey and its docks, emotions got the better of him. Dancing, leaping, and shouting for joy, he finally felt protected from the clutches of American law. He was free at last.

* * *

Although the flag yard was predominantly Irish, there were two Methodists amongst their number. While most in the yard detested the Orangemen, the Methodists were tolerated, albeit open religious discussion amongst the two communities rarely took place. What was known were the thoughts of one of Liverpool's more prominent Methodist opponents of Catholicism, the Reverend Dr McNeile. Even outside the Methodist community he was known as a formidable orator, though engagement with any non-Catholics was not encouraged; indeed, it was actively discouraged by Austin's new parish priest. The Catholic Church was the one and only true religion.

It was Donal who discovered that a lecture was to be given by a former slave, John Watkins. Had it been organised by Catholics, they were certain that priests all across the city would have encouraged attendance in their sermons. But Rev. McNeile's involvement, and that of other prominent Methodists, rendered no tangible mention. The meeting would be held at St. Jude's Church on Hardwick Street, and no priest of the Catholic faith would advocate visiting a Methodist institution.

Donal announced he would be attending and managed to enlist two or three others who he thought might be of like mind. Austin's interest had been piqued. He had seen many black sailors in the beerhouses and on the Dock Road, but he had never met a slave, or more accurately a former slave, before. Like many of the others, he had difficulty conceiving that the life of a slave could be much worse than that of the Irish pauper. He therefore very much wanted to hear what the man had to say.

The meeting had been set for a half past six on a Saturday evening, March 22nd. When their small group of four arrived at the church, it was already packed. There was no seating, so all four had to stand at the back near the entrance, together with two dozen or so others. After a short introduction by a Methodist minister, welcoming those present and introducing their guest, James Watkins stood up from a pew at the front of the Gothic-style nave. He walked to the centre of the altar area and climbed two steps, before turning to face perhaps a hundred and fifty or more expectant faces. His audience fell into silence as they waited for him to speak.

'My name is James Watkins. I was not always James Watkins, but was once "Ensor Sam" after my owner, Mr. Abraham Ensor. This is my story of how I came to be in your fine city...'

Clearly a little nervous at first, he soon found his footing. Whereupon, he began to talk of his life in Maryland, being a slave, his two escapes to freedom, and the 'atrocious and abominable law' that had recently been introduced – the cause of his flight to safety in England. He praised England and its pursuit of abolition, contrasting it with the dark world he had just left. While not wishing to traduce the country of his birth, he earnestly appealed for help in delivering America from the curse of bondage.

Austin began to feel uneasy. Had Catherine been with him, she would have no doubt taken note of what this James Watkins had to say, and used it in argument against a new life in America. Indeed, after hearing what he had to say, she might have had some sound reasoning. As Austin's mind drifted on thoughts of America, and their own future, their speaker concluded. He had stood for over an hour before inviting questions.

After listening to a couple of technical enquiries on the nature of slavery and punishment, Donal decided to speak up. He began to ask the questions that at least a few of the Irish working men present were no doubt thinking.

'Sir, I would like to ask if you know of the Irish enslaved, the paupers, and the starving in Ireland?'

'You are Irish? Are you Catholic as well?' interjected a Methodist minister before James Watkins could reply.

'I am, sir. What of it? Am I not allowed to speak?' replied Donal, ready for a verbal struggle.

The minister hesitated, obviously unhappy with the presence of Catholics, but unable to take action given the presence of so many.

'You are. But ask judicious questions and don't take too long.'

Though irritated, Donal elected to keep his silence and wait for their visitor to reply.

'I know of the Irish, and there are few who have not heard of the famine. I met Irish people in Hartford, and I know of your struggle against starvation. I know you call it "The Hunger". This much is clear to me. But you are not enslaved as we black people are. You are free men,' replied James Watkins.

Donal was not prepared to let it rest at that.

'How can you call us free? We work hard and long for little pay. In Ireland I had a smallholding, three acres, and had to work for the landlord for two-thirds of the year, every year, to pay the rent. When I couldn't pay, the landlord just threw me off. I had no rights. In my father's father's time, the English treated us worse than they would their dogs and cattle. We were not people. My father's brother was struck down and killed for speaking back. It was not murder, they said, because he was Irish and of no value. Even here, in Liverpool, we are hardly treated better. And you tell us of this slavery because of the colour of your skin. Well, I say there is slavery here, still,' said Donal.

'What is your name, sir?' asked James Watkins.

'Donal O'Hare,' replied Donal.

'Well, Donal. You are clearly wronged, as was your father and his father. But you cannot compare your lives with true slavery. I can tell you why this is so. When you have stood on an auction block and been sold to the highest bidder, with the same or less consideration as you would give a pig, then you can call yourself a slave. Though you might not like your job, and your pay, you can give notice and leave. You cannot do this as a slave. When you are punished and whipped for the smallest of misdemeanours, without appeal, then you are a slave. When you are told who you can marry, and when you can marry, then you are a slave. I've seen little of this in England so far. The Irish have had it very bad these past years. I know thousands upon thousands have been lost, and many have flown your fair island. But even so, I still have this to say to you. The difference between the working man in England and Ireland, and a slave in America, is this: as a slave I hold no key to my jailer's door. You do. You can leave. Even indentured, there is still a path to freedom. This is what I ask you to consider and to comprehend.'

Many in the audience began to clap as James Watkins closed his reply. Some turned round towards Donal to see what he might say, but Donal remained silent. He was unaccustomed to being defeated in argument, but defeated he was. Gracious in accepting the power of James Watkin's counterpoint, he had few more words.

'Thank you, Mr Watkins. I understand, and would not wish to diminish your life as a slave. I will speak no more.'

At that, the minister stood up, clearly satisfied with his guest's answers, and perhaps not unhappy that one of the Catholics present had been frustrated at trying to better him. More questions were asked, and answered; some important, some frivolous, some irrelevant. But at the end of the lecture there was satisfaction that it had achieved its purpose. Donal, Austin, and friends included, all left the church that night convinced that existence of slavery was an evil that the world could do without, to be despised and fought against.

* * *

Outside the church, Donal had more to say, more to disclose about his own family's plight in Ireland.

'I could have said much more, much, much more. But the night was his. He's right about slavery, but as he thinks I don't understand American servitude, so he also knows little about Ireland.'

'What are you saying, Donal?' asked Austin.

'"The Hunger". There's more than meets the eye. There's been blight; sure, there's been blight, but "The Hunger" was down to the British Army. I know it was. I see what many did not. They took the food. They starved Ireland. They starved our people, the Irish. The black men are slaves, but they are fed and sheltered. What of us? None were fed and none were sheltered. Are we worse than dogs?'

Donal's anger swelled up. When he spoke in the yard, most around him took only a little notice, not wanting to cause the ire of the stonemasons. At times he was regarded as a figure of fun, a politician without a constituency, a rebel with a cause, but no followers. But this was different. This was not simple political rhetoric. It was raw emotion swelling up. Something suppressed finally finding release.

'We've all had to leave, Donal. Every Irishman in Liverpool has had cause to leave Ireland. But James Watkins was right. I've never been sold like a pig, nor did we have to stay in Mayo against our will,' replied Austin.

'Perhaps not. But was your treatment any better? The truth was you were a non-person in Ireland, not worthy of saving. When the blight struck, the landlords didn't care. They shipped food to England when it was desperately needed in Ireland. Perhaps if they had fed us, forgiven some rent, then our kin would still be alive. They may shackle the black slave, but they feed him. The Irish slave, huh! The Irish slave is worthless,' said Donal.

'You know if we rise, Donal, the British Army will just strike us down. You know they will,' replied Austin.

'If every man thought as I did, and if every man stood up for his right to live a decent life, even the British Army could not stop us. One day people will see the injustice that has been inflicted on us. One day we will hold our heads up high, as equals to the masters, the landlords, the aristocracy. And soon may it come,' said Donal.

'But until that day we have to eat. We have to survive. We should be thankful for small comforts. I told Catherine I would go to the beerhouse and fetch some kegs on my way home,' replied Austin.

'Aye. To the beerhouse then. We'll talk some more there about what can be done,' said Donal.

'To the beerhouse it is then. We should go to Leeds Street,' replied Austin, closing their brief but interesting discussion.

* * *

Less than two weeks later, March 31st, there was a knock on the door. Rumour had preceded who this knock might be; rumour provided by Donal as it usually was. Donal called it the 'Census' and told everybody that that the 'government' had decided to count everybody again, just like they had ten years earlier. Austin had a vague recollection of something similar taking place in his father's time and being sent out to find out more. Ten years earlier he had been told that there was nothing to be afraid of, but like his father then, he was none too sure about it. Irish Catholics in Liverpool were now a formidable share of the total population, but they were still in the minority, and still despised by the Orangemen and the wealthy. Even the Irish who had prospered in Liverpool now wanted to distance themselves from those of 'low birth'.

As a precaution, he decided to be out on the day of the count, instructing Catherine and Thomas – a cousin of Austin's who had recently come to live them – to provide the minimum of information: 'I'm Austin Melia and I was born in Ireland.' That was the top and bottom of it. As it happened it was Timothy Kayne, the head of their household, who spoke for everyone, including other lodgers like themselves. Fearful for some considerable time, it was weeks afterwards before he finally accepted that there were to be no unexpected visitors.

Life for Austin returned to normal. It seemed to be as true now as it was then; all they wanted to do was to count people. Why they would want to do such a thing remained beyond him. Even Donal's somewhat vague explanations appeared somewhat wanting.

Thomas seemed to hit it off with Catherine. So much so that she agreed to help him buy some more respectable workwear, much like Austin's. Austin had managed to secure Thomas some regular work at the flag yard, on a trial basis at first. After four or five weeks, they seemed content with his efforts and agreed that he should be taken on full time, five days a week and Saturday mornings. It was Catherine who recognised that his clothing was inadequate for such hard labour, so she suggested that she could loan him the money to purchase a pea coat, and a less worn pair of moleskin trousers. He already had a waistcoat and necktie, albeit the former was already looking a little worn.

Decked out in a woollen navy pea jacket, blue plaided moleskin trousers, and a contrasting red necktie, Thomas looked the part. At sixteen he had been working for several years, but it was only now, dressed up in the uniform of an adult, that he felt like a man. With a full wage, a good set of clothes, and a roof over his head, he could start to make his way in the world, and have some fun along the way.

* * *

Austin arrived back home in Collingwood Street at his usual time, expecting to find his nephew waiting for him. It was Friday night, and both had talked about going to visit some beerhouses, or even a better class public house. As it was, Thomas was keen to thank his Uncle Austin for taking him in, and helping him secure some reliable work on decent enough pay.

'Where's Thomas?' asked Austin, minutes after arriving home.

Catherine shrugged her shoulders.

'I don't know. Your Uncle Patrick visited. They talked about something or other, and then they went off together,' replied Catherine.

'We were supposed to go out for a drink tonight. He invited me. I'm surprised he's not here,' said Austin.

'And what about me?' replied Catherine.

'I'll be staying in. I'll get a keg or two and we'll have some ale at home,' said Austin, wise enough not to get into a debate about the wisdom of visiting a beerhouse with Thomas.

'Huh!' Catherine grunted, not exactly pleased with her husband's response.

For a moment or two Austin considered going looking for him, but then thought better of it. After all, there was Saturday afternoon after work, and Sunday after Mass.

'Did Patrick say what he wanted? You know his reputation. I don't want trouble brought to our door,' said Austin.

'He said nothing. I was busy with your food. And I've been thinking about Edward. He's eight now, nine in December. He can work. It's good he helps me with the fish, but I can't pay him. He needs to earn his food like the rest of us. You know he does. And he's old enough to start learning the ways of the world,' replied Catherine.

'No work, no food. It's not hard to learn that. I would have had him earning his way before now, but for that damn law. You know, all over Liverpool they now take your age before they will take you on. Think of it. I could say anything,' said Austin.

'It's not you they want, Austin. It's the children. I've been asked about Edward by the constables. They asked me how old he was, and then told me that the law says no child under nine years of age will be permitted to work. They soon shut up when I told them he's my son and that he's not working; that he's helping me. But in my family, everyone had to work. No slackers. Edward knows it, and he's no longer a babe,' replied Catherine.

'You'll get no argument from me. But there's no work in the yard for a child. Even Thomas had to prove he had the strength. Stonework is back-breaking. You know it is,' said Austin.

'Don't be silly, Austin. He needs to work, but not at that. Maybe with oakum, or selling wood. He could do that next to me on Scotland Road. Now there's an idea. I could keep an eye on him. And he'll do as he's told,' replied Catherine.

'I'll leave it to you. When he's old enough, I'll sort him out with a proper job, just as I did with Thomas. I just hope Uncle Patrick doesn't show him any bad ways,' said Austin.

'He's old enough, Austin. You can't make his decisions for him,' replied Catherine.

'I know it, but...' said Austin, leaving his sentence unfinished.

The discussion over, he left to buy some ale as he had promised, though calling into a few more of their regular beerhouses to check for Thomas. Disappointed in not finding him, he returned home for the rest of the evening.

* * *

Thomas was known to Patrick, and was effectively his great uncle. Though kin to Austin, and notwithstanding the extra coin that had landed into Austin's lap via his uncle some five years earlier, he had decided to maintain some distance from him. Uncle Patrick was trouble. Austin knew that, and so did Catherine. He would be invited to family occasions, as was expected, but going out to a beerhouse on a regular basis was not considered a good idea. Had he been at home when his Uncle Patrick called, he would certainly have dissuaded Thomas from joining him.

But it was too late. Patrick had a reason for calling on Austin, and it was not a social call. The presence of a strong young man, and a relative – one who could be trusted – was a gift not to be ignored. Patrick had taken Thomas down to Bath Street, 'for a beer or two' and a 'bit of fun'. He was a familiar face in those areas and knew his way around in more ways than one.

'Ahhh, you're a man now, I can see it. We'll have a bit of fun with the girls later, but first I've got a bit of business to deal with. Maybe you can help me with that. There'll be a bit of coin in it for you as well, young Thomas,' said Patrick. They had already consumed two jugs of ale between them, and Thomas was starting to feel relaxed with his relatively unknown great uncle.

'I could that, Uncle Patrick. It's all above board, isn't it?' replied Thomas.

'Don't you worry about that. I need to see that man over there. You get another keg. I'll be back before you know it. And call me Paddy. Everyone calls me Paddy around here,' said Patrick.

Patrick trod over to the other side of the beerhouse, and after exchanging recognition greetings, sat down to talk. Ten minutes later he was back with Thomas.

'I need a bit of strength tonight. There's another lad, you, and me. We're to move a few bales of cotton from the docks to a storeroom. It won't take long. Maybe an hour and we'll back, right as rain, and ready for some fun. There'll be five shilling in it for you, Thomas. It's good money for little work. You know it is,' said Patrick.

'At night, Paddy. Why at night?' replied Thomas, suspicious even in his mildly inebriated state.

'Aye. It's needed there for a morning train. Don't you worry. Think of the money,' replied Patrick.

Thomas hesitated.

'We'll need to go now. Are you coming? It's better with three. It will be longer before I get back if there's only two of us,' said Patrick.

Thomas examined Patrick's eyes, looking for clues as to what he should do. He was not at all sure. His Uncle Patrick looked like fun, but he had also heard a little from Austin about his reputation. But then again, five shillings was a lot of money for an hour's graft. He could pay his Aunt Catherine back.

'I'll come,' replied Thomas.

'Good lad. Let's get down to the docks then,' said Patrick.

Fifteen minutes later, all three men were standing only yards away from where Austin had first recognised his uncle all those years earlier. Unknown to Thomas, his great uncle was at it again. That, or something similar.

'Martin, leave the lantern. Go keep a lookout over on the corner. Thomas and I will put the cotton on the cart. Be quick now,' Patrick said to the man Thomas now knew as Martin.

'Paddy, you said it was legal. I don't want trouble with the constables,' said Thomas, when Martin had disappeared out of earshot.

'I said no such thing. Five shillings and an hour of your time. We're here now. The sooner it's done, it's done,' replied Patrick.

Thomas began to get nervous, shaking at the prospect of getting caught. It could be prison or being shipped back to Ireland. They had only recently stopped sending prisoners to the colonies. Thoughts of capture raced through his head.

'Thomas. Let's do it quickly. Get as many bales on the cart as you can. We don't have much time. Quickly!' said Patrick.

Thomas, strong as he was, started lifting bales off the dockside and virtually throwing them on the cart, disturbing the horse as he did so. Inside twenty minutes the cart was full. Loose covers were replaced over the remaining bales, with Patrick then climbing on the cart to get the horse to move it.

'Get on. Both of you. Get on,' instructed Patrick.

Martin and Thomas climbed on next to Patrick. As they did so, Patrick encouraged the horse to start pulling the cart. Minutes later, they were near the railway terminus on Crosbie Street, when they heard a commotion emerging from the direction of where they had just left.

'Stay calm. If anyone stops us, it's our stuff we are moving for the train tomorrow,' said Patrick.

'So that much is true then,' replied Thomas.

'We're nearly there. There's a shed up on Sparling Street. It won't take long. And then it's five shilling to you both,' said Patrick, ignoring his great nephew's barb.

Forty minutes later, Patrick and Thomas were back sitting on the same seats as earlier, in the same beerhouse on Bath Street, both holding a mug of ale.

'Do you do this a lot, Paddy?' asked Thomas.

Patrick laughed.

'Enjoy the night. I told you it would be safe. I'll buy the drinks. You keep your five shillings,' replied Patrick.

Not wishing to look a gift horse in the mouth, and now starting to relax, Thomas sipped all the beer that his great uncle offered.

'We'll find a girl for you later. But now let's drink to a profitable evening,' said Patrick.

And drink he did. By ten, Thomas was as close to blind drunk as a man could be. Patrick, more experienced and a little wiser, had paced his drinking.

'I'll get you a girl and a room. You should stay here. You can meet Austin at the yard tomorrow morning. I'll sort it out,' said Patrick.

'No. I need to... I neeeeed to...' started Thomas, already slurring and losing coherence.

'You need to stay here. I've got to go, lad. But I'll stand my word. I'll pay for a room, though I think a girl... well, perhaps another night,' replied Patrick.

Thomas sat back, closed his eyes, and started to doze. Patrick, meanwhile, had gone to the bar and paid for a room for the night.

'Take him upstairs, will you, John? He's not in any state to go home. I don't want any more trouble with his cousin,' said Patrick to the beerhouse keeper.

Accepting Patrick's money and instructions, the man left Thomas dozing on a bench, oblivious to the noise and activity all around.

At around eleven Thomas woke, startled and unclear where he was. A jug had been dropped feet away, noisily smashing into pieces as it did so. It was a couple of minutes before he realised where he was. Still drunk and unsteady, he rose to his feet and headed for the door. John, the beerhouse keeper, failed to notice that his temporary ward had left until it was too late.

Thomas emerged onto Bath Street and staggered for a few yards before tripping over raised stone in the road. He fell flat on his face into a pool of rainwater, residue of a shower earlier in the day. He groaned in pain. The trip had no doubt caused some bruising, and for a moment he felt like he may have broken something. As best he could, he checked himself for obvious injury then lifted himself off the road. He staggered on, quite obviously drunk.

Unknown to Thomas, and unseen by him, four men were watching the floorshow from the shadows of some recently erected gas lamps. They laughed as their prey staggered on.

'I'll have that. He's about my size,' said one.

'He's had a skinful. He won't remember a thing tomorrow,' laughed another.

All four walked over towards Thomas, two grabbing him and then pinning him to the ground.

'Search him,' said another.

Thomas tried to fight back, finally coming to his senses and beginning to realise what was happening. He was being robbed. He tried to bite the hand of one of his attackers, but then everything went black.

* * *

Seven hours later he came round again. His head banging, both from the effects of the beer and the punishment he had apparently taken. His new jacket had been removed, and the five shillings Patrick had given him was no longer anywhere to be seen. In fact, he had no money at all, merely a shirt and some trousers to his name. He looked around. Bars. He was in a cell with a dozen others, many in a worse state than him. The room stank of urine, filth, and vomit, its smell alone causing him to retch. What had he done? He felt thirsty but could see no water to hand.

'Hello,' he shouted out.

'They'll come for you on the stroke of eight,' announced a voice behind him.

Who would? What was going on?

'What...?' Thomas started.

'You'll be in front of the magistrate. A few days in gaol.'

It was the same voice. Thomas turned round to face an old grey-haired man, who looked more like a vagrant than a workman.

'Why am I in here? How did I get here?' Thomas asked.

'Drunk. The constables would have got you. Asleep on the road. They don't like that sort of thing. That's my guess. That's why most of us end up in here. It's not the first time,' replied his fellow inmate.

'I wasn't drunk. I was attacked and robbed. What's your name?' asked Thomas.

'That'll be James O'Hare. And you?' replied James.

'Thomas,' said Thomas, declining to give a surname.

'You'll have to tell your story to the magistrate. Good luck with that. There's few that'll believe such a fanciful tale,' said James.

As the chimes of an outside city clock struck eight, their jailer appeared and picked out the six closest to the barred door, including Thomas. He then unlocked it and led all six straight up to the magistrate court.

* * *

'Seven days penal servitude in the Borough Gaol.'

The magistrates did not believe a word of Thomas's explanation, apparently viewing everything he said as artifice. As Austin had once said to him, 'They never believe the Irish.' He had been given a week inside one of Liverpool's notoriously awful prisons, Kirkdale Gaol. Austin had warned him about falling foul of the constables, and about his Great Uncle Patrick, and this is where it had led him to. How would he explain it to his uncle and Catherine? How would he explain his absence from work? Would there be any work for him when he came out? As these thoughts passed through his still clearing head, they would prove to be the least of the ordeal he was about to face.

Kirkdale Prison was a good walk from Collingwood Street, perhaps a mile and a half, or even a bit further. Thomas was not too sure. Not that it mattered. Austin would have no idea where he was unless Paddy told him, and he doubted that he would. He had finally got the measure of his great uncle, and reliable he was not. He was a rogue, good and true.

A dozen prisoners were packed into a closed and locked wooden carriage, two tiny barred windows in the doors for fresh air and minimal light. Thomas was chained to his seat, as were his companions, on the short transit from the court to the prison. They were silent for the journey, with only the muffled sounds of nearby street life for company. As the carriage reached the edge of the city, the outside world also fell silent, with only the squeaking iron-edged wheels adding audible repetitive rhythm to their progress. They reached their destination before ten, whereupon all twelve were removed from their conveyance, still chained together, and stood in a line ready to be processed. Thomas was third out of the carriage. He had to immediately shield his eyes from the relatively bright sunlight as he stepped down from his confinement.

He had a couple of minutes view of the Mersey before being ordered through the main gate. Kirkdale Prison stood in an elevated position with an uninterrupted view of the river. For a brief moment he could see activity on the Leeds Liverpool Canal, the railway, and the Huskisson Dock, still under construction. The latter resonated in his thoughts. Only last week he had been carrying stones destined for those very same docks. His heart sank as he faced the reality of his predicament. He was innocent of the petty crime he had been accused of and should not be here. There was no justice.

The twelve walked through the gates of the gaol to a reception room. The doors behind them were locked and another half dozen jailers appeared. The first three men, including Thomas, were released from their chains.

'Strip. Take everything off!'

Each man did as he was told and was given some new items to wear, all of which looked like it had been previously used. A coarse shirt, almost threadbare trousers, cap, a jacket with a blue stripe, and a pair of battered wooden clogs. An even coarser woollen nightshirt was given to him for sleeping in. It was only later when he asked another prisoner that he discovered the significance of the blue marker on his jacket. As a petty offender, he would be seen by his jailers as a lower risk, unlike others in his company wearing grey, yellow, or red and blue. Except for this tiny differentiator, all the prisoners were treated equally, be they murderer or drunk. He went cold at the prospect of having to share a cell with a murderer, even if only for a week.

'You three, follow me,' instructed his jailer.

In blind obedience, Thomas followed two other men and the jailer to their shared cell. It would be his home for the next seven days. As the door of his cage was locked behind him, Thomas's last thoughts were that he hoped they remembered he was just in here for seven days, and that he would still be alive to tell the tale of his captivity.

* * *

As Thomas was being locked in a cell, Austin was being questioned about his nephew's absence. Unaware of Thomas's predicament, he had to think of something.

'He's a fever. Too unwell to work.' It was all he could think of.

'There's plenty others that need the work, Austin. I know he's your kin, but we have a business. Customers won't wait for the sick. I'll take on another for a few days, but if he's not back in a week he'll have to labour for another,' replied Kevin.

It felt harsh and uncharitable, but then again Austin could not defend his nephew. He had disappeared without thought or word of warning. A mix of guilt and anger, emotions he necessarily had to hide from his employers, briefly dominated his thinking, before rationality returned. He would have to find his Uncle Patrick and get an explanation.

He wasted little time getting home that evening. A quick meal, a few words with Catherine, and he was off to find Patrick. It was not difficult. A couple of questions at Patrick's home and he was directed to a beerhouse on Bath Street – the same one Thomas and Patrick had been in.

Patrick was sitting with another man, laughing and quite obviously enjoying an ale.

'Patrick!'

Austin shouted his uncle's name. Patrick waved and shouted back.

'Come over, Austin. Join us for a drink. It was only last night we were here with Thomas,' replied Patrick.

'It's about Thomas I'm here. He didn't come home last night. Where is he?' asked Austin.

'I can't help you. I don't know. He stayed here last night. You know, a bit the worse for wear. I paid for a room. I'm sure he'll turn up, probably with a sore head,' replied Patrick, laughing off Thomas's absence.

'You sure he stayed?' asked Austin.

'As sure as I'm sitting here. Ask John over there. He looked after him after I left,' replied Patrick.

Austin sauntered over to speak to the beerhouse keeper to ask him a few questions. Yes, Thomas had been there. But no, he had not stayed the night, but had left. The beerhouse keeper did not see him go.

Austin returned to Patrick. 'He didn't stay here. He's missing. I'm worried. I just hope he's not in the docks or the canal. He's a good lad, you must know that,' said Austin, while giving Patrick a questioning look.

'He had drunk a lot, but you know, not enough for an accident. I'm sure of it,' replied Patrick, now looking uncomfortable.

'I need to find him, Patrick. Will you help?' said Austin. It would not be the first time he had been looking for someone in Liverpool's nightlife. But this felt more urgent, and he was family.

'Of course. I'll put word out on the Dock Road. I'm known in these parts. We'll find him, Austin,' replied Patrick.

Only slightly relieved, Austin, with Patrick contributing, developed a search plan to be started immediately.

It took only a day before Patrick worked out what had happened. Thomas had been spotted in Liverpool's magistrate court and sent down for being drunk and causing an obstruction. Contacts were always useful, thought Patrick, as he made his way to Collingwood Street. He knew Austin would not like it, but at least the lad was alive. That must be seen as good news.

As Patrick had guessed, Austin was not at all pleased. He blamed Patrick for Thomas's drunkenness, and therefore his current situation.

'What are you going to do about it?' asked Thomas.

'Nothing. He'll be out in days. He'll survive. Six months or a year and you don't always come out of Kirkdale, except in a wooden box. But seven days? He'll be as right as rain,' replied Patrick.

Austin remained unimpressed, but he also knew his uncle was right. It was not even worth visiting the boy. But if he was not out in a week, Austin would be complaining to the magistrate. Relieved at knowing where his nephew was, Austin's main challenge now was to secure the job he had worked so hard to get. He had no choice but to lie about Thomas's medical condition, that it was improving, and promise that he would be back the following week.

* * *

Thomas did as he was told for the full seven days. As it happened, his two cell companions were not murderers but merely thieves. He knew he could not criticise given his own involvement in matters that were not exactly legal. So, he elected to try and get on with them, which he did. His stay could not be described as anywhere near pleasant, but it was tolerable. Tolerable that is, but for the food. Bread and gruel for breakfast; a broth, either scouse, cow's or pig's head, more bread; and maybe some rashers and vegetables for dinner. It was sustenance, but that was about it. Badly cooked, and using the worst ingredients, Thomas more than looked forward to his aunt's cooking. He counted down the days, making a faint mark on his rudimentary pine bunk as each day passed.

At last, day seven. Thomas waited. He was first taken for breakfast as usual, but then returned to his cell. Fear instantly took hold as his jailer turned the key – a fear that his jailers had forgotten that this was the day he was to leave. Unsure what to do, he remained silent, considering whether to call out. But then he did not want to antagonise his jailers. After all, they had complete control. By mid-afternoon he resolved to speak to one of them, politely. He just hoped that it would work.

As the prison clock chimed for four, his cell was unlocked. It was too early for dinner; Thomas's hopes were raised.

'Thomas Melia.'

Thomas stood up.

'Follow me.'

Thomas followed without saying a word.

Thirty minutes later he was outside, his prison garb removed and wearing his own clothes – what was left of them. He took a last look at the prison gates and resolved never to get into a situation where he might mind find himself back in there. It had been a life lesson. He had been unlucky to be jailed for a week and to lose his five shillings, but lucky not to be apprehended by the constables for theft. Great Uncle Patrick would not be one of his close drinking friends in the future, and whatever the attractions of a few easy shillings, he would not be one to take more coin off his uncle. Austin had been a good guide.

Now all he had to do was to work out what to say about his temporary absence. And how was he to explain the loss of his new jacket to Aunt Catherine? He still owed her the money.

But he was out. Life was hard, but not as hard as the one those poor souls inside faced.

Chapter 8

BROWNLOW HILL

Thomas's explanation garnered more sympathy than had been available in the magistrate court, more so when he told of the attack and robbery. He talked of 'all his money being stolen, and his jacket', and of being knocked unconscious by four 'loafers, or crimpers', who left him for dead, 'for all they cared'. Austin had a loathing for these types, and had already made his mind up as to was to blame: Patrick.

Feeling safe in the knowledge that Patrick would not be a regular visitor to Collingwood Street, Thomas left out a bit of detail about the evening: his participation in the removal of several cotton bales and the money involved. He had heard the story, or at least some of the story, of the time Austin had worked in the docks as a watchman, and what had happened. Thomas knew Austin would certainly not have approved of his own 'dock work', and divulging this might even significantly change his opinion of him. What each man did not know about the other, was that both had accepted payment from Patrick for services rendered. It was an irony, and neither Thomas nor Austin saw much value in raking up the past, recent or more distant. Neither event was ever talked about in any detail ever again. As for Catherine, she still wanted her loan repaying, but in acknowledging his difficulty she gave him a lot more time.

The return of Thomas to the flag yard raised a few eyebrows, but his employer's circumspection did not seem to last. He seemed to have got away with it. A few mentions of a fever, and a rapid recovery, apparently did the trick. Indeed, at least for a short while he developed a reputation as someone who could get seriously ill, but then quickly recover. If anything, his reputation as a reliable worker gained additional traction. It was irony indeed.

1851 passed into 1852. Life became routine; hard but routine. Spring rolled into summer, and the warm weather lifted everyone's mood, as it always did. Donal kept the yard informed of outside events as he always had, more careful and less inflammatory with political comment than he had been, but he still made his points. Most of the time the rest of the men paid no more than lip service to his protestations, his constant and repetitive criticism of the aristocracy and the rich, but on occasion he talked about something which attracted a little more attention.

'I have some news,' announced Donal.

He always had some news, interesting or otherwise. Many had heard him say this before, only to be disappointed by what he actually said. It was therefore not a surprise to find that most of the men simply continued chattering away to each other, essentially ignoring Donal. Austin tended to be a little more polite. He stopped talking to Thomas, thus providing Donal with the audience he sought.

'There's been a riot in Stockport. The Protestants, Orangemen types, have attacked the Catholics. They've destroyed two chapels, injured scores. An Irishman named Michael Moran is dead. It started in a public house, so they say. They attacked us Irish. They rioted.'

'How do you know this, Donal?' asked Austin. He knew Donal could not read, so he was always interested in where he got his information.

'I know people, Austin. I know people in every town in these parts,' replied Donal.

Austin knew that to be an exaggeration, but he let it pass.

'How do you know the truth of it? That's what I mean to ask,' said Austin.

'It's the truth, Austin. And what's more than the truth, my belief is that it will come here. One day it will come here. We will have to defend ourselves,' replied Donal.

'That's the job of the police,' interjected Kevin. Hearing the word 'rioted' seemed to get his attention and those of others eating breakfast.

'That may be. But we should still defend ourselves. Will the police really defend us?' asked Donal.

'It's their job. Besides, there are tens of thousands of Irish in Liverpool. There are too many of us,' replied Kevin.

'Not all of the true faith,' replied Donal.

'That may be so, but most are,' said Kevin.

'All I'm saying is that we should be ready for trouble. Then when it happens, well, you know, we will be ready. You may be mason here, and us just doing the labouring, but the Orangemen won't care about that. They'll come for you as they would us. You know that to be true,' replied Donal.

'What I know to be true is that we have work to do, and customers for our stone. Orangemen or Irishmen, they've given us their custom. Now, let's get back to work,' said Kevin, clearly wanting to draw the discussion to a close.

As the rest of the men prepared to move, Donal could not resist a final word in Austin's ear.

'I'll be listening, Austin. Don't you worry. You'll be the first to know if I hear of Orangemen on the march.'

'Aye. I'll be sure to be ready, Donal,' replied Austin, giving him a wink as he did so. Donal had always been a bit of a fearmonger, but that did not mean he was always going to be wrong.

* * *

Christmas was always bittersweet. It was a time of abundance for some, the rich and wealthy, but for most all they could do was gape at what was on offer. Darlington's shop on Scotland Road, with its offerings of the meat of fat sheep and heifers, would have tempted anyone who passed. But the prices were far beyond what most could afford. Geese at four to eight shillings, turkeys at four to fifteen shillings, pheasants at seven shillings, capons at five to seven shillings; the list went on. Perhaps they could have bought a goose or a turkey, but then they would not have been able to buy anything else, and perhaps not eat again for days. What little they still had in savings could have been spent, but then that would have been the end of it. If any misfortune came to pass, there would have been more than regrets.

Catherine managed the family finances as best she could, and Christmastime was no different. Some little luxury might be allowed, but excess would never be permitted. And so, the Christmas feast would again be a couple of rabbits at two shillings, and a good-sized hare at about the same. A pie or a stew would be baked with seasonal vegetables and whatever else was on offer and could be bought or traded against some fish. It would not be the first time that some of her stock would have been bartered for a change of diet at home.

Other than a great storm, which damaged property up and down the Lancashire coast, Christmas 1852 passed without incident; as did the new year festivities. It had almost become a tradition on New Year's Day for Austin and Catherine to revisit a discussion about moving to somewhere with better prospects – another town or city, or even America. It was inconclusive, as it had been for some years now. Change, and change for the good, was always anticipated as Liverpool's church bells tolled on January 1st, but no-one in the household could have anticipated what was to happen next.

* * *

The year started ominously.

Austin paid little attention to the daily news of ships. There were always ships coming and going; there was always something to say about shipping, launches, races, fires and accidents, and sinkings. Once he left dock porter work, the seasonal nature of ship movements, the port's arrivals and departures, became far less important. He was no longer in thrall, from a work perspective, to the vagaries of ship movements. His pay relied on the demand for stone, and not the demand for the loading and unloading of ship goods.

But there was one report that did attract his attention.

February 1853's weather had been cold, damp, and miserable, with winter still unwilling to loosen its grip on the people of Liverpool. Day after day, Austin and his fellow workers toiled in rain-soaked clothing, heaving recently hewn stone across the yard and into carts. On occasion he would accompany a cart to a customer on the other side of the city, unloading in accordance with instruction. There were fires in the yard, around which the men would huddle for a time in an attempt to get warm, but on the whole it was a losing battle. Most were constantly cold, chilled to the bone in driving rain, and always hungry as their bodies sought the energy to keep going. At the end of a day's hard graft, it was no wonder almost every man in the yard would seek instant relief from their labours in a jug or two of ale at a beerhouse.

Austin did not drink as much as some, but in winter he and Thomas might accompany the other labourers more often. It was a Tuesday night in the middle of February that Austin heard some news that gave him a fright. He was not particularly superstitious, but this particular report resonated, upsetting his mood and imbuing an irrational fear about what was to come.

Donal chose the beerhouse that night. He chose it because it was an evening where he would receive news of the outside world. At last, Austin and his fellow workers would get to find out where Donal sourced his rich seam of general news, political insight, and knowledge.

'It's a Threlfall beerhouse on Naylor Street,' announced Donal, as he led a small troupe of weary workers up Leeds Street. Naylor Street was not too far away, just a brisk walk up Leeds Street to Vauxhall Street.

Some questioned why they had to go so far when there were plenty of places more local to the flag yard.

'I have a surprise. You are always asking me where I get my news. Well, tonight you will know,' he added.

In presentation, the beerhouse was typical of those on almost every street in Liverpool. But what was not typical was the noise, or lack of it. This was different. There was a man talking, and apparently reading from notepaper to a clearly captivated audience. The same thoughts crossed every man's mind as they finally understood the source of Donal's insights. It was a storyteller. Perhaps a man of their class who could clearly read, and could probably write.

Donal, Thomas, Austin, and two others, ordered some ale before finding some seating and sitting down. Though impatient for conversation, they seemed to know what was expected and remained silent. They were, after all, about to be entertained.

'Welcome all, Donal.' Their host, recognising Donal, was obviously known to him.

He did not appear old, but was not young either. More smartly dressed than Austin, his clothing was not that of a worker, but he was also not obviously a member of a better class. The man was already a mystery. His hands were not visibly calloused or leathery, suggesting perhaps a merchant, and yet his manners were that of the labouring classes. From time to time, in between sentences, he smoked a French-style tobacco pipe. Austin was intrigued.

'He's a Chartist,' whispered Donal, apparently reading their puzzled expressions. He clearly saw this as adequate explanation.

'I'm John Evans, for those who do not know me.'

His accent had no more than a hint of Irish. Still more of a mystery. A 'foreigner' reading to a bunch of Irish Catholics.

'I'll tell you first a story, the story of the mermaid.'

'He'll tell of news later. John likes to tell a story, and they're usually good ones,' whispered Donal, again attempting to explain.

The man they now knew as John Evans looked down to his notes and began.

'And here the strange tale of John Robinson, mariner, who spoke with a mermaid on Black Rock, nigh Liverpool. Who was tossed on the ocean for six days and six nights and was preserved by her. I'll tell of what was spoken of and what became of John Robinson five days after his return home. I will speak as best I can in the tongue of the time.'

Austin and his associate workers remained silent, though somewhat bemused by the situation they found themselves in. It was not quite the evening expected.

'But then to his amazement he espy'd a beautiful young lady combing her head, and tossed on the billows, clothed in all green. Then she with a smile came on board, and asked how he was. John Robinson, being a smart one and a scholar, replied, Madam I am the better to see you in good health, in great hopes trusting you will be a comfort and assistance to me in this my low condition. And so caught hold of her comb and green girdle that was about her waist. To which she replied, sir, you ought not to rob a young woman of her riches, and then expect a favour at her hands. If you return me my comb and girdle, what lies in my power I will do for you.'

As John Evans spoke, the trials of the day began to ebb, and the relative warmth of the beerhouse, and its ale, started to flow through Austin's being. The unusual circumstance he found himself in began to feel natural. Without realising it, he was beginning to enjoy the words effortlessly pouring out of a natural storyteller. He took another swig of ale and listened on.

'At her departure the tempest ceased and blew a fair gale to the Southwest. And so, he got safe on shore. But when he came to his father's house, he found everything as she had told him. For she told him also concerning his being left on ship board, and how all the seamen perished, which he also found to be true, according to the promise made him. He was still very much troubled in his mind concerning his promise, and while he was musing, she appeared to him with smiling countenance. She got first word of him, such that he was struck dumb but could understand all. He took notice of the words she spoke and then she began to sing. After which she departed out of the young man's sight, taking from him the compass. She took the ring from her finger and put it on his, and said that she expected to see him once again with more freedom. But he never saw her more, upon which he came to himself again, went home, and was taken ill and died five days after.'

Most listening to the tale had the same questions as Austin, but dared not ask.

'I can see a question but that no-one wishes to ask. The tale is true. As true as I'm standing here in front of you. There are wonders in the sea, wonders that only few men have seen. And there are mermaids and sirens of the sea who will catch the unprepared. John Robinson was not as smart as he thought. A mermaid got the better of him, not far from what is now Black

Rock Lighthouse. The light of thirty lamps may guide the wise but...' he left his sentence unfinished.

A short silence followed.

Donal then stood up and made a request. 'Can you read the news?'

It was what he had been waiting for. While stories and tales were fun, what he wanted was news of the world outside of their tiny frontier of home, work, church, and the beerhouse.

'I can, Donal. I have the *Mercury* with me,' replied John Evans.

It was his usual practice to tell at least one, and often two or more, Lancashire stories before concluding a performance by reading out the news from a local newspaper, usually the *Liverpool Mercury*. He read the national headlines, but then quickly came to a story that shocked Austin.

'The Wreck of the *Queen Victoria*. Dreadful loss of life.'

He waited a second or two before proceeding. 'The City of Dublin Company's steamer *Queen Victoria* ran ashore on Howth, in a snowstorm, this morning, at 1.40 a.m.'

Austin listened in shock; a shock of the familiar. Accidents happened all the time at sea, but few made such an impression on him as this. He knew the *Queen Victoria*. It was the paddle steamer that had aided his family's escape from Ireland all those years ago. He reflected on those times and shuddered at the thought of the likely many who had lost their lives earlier that day. Thirteen years ago, it could have been him, his father, mother, brother, and sisters. It was not an agreeable contemplation; it was entirely disagreeable. He began to wonder why he had agreed to come here. It all seemed to be about drowning and death, either folklore or news of the day. The hairs on the back of his arm bristled, just as his body produced an impromptu and incongruent shiver. The room was warm, the beer was good, and the company agreeable. And yet he felt cold, in body and spirit. An irrational fear seemed to have gained the upper hand.

'Austin. Austin!'

It was Thomas. He had noticed that his uncle had slipped away into vacant reflection and had decided to bring him back before others also noticed. Austin turned to face him, a blank expression still on his face.

'Austin. Perhaps we should go. You look unwell.'

Austin blinked and then looked around. It took another minute before he remembered where he was. 'I must have dozed. I'm awake now.'

Thomas examined his uncle's face again. Its colour seemed to be returning, but he still did not look like his usual self. He made a decision.

'Let's go home. Catherine will be waiting.'

'Yes. Yes. Yes, of course. We should go. I'm tired. And the beer. I need to get to bed,' replied Austin.

Both men rose from their seats, made their farewells, and set off towards home. Though feigning alertness, Austin's mind was elsewhere on the walk back. The story, the news of the sinking of the *Queen Victoria*, was certainly on his mind, but it was the intangible sense of doom that nagged his sentience, a feeling that something terrible was about to happen.

* * *

The weather steadily improved during March, and by April spring was in the air. Austin's mood had lifted, especially with what he had once seen as ominous portents now a receding memory. Business at the yard had also improved, and there was growing optimism about Ireland's future potato harvests as the blight infestation further retreated. Competition for work was always there, but the numbers seeking it were fewer than in recent years, and measurably less than in 'Black 47'. Liverpool's apparently inexorable growth was already beginning to absorb its surplus labour, and the threat of any further reduction in wages had faded. The year's less than promising start had apparently transmuted into something entirely different. Or so he thought.

'You two. Load them flags, and that stone, and take it to Huskisson. It needs to be there on the stroke of noon. You need to be sharpish,' said Kevin. He had chosen Austin and Thomas to carry out the task, for no reason other than the fact that they were the nearest.

Both men began immediately. Within the yard they were lucky in that there was additional help. Two other labourers were called for, and then the four of them lifted four heavy flags, and as many stones, onto the cart as it and its single horse could reasonably manage. Their load was a drop in the ocean given the size of the dock building project, but the yard's contract had been steady and long; deliveries had been regular, almost daily. Both men had carried out the same task many times before, with each knowing that the harder part was loading, easily a four-man task. While care was needed with unloading, it was a considerably lighter job. Not something to enjoy, but at least it was tolerable.

The journey to the recently opened dock was almost a break from work. It was a ride, a trip down Barton Street to the Dock Road, and then a drive by the docks themselves: Waterloo, Victoria, Trafalgar, then Clarence. Austin always thought of his early life in Connaught when he passed Clarence. And then Collinwood, Stanley, Nelson, Bramley Moor, and then Sandon, before a turn to Huskisson Dock. The journey did not take long, perhaps a half hour. They arrived at their destination a good ten minutes before the appointed time, experiencing a sense of relief as the works overseer recognised them.

'Unload over there.' He pointed at a loosely stacked pile of flags and stones five or six yards away from the edge of the dock basin. From Austin and Thomas's perspective, there was no obvious use for their materials, but then they cared little; they had a job to do.

'Will there be any help today? They're as heavy as they usually are, sir,' asked Austin.

'No. You'll have to do it yourselves. That's what I pay you for,' replied the overseer. It was a surly response, a little out of character. They knew the man, not so they could call him by Christian name, but he was usually a friendly face.

'We'll do it now, sir,' said Austin, encouraging the horse to move, and not waiting for another reply. It was better they got on with it and left if their reception was not going to be more welcoming.

Halting by the pile of materials, Austin decided on the plan.

'Half the flags and half the stones, and then the other half. Think of the weight, Thomas.'

'Stones first?' replied Thomas.

'Aye,' said Austin.

In another half hour most of their load had been despatched to the ground, leaving only two remaining flags to unload. It had been tiring work already, but both could see an end to it with another ten minutes or so of graft.

'I'm hungry already,' said Thomas. He knew it would be hours before they would see a plate of food, but he felt it helped to share his pangs. Heavy work demanded more of the body.

'Let's get this done. I've got enough for a bit of bread. We're early; we could stop on the way back. No-one will see,' replied Austin, to a surprised but delighted Thomas. With the prospect of an early meal, Thomas's enthusiasm for finishing quickly had been rekindled.

'This one next. You climb up here. I'll catch the last two this time,' said Austin, as he jumped off the cart to the floor.

Thomas leapt up and began to heave the penultimate flag to the end of the cart. It was an awkward one, some additional stone ridges hindering its journey over the relatively lambent wooden surface of the cart. It had not been cut as well as others. Austin, meanwhile, had been patiently waiting for it to arrive to a position where he could begin manoeuvring it to its resting place. It took at least twice as long to move it than expected, but at last Austin felt he could take control.

'It's a heavy one,' said Thomas.

'No. It's just a bad one. I wonder who cut it,' replied Austin, musing on who might be guilty of poor finishing.

'It's all yours. I'll start on the last one,' said Thomas, moving over the last flag.

Austin pulled the stone into position. Another gentle heave and it would be on the floor, possibly in pieces, without him easing it to the ground. It was rougher and heavier than most, but he felt he had the strength to slow its move to the floor. He knew he could never lift it from ground to floor, but the other way round was a far easier proposition; better with two, but if they were to finish and get some bread, he needed to get on with it.

He heaved. The flag fully in both his hands, Austin lifted it off the cart. All was well for the first few seconds but then...

'Aaaaaaaaaaaaaagh!'

In an instant, his left-hand grip failed. A combination of a wet mossy surface underneath the stone, and its unusually heavy weight, had led to Austin underestimating the task. The flag slipped from first his left hand, and then his right, and then instantly dropped to the floor, crushing his right foot as it did so. A sharp searing pain rattled through his frame; all he could do was scream.

Thomas rushed over and jumped off the cart, almost as shocked as Austin. He quickly removed the corner of the flag still compressing Austin's foot, causing him to scream again. It was not a sight either man wanted to see. Austin had clearly been badly injured, possibly maimed by the accident.

'Finish it. Get me on the cart,' cried Austin, his face looking dazed, and still writhing in pain. Not only had the stone crushed his foot, but in losing his balance his temple had caught the side of the cart.

'I'll need to get you to help,' replied Thomas.

'Get the last stone off. Five minutes makes no difference. Throw it off,' said Austin, now uncaring of whether the flag broke into pieces or otherwise.

Thomas complied, and then helped raise Austin back onto the cart.

'Where will we go?' asked Thomas.

'The Northern. Then drop the cart off, tell them of the injury, and go and find Catherine,' replied Austin, still coherent despite his obvious pain.

Relieved of most of its burden, the horse was able to carry them back to Great Howard Street at speed. It was fortunate that the Northern Hospital was situated only yards away from the flag yard, a coincidence that none ever wanted to take advantage of. Thomas changed the plan on the return journey, just as Austin seemed to be on the verge of possibly losing consciousness. He drove back to the yard for some additional help. At the yard a makeshift stretcher was rapidly constructed from materials littered about, whereupon Austin was then carried by hand to the doors of the Northern Hospital.

In the days following the accident Austin received some rudimentary treatment, but the news was not generally good; his foot had been crushed beyond repair. Though the doctors deemed an amputation unnecessary, they informed him that it was unlikely that he would walk properly ever again. The news was devastating. If he could not walk, he could not labour, either in the yard or on the docks. His fear of some physical incapacity was now a fear of hunger. With Catherine's income from selling fish, they might survive for a time, but without his wage from the yard they would likely face a very bleak future. In time it would come down to using what they had to buy food, or using it to pay the rent. They could end up out on the street.

* * *

'We'll get by. Thomas will help. We have a little saved,' said Catherine optimistically.

Despatched to home after only two days, and with little more than a few bandages and a stick, Austin spent his time sitting at his usual place by the fire. He knew Catherine would try her best, but he also knew that the time they had in this house was borrowed. In a matter of weeks what remained of their savings would be depleted. Thomas could not pay the rent for all, and what Catherine earned would be needed for food; it was, after all, a supplemental to their usual needs. Relatives would help, but even that could only be for a time; each had their own to feed and house. It was a disaster. He soon began to think that the portents of February had indeed been true.

May arrived without an obvious solution. They would not have a roof over their head by the end of the month if one was not found. Austin's mood declined into black. He stopped talking to other residents and merely grunted responses to Thomas, Edward, and John. After a time, even Catherine was ignored.

'Nothing for me.'

And then he stopped eating at regular intervals. Nobody was sure why, though Thomas surmised that perhaps he wanted the others in the family to eat. By mid-May he had taken to bed, now unwilling to move his weakening contorted body. What hope Catherine had of finding a fix for their predicament also began to ebb. Other members of the household offered modest help, as did her own family, but these could only be temporary aids; perhaps a week at best. If their share of the first week of June's rent was not in hand by the last day of May, they would have to leave, irrespective of Austin's situation.

'I'm sorry to you all, but there's nothing I can do,' said Timothy Kane, generally recognised as head of their household. As usual, he was collecting the following week's rent. It was his job to collect off other lodgers and submit a total to the landlord each week, in advance.

Catherine stared at him. There was little point in tears; she knew it was coming. She turned towards Thomas, who wanted to support her as best he could, though there was little he could do. Everyone knew that if their share of the rent was not there, then they would have to leave.

'You stay, Thomas. There's nothing to be done.'

Thomas responded with a pained expression. He had no words. Catherine was right; there was nothing that could be done.

'I'm sorry. If you can find the money, then our door will be open to you,' said Timothy Kane, repeating his apology and making an offer which he knew could not be met.

'I'll fetch Austin,' said Catherine.

'I'll help you lift him onto the cart,' replied Thomas.

The cart was all they had left. What little furniture they owned had been 'sold' to other household and family members. It was really a form of charity, though everyone participated in the pretence of a commercial transaction. At best it had bought them a couple of weeks.

Thomas helped Austin down the stairs, and onto a hand cart that was not designed for carrying people. Catherine doubted she could manage it alone.

'You know what we'll have to do, don't you?' said Catherine.

'I do.' Thomas nodded his head.

'I'll need you to push him there with me. I can't do this alone,' said Catherine.

'I'll help,' replied Thomas. Guilt rippled through his being. For a moment he could not look Catherine in the face.

'Brownlow Hill it is then,' said Catherine.

It was Tuesday, May 31st, 1853. Austin, his foot deformed and unable to work, Edward, John, and Catherine, were having to make the short trip that no man, woman, or child ever wanted to make. The short trip down Scotland Road and Byrom Street to Shaws Brow, and then a walk up towards London Road and Pembroke Place would take them to Brownlow Street, and to within sight of Brownlow Hill, their destination.

Misfortune was common in Liverpool, and so the sight of a family group pushing, and encircling, a hand cart, attracted little attention or interest. Catherine stopped halfway on the journey outside the new Assize Court. The building, in all its neoclassical magnificence, fostered no admiration.

'But there is no bread for the likes of us, only the workhouse.'

'Let's move on,' replied Thomas. There was little to be gained by comparing their misfortune with the luxuriance of the wealthy.

Oblivious to their fate, Edward skipped on ahead, with John following. Neither child could know what the next few months, or even years, would have in store for them. Catherine, Thomas, and Austin, knew only too well, but no-one wanted to talk about it. At the gates of their new home, Thomas and Catherine helped Austin down from the cart. He could still walk, but the weeks since his accident had depleted his strength, his mood and unwillingness to look after himself exacerbating an already impaired state.

'Take the cart to my mother. One day perhaps we will leave this place,' said Catherine, more in hope than expectation.

'I will. I don't know what to say,' replied Thomas.

'Say nothing. You've done what you are able. Now go. Look after yourself. I don't want to see you in here,' said Catherine.

'Goodbye, Catherine, Austin. Be well,' replied Thomas, grabbing hold of both handles and moving the cart.

Within a few minutes, he was out of sight. With a stick in one hand and his arm over Catherine's shoulder, Austin finally had something to say.

'Now we must face our ordeal.'

With the children in tow, they walked up to the main doors and knocked.

* * *

'Brownlow Hill', 'Mount Pleasant', 'Liverpool Workhouse'; their new home had a number of names, but the one familiar to Austin and Catherine was 'Brownlow Hill'. The door opened in response to their knock. A stern looking elderly man appeared.

'What do you want?' It would have been obvious to anyone what they wanted, but he clearly felt the need to ask.

'We have need of help,' replied Catherine.

'The governor's ill. Follow me,' replied the doorman.

Austin tried, then failed, to follow. With an arm around Catherine, and a stick in the other hand, he fell over on his third step, dragging Catherine down with him. The doorman instantly turned round and assessed the situation.

'He'll have to go to the men's lying-in ward. If he can't stand, he can't work, and everyone who is able works for their food here. A man who can't work must be ill, or a cripple.'

'He's not a cripple, just injured. He'll be better with some rest. You'll see,' replied Catherine.

'Huh. I doubt that. He looks half gone to me already.'

The workhouse doorman expressed little sympathy for Austin's condition, obviously inured by the experience of seeing so many in a wretched state walk through Brownlow Hill's doors. Only the desperate crossed the threshold of the workhouse.

'What about us?' asked Catherine.

'Mrs Kendall will see you in a minute. I'll take him.' replied the doorman. He left their sight for a couple of minutes, and returned with two other burly looking fellow employees.

'I'll see you soon,' said Austin, as he was brusquely removed, almost dragged, from the reception area.

Once Austin was out of sight, Catherine had another question. 'When will I be able to see him?'

'I don't know that. Not many visitors allowed, especially women, on the men's ward. Perhaps on Sundays,' replied the doorman, finally realising that what he had said was perhaps a bit too harsh.

'Ah, Mrs Kendall. A woman and two young ones for you,' said the doorman to an older woman who had just appeared from an ante-room.

'I'll take them now, George. You three follow me to the receiving house,' instructed Mrs Kendall.

Catherine, Edward, and John dutifully followed. Without the comfort of familiar faces, her increased anxiety and nervousness was now getting the better of an already apprehensive mood.

Mrs Kendall led them into a small cottage, within which various questions were asked, including the children's ages and the former occupations of both Catherine and Austin.

'When will I see my husband? He's been taken to the ward,' enquired Catherine.

'I can't say. That's not up to me,' replied Mrs Kendall.

'Can anyone say?' pressed Catherine.

'You'll be told when the time's right. But for now, you have to bathe. We need to rid you of them creepin' ferlies. We can't have people bringing more in than we have already,' replied Mrs Kendall.

She then led the three of them to a bathhouse.

'You first, then the boys,' said Mrs Kendall.

The room was warm, as was the bathwater. After bathing, she was sprayed with a sulphur compound in an effort to rid her of nits and other body-hugging lice. Once finished, she was issued with an ill-fitting workhouse uniform, her own clothes having been removed for cleaning and storage. A strong smell of sulphur now replaced the usual odours of life in the Irish Quarter. Edward and John were then subjected to a similar process.

'You'll get your clothes and belongings back when you leave. I've also had word that your man is regarded as being in a bad way. If it gets worse, you'll be allowed to see him some more. We're not heartless, but every one of the nearly two thousand in here has to work. That is unless they are ill or injured. Your husband has been spared that, for now. You and the children will have to work in here. The Vestry expect it if you are to stay,' said Mrs Kendall, after Catherine and the two boys had completed the initial admission process.

Catherine more than understood the message. She and the boys would have to work for their food. And, she assumed, they would do as they were told. She was under no illusions about the workhouse. Everyone knew it was a hard place to be, but then what choice did she have?

'I… we understand, Mrs Kendall,' Catherine replied meekly.

'You two. You'll go with him to the boys' area,' instructed Mrs Kendall.

They were to be separated. Catherine knew that this was the rule, but that knowledge made it no less painful.

She shouted as her two sons were whisked off out of sight. 'Look after him, Edward. Look after your brother. I'll see you soon, John.'

She could hear John starting to scream, his voice echoing down a nearby corridor.

'I don't want to go! Ma! Ma! Ma! I don't want to go! I want to go home! Ma!'

And then silence.

'This way.'

Mrs Kendall began to lead her in a different direction.

'When will I see them?' asked Catherine.

'There's no mixing. Those are the rules. The children will be fed and clothed so long as they work. They'll go to church on Sundays, and some will learn a trade,' replied Mrs Kendall.

This was now her life. No freedom, not even to see her family. All she could do was to follow instruction and work. The enormity of the decisions and actions she and Austin had taken finally sank in. It already felt no better than the slavery Austin had talked of when he had gone to see that John Watkins fellow. She began to pray, in silence, that somehow there would be some relief to their situation, and that they might be reunited.

* * *

The workhouse was hard; harder than she had expected. It was not so much the work, but the loss of freedom that hurt the most. No-one was allowed out of the workhouse without permission, nor was she able to see Edward, John, and Austin, without approval. The scarce occasions when Catherine was able to see her children were fleeting and supervised. The Vestry seemed to want to make the workhouse experience as unpleasant as it could be. She hated it from the minute she entered Brownlow Hill's 'doorway of despair', as she thought of it.

Life now seemed to revolve around three or four rooms: a day room for use when not working, a work room, a sleeping room, and a dining room. Though austere, the rooms were relatively clean and dry. Cleaner and dryer than Collingwood Street, mused Catherine, on her third day as a pauper inmate. Yes, she was of no status now. No longer a fish dealer, but a 'pauper' – almost the lowest of the low. For most of the women, work consisted of picking oakum, or hair, cleaning, washing or doing laundry work. Some of the weaker women would mend clothes, or work as pauper assistants in the infants' and very young children's wards.

'You'll do laundry work today.'

Catherine was never sure what work she would be assigned. She did not really care, although strangely, working with oakum seemed to relax her. Repetitive and boring, it allowed her mind to drift into better times.

'Keep your nose clean, or you'll be out there.'

It was good advice from a woman called Sally, whom she had befriended soon after arriving. The 'out there' was a reference to who the workhouse regarded as the worst characters – 'the class'. They were the most violent, the women of the street, and those who had children out of wedlock. The Vestry, the Guardians, hated that. They gave those women corn to grind. They were kept in a yard spinning fly wheels and expected to grind dozens of pounds of corn every day.

'Oakum is easy. Laundry is easy. You don't want to grind corn. It'll nigh kill you with weariness, Catherine.'

Catherine had no intention of grinding corn, and every intention of keeping on the right side of the Superintendent and overseers. She knew it was her best chance of seeing Austin and the children.

* * *

'What's to eat?'

It was John's first question on the second day of his internment in the workhouse. They had been lucky. Edward and John had been allocated beds in the same children's ward. John had climbed out of bed early and had walked over to question his brother.

'Back to bed, boy.'

A man's voice boomed from the entrance to the sleeping room. John had been unlucky; caught on his first morning, just as an overseer was doing his early hours rounds. Edward feigned no knowledge of John, ignoring him, should they decide that the two brothers could not share the same dormitory. Startled at the loud instruction, John scampered back to his bed and climbed back in under a blanket.

But the mild altercation had wakened every boy within earshot. Many began to sit up, some climbing out and starting to use pots placed under their beds. It was as if the morning had started early. Hearing the muffled sounds of early morning risers, the overseer returned.

'Back to bed, the lot of you. I'll tell you when to be up, he repeated his instruction.

'I'm hungry, sir. When will we eat?' asked John.

The overseer walked over to John's bed and gave him a light cuff on the ear.

'When I say so.'

One ear red and smarting with pain, John lay back and pulled his blanket over his head again. He began to whimper. Edward could hear his brother's sounds, but recognised his helplessness. It was a hard lesson for his brother, but perhaps better he learn it sooner than later. They both needed to understand the rules.

An hour and a half later both brothers were sitting at the breakfast table. Porridge was served with buttermilk, a meal they were soon to find out would be served at supper as well.

'Who are the new ones? Who arrived yesterday?'

It was obvious really. After breakfast, most of their new companions had gone to a work room, leaving Edward, John, and a handful of the other boys in the dining room, unsure what to do. They all placed their hands in the air in response to the question.

'Follow me. All of you.'

They were a group of eight boys, ranging in age from six to about thirteen. In the workroom they were all allocated the task of picking oakum, standard fare for new arrivals. In time they might be allocated to one of the trade rooms, but oakum it was for now.

On the stroke of noon all were trooped back into the dining room to be given rice pudding and milk. One of other boys said it would be the same every Wednesday.

'And what of the other days?' asked Edward.

'Thursday, potatoes and pork; Friday, soup; Saturday, scouse; Sunday, meat and potatoes, and Monday, soup and bread. It's the same most weeks, except on Christmas Day,' came the response. It was left to Edward's imagination to guess what Christmas Day fare might be.

In the weeks that followed, Edward learned of the pigs that were reared on site, the bakery, and the corn that was ground by some of Brownlow Hill's pauper women. He also learned the stories of some of his fellow inmates; some with tales worse than his. Fatherless and motherless boys, parents who had abandoned them to their fate on the streets, some who had been beaten; even some who had skirted on the edge of Liverpool's community of crime. He felt sympathy for his companion unfortunates, but reserved his strength, and thought, for working out how he and John could escape the clutches of the workhouse. Without his mother, he knew that he would have to be the one to make decisions for both of them, should it ever come to that.

As he drifted off to sleep at the end of another day in the workhouse, much the same as the one yesterday and the one before that, he thought of his father and mother, and of better times. They were so close and yet so far away. The brief glimpses he caught of Catherine were hardly better than none. His sole thoughts became of how he, John, and his mother and father, could leave, alive, and perhaps refreshed with a new vigour for life outside. One day he would no longer be here. One day he might even leave Liverpool, as he had often heard his parents discuss.

* * *

For the first few days of his confinement on a medical ward, Austin simply slept. Weakened by a loss of interest in life, and a reluctance to eat, he had determined that his life was no longer worth living. Weeks ago, he had decided that Catherine would be better off without him. Unable to work, he felt a dead weight on the family, consuming what little resources they had and contributing nothing. The more he thought about it, the more depressed he became. Everything had become an effort and a drudge. Even conversation became tiresome. What had he of any use to say? He was a dead weight, an embarrassment, a person worthy only of charitable attention. Austin knew Catherine and Thomas thought differently, but it was just so pointless. His foot would never recover. He knew that then, and he knew that now, here in the workhouse. He had brought his family to total destitution. Would they ever leave?

'Porridge, Austin,' said a female nurse. She had brought him breakfast as usual.

Austin turned over to look at it. He knew that if he didn't eat it, there would be plenty who would. But today, the pangs of hunger had got the better of him. He would eat.

Over the months since the accident, the pain around his foot had faded. It had become intermittent, almost painless even, that is until movement aggravated any latent discomfort.

But something else had started. Ever since the accident he had also started to become forgetful, having trouble concentrating on matters at hand. These symptoms exacerbated his depression. He did not want to talk to people, even Catherine. But that was not just because of his foot; he now seemed to have difficulty forming the words. It was better that they think he was unwilling to speak than they know for sure that he was having difficulty communicating. He was not mad and did not want others to think that either.

'Austin. Austin. It's noon. Time to eat.'

It was the same nurse again. Austin turned to look at her. It did not seem more than a minute since she was there giving him breakfast.

'Austin. You're back again. You must eat. It's been days since you last ate anything.'

She was saying stuff that made no sense. He had only just eaten breakfast. Austin stared at her and the food left at the side of the bed. He then began to drift again, back into a world without pain and suffering.

'Austin. It's me, Catherine. Austin, talk to me.'

Austin turned to face the voice. It sounded like Catherine, and the face looked like Catherine, but he was not so sure of it. Was it a dream? He could no longer be sure.

'Austin. It's me. Don't go back to sleep. Please, please eat something.'

The voice was breaking up, breaking up into distant and muffled tears. What he was hearing must be a dream. From his dream state, he tried to talk back to the voice.

'Caaaaaathhhhh.'

It was too much effort. He drifted back into the solace of the other world he now lived in. A faded, blurred, and fuzzy world of shapes, sounds, dismembered voices, and abstract incomprehensible conversation. It was pleasant to be back home.

* * *

'He's dying. I'm sorry, but that's the truth. He can't or won't eat. He doesn't seem to want to get better. We can't help him. I'm sorry.'

The nurse told Catherine how it actually was. It was no surprise. She had been allowed to visit him more frequently during the warm summer weeks of July, and it was obvious to her that the man she once knew had evaporated into the thin frame that lay in front of her. His personality and character had achromatised into blank expression; he seemed oblivious to Catherine and the world around him. The workhouse, notwithstanding the better medical care, had done nothing for him. All that Catherine had left was prayer to a rediscovered divinity, a God that had always been there, but not always present within her.

August followed July. Catherine had been given special permission to attend Catholic Mass outside the workhouse on Sundays, and had called on the services of a priest. She knew Austin had little time left, and wanted the priest on hand to give the Last Rites.

The end felt very close.

On the night of August 10th, Catherine was called from her bed.

'You should call on your priest. The doctor thinks the end is close.'

It was not a wakening that anyone would want.

She went straight to the medical ward where she was told of Austin's condition. But she could see it. His breathing had become erratic, apnoea-like.

'I'll fetch the priest,' said Catherine.

'Quickly now. He's not long for this world,' replied the nurse.

Within an hour she had returned with Father Nugent. He was not her usual priest, but had been covering for an illness absence. Father Nugent could see straight away what Austin's condition was, and immediately commenced with the ritual.

'Be at peace, Austin. May God be with you.'

The priest blessed Austin, and then turned to Catherine.

'It's in God's hands now, Catherine. His pain will soon be over, and his soul will soon be admitted to the glory of Heaven. I'll wait with you awhile.'

The priest and Catherine sat by Austin's bedside for the next two hours. Few words were exchanged, though many prayers were said, both out loud and in silence. A few minutes after the hour struck two on the somnolent sound of distant chime, Austin drew his last breath.

For five minutes, total silence beset the room.

'He's gone, Catherine. Gone to the glory of God. There's nothing more those of us on earth can do for him, but I will pray that his passage is good.'

Catherine was unsure what he meant by that, but thanked him nonetheless.

'I'll go now. Stay awhile until they collect his body. But remember, what is left is no longer him. He is no longer with us. I must go.'

At that the priest departed, leaving Catherine to her thoughts. A few minutes later a nurse appeared and encouraged her to leave.

'You should get some sleep. I'll tell the overseer. He'll be easy on you tomorrow. Don't you worry about that.'

Catherine got off the wooden bench she had been sitting on and left the room. Austin, her husband, had gone. It was now just her, Edward, and John. Sad though she was at Austin's passing, she was now more concerned with the living. She knew her grief must not shroud what she had to do. And that was to think of a way of getting out of the workhouse, and being able to earn enough to feed her and the children. Her own dreams were confused and erratic that night. She dreamt of being with Austin, and the children, in their ancestral home of Mayo. It was strange and otherworldly, though reassuring. Austin had left in body, but would always be with her in spirit.

* * *

Catherine was given a certificate of death the following day. Being unable to read, she had to ask what it said of Austin.

'He died of... It says Hemiplegia,' said Mr Evans, the governor of the workhouse. He had been visiting the medical ward where Austin had died the previous evening, and was therefore on hand to answer questions. He handed the document back to Catherine.

'What's that?' asked Catherine.

Mr Evans turned to an attending doctor for some help.

'It's a disease of the brain. Did your husband get hit on the head?' asked the doctor.

'It was said he banged his head falling over when a flag he was moving crushed his foot,' replied Catherine.

'Yes, a bang on the head can cause many symptoms. I've seen some patients unable to speak, others experience black moods, spasms, tiredness. A crushed foot alone would not cause it,' replied the doctor.

Realisation dawned on Catherine. Austin had become withdrawn in the weeks following the accident; he had also refused to speak and to eat. She felt a pang of guilt, wondering whether there might have been anything she could have done.

'Thank you. What do I do with this?' she then asked.

'It's yours to keep. For officials to look at if they need to,' replied Mr Evans.

Catherine took the document, said her goodbyes, and left. She still had a burial, and perhaps a service, to sort out. Again, guilt rippled through her body. There was no money; it would be a pauper's service. She could not even give Austin a decent burial. The workhouse was no life. She had to get her and her sons out, however long it took.

* * *

It would be a year or more before she managed to get out. Even then, it was without her sons, Edward and John. After Austin's death, Catherine's father, Darby, had said she could come and stay with them on Collingwood Street, not far from where she had lived with Austin. Alas, there was a problem. He suggested that with the income Catherine could raise selling fish, they could give her a roof over her head, but that he could not afford to feed the children as well. They would have to stay in the workhouse, until either Catherine remarried, or they were of an age to earn their own keep. Catherine was naturally unhappy about it, but it was not much different than her situation as a pauper in the workhouse. She could only see them with permission, and not very often at that. She consoled herself with the thought that, despite the rigours of the workhouse, at least Edward and John would be clothed, fed, and have a roof over their heads. And it did give her a chance to put her own life back on the right foot.

Leaving the children in the workhouse would be a delay to resuming life on the outside, not final, and she might even get to see them more often. She even thought of seeking permission to take them out on Sundays to attend Mass.

Perhaps the arrangement would not be so bad after all.

* * *

Edward's age did seem to work against him, but John was considered young enough to learn a trade inside the workhouse. Within months of him arriving, it was decided that he be apprenticed to a weaver. The Board of Guardians had decided to acquire a number of looms and add flannel weaving to the list of workhouse occupations. John had been lucky in the sense that the more experienced weavers had been looking for a handful of plucky young lads, just after he entered the institution. So that became his life, and his trade. Fifteen years later, he would travel to America as a skilled weaver, finally fulfilling the dreams of his father and grandfather.

Edward continued to work on less skilled and less demanding tasks until Catherine found the means to release him. It took far longer than she had anticipated. He was nearly three years in the workhouse, and by the time he left, aged fourteen, he was deemed old enough to earn his own living on the outside. Without the skills of his younger brother, he followed in the footsteps of his father and grandfather as a general labourer working in the docks, on buildings sites, and wherever there was need of muscle power. In time he would decide for himself whether Liverpool was the place for him.

John was last out of the workhouse. Though youngest, the skills he was obtaining as an apprentice weaver were considered worth the unpleasantness of institutional life. His father and grandfather would have been proud of him. The first in the family to learn a skill; a first step on the long journey out of abject poverty and Liverpool's Irish ghetto.

As the pain of the of loss of Austin finally began to fade, Catherine drew some hope that her sons, and perhaps one day her grandsons, would escape the misery of what their families had endured before, during, and after the famine years. Perhaps one day they would look their English masters in the eye as equals.

EPILOGUE
1860

There was no time for Edward to grieve.

John had been taken in by his aunt after their mother's death, but there was not enough room for him. And they certainly could not afford a passenger, another mouth to feed. He had to find his own way, earn his own living. It wasn't that he disliked Liverpool; it was simply the competition for work. There were just too many of his fellow Irish chasing the dock and labouring work, and what work there was, well, the gangs had it all stitched up.

Many of the lads he had grown up with still had fathers, dockers with connections. It was true that his uncle had helped from time to time, but that could not last. He had his own to consider, and was bound to put them first. Edward had to be grateful for the scraps, the rare occasions where the demands of unloading the ships required some extra hands. And those days seemed to be becoming scarcer.

He would have to look elsewhere.

'The mines, lad. There's work in the mines. Lots of it.'

Outside of Liverpool, Lancashire was booming. The textile mills and the mines were crying out for labour. Alas, he had no skills to speak of. It had always been labouring of one form or another, so labouring it would have to remain.

'You need strength and no fear of the dark. It's paid well enough, lad.'

That was all he needed to know. It would be the mines. But where to go?

'Everywhere, lad. There's work across the county from here to Manchester. You could take a brisk walk to St. Helens in day, and have work in two. I promise it.'

Thus, it was a conversation in a beerhouse that set Edward on a path away from his birthplace, and what remained of his family, to a new life. Not far. Perhaps a day, or maybe two days' journey from Liverpool. But it was further away than he had ever been before. Nothing like the stories of his grandparents' journey from Mayo, but it seemed like no less of an adventure to Edward.

* * *

There was a hint of rain in the air as he set off on his walk to St. Helens. Edward had money in his pocket, but not much of it, perhaps enough for a week's lodging somewhere and a little extra for food. But that was it. He would have to find work almost as soon as he got there, he mused, hoping that he had heard the truth the previous week.

But this was no time to doubt. His decision had been made and the first steps taken. He looked up, just as the clouds parted and a shaft of sunlight punctured through, bouncing off the damp gleaming stone of the recently cobbled road. Transient though it was, it seemed to mark the path to a better life.

Perhaps it would not rain after all.

Raithe an ocrais

The hungry season.

Gombeen man

Old Irish reference to a usurer or moneylender.

Chlann

Children.

Culchie

An old term for people from rural parts of Ireland. Probably originating in Mayo, it is still used as a derogatory reference.

Oíche na Gaoithe Móire

'Night of the big wind'. Starting on January 6th 1839 it caused considerable damage and several hundred deaths across Ireland.

Striapach

Pejorative term for a prostitute.

Sleeveen

Old Irish for a trickster; a sly or obsequious person; an unreliable clown.

Cead mile failte

A warm welcome to you all.

Má ithis, nar chacair

'If you eat, that you may not shit!' or 'Having eaten may you not be able to pass it'. An old Irish curse referring to someone who always wants more.

An Gorta Mór

'The Great Hunger.' A reference to the Irish Potato Famine.

An té a luíonn le madaí, eiroidh sé le dearnaid

'He who lies down with dogs, gets up with fleas'. A pretty clear reference to being careful of the company you keep.